BROWSING COLLECTION
14-DAY CHECKOUT
No Holds • No Renewals

THE FOURTH RULE

THE FOURTH RULE

A NOVEL

JEFF LINDSAY

DUTTON

DUTTON
An imprint of Penguin Random House LLC
penguinrandomhouse.com

DUTTON and the D colophon are registered trademarks of Penguin Random House LLC.

LIBRARY OF CONGRESS CATALOGING-IN-PUBLICATION DATA
has been applied for.

ISBN 9780593186251 (hardcover)
ISBN 9780593186275 (ebook)

Printed in the United States of America
1st Printing

BOOK DESIGN LAURA K. CORLESS

For Hilary, as ever

THE FOURTH RULE

*I*t all looks a lot different when it's over, doesn't it?

While things are happening, it seems like number one leads to number two, and two leads to three, and it's all moving in a straight line, just like you planned it. But afterward? When it's over and you're looking back on what was really happening at the time while you thought something totally different was going down? That's when you get bruises on your forehead from smacking yourself and saying, I should have known. Yeah, you should have. But you didn't. Because you're not half as smart as you think you are. Nobody is. Not even me.

I always thought I was way beyond smart. Looking back, why wouldn't I? I stole Iran's crown jewels, and I lifted an actual freaking fresco off a wall in the Vatican. And I got inside a fortified, heavily guarded death trap and stole a flash drive holding plans for an end-of-the-world weapons system when all the Russian and Chinese and US black ops guys had given up. Nobody else in the world could have done that, or half the other things I pulled off.

So I had a right to think that I am the very best in the world at what I do, which is stealing things that are impossible to steal. I start where everybody else quits. Nobody else comes close. I am it. And I've been the best for a while now. I mean, nobody took a survey, fans didn't vote, scholars didn't study it and make a list. But who else could have done what I did? So yeah,

I am the best, and that's all there is to it. If there was somebody else in my league, I'd know about them. And I hadn't seen it yet.

It's just me, alone on top. I never thought about it a lot. I just am, and I know it, and anybody who knows anything at all about working on my side of the street knows it, too. Riley Wolfe, top of the heap, the best there ever was. End of discussion.

It wasn't easy getting there. It never is. And it's just as hard to stay on top. There's a lot that goes with being the best at anything. You have to try a little harder every time. You have to keep getting better, and you have to evolve, too, be different each time out so you don't develop a pattern that the guys on the other team can read and predict. I've always done all that, no problem. But there's one more thing about being ichiban, something that should be obvious and never is. And I know it so well I made it part of the rules I live by, Riley's Laws.

Riley's Fourth Law says, Even if you're the best there is, watch your back. Because somebody better is coming.

People have taken their shot at me before, plenty of times. I'm still here, and I'm still on top. But I knew someday, somewhere, somebody better was coming for me. It just makes sense, because when you're way out front, everybody else has a clear shot at your back, and somebody is going to take it.

That's a fact. It's like a law of nature. Eventually there's going to be somebody better than you, and if they aren't coming at you right now, that just means they will be someday soon. Just about the time you start feeling like you've settled in as king of the hill, maybe even saying out loud that you're the best in the world, somebody shows up to let you know it's their hill now and you're headed for the dungeon. It always happens, every time, and you better remember that.

I know I should have.

It had been a couple of months since I pulled off an insane heist that had been a lot easier than it should have been. I stole the Irish crown jewels. Not from Ireland, because Ireland didn't have them. They did once, sure, but the whole collection disappeared over a hundred years ago and hadn't been seen or heard of since. Until now, of course, because I got 'em.

Most people don't even know there's any such thing as Irish crown jewels. Partly because, like I said, they went missing over a hundred years ago. But there's more to it than that. Just say it out loud: "Irish crown jewels." It kind of sounds like the punch line to an old joke. I mean, we don't think of Ireland as a kingdom, right? And there's never been any exhibition of the jewels, or a *National Geographic* special on them. And no third world country has been yelling about how Irish colonialism stole the jewels and ought to give them back. Nothing. That's not just because the British jewels are so flashy they hog the spotlight. It's mostly because when the Irish jewels disappeared, they stayed disappeared. A hundred years and nobody knew where they were. Totally gone, and nobody was even sure how it happened.

It raises a couple of questions. Like, how do you lose crown jewels, which are, after all, kind of important for national pride, as well as being worth a ton of money? Well, actually, that part was easy. First, the jewels had been kept in a *library*, in a safe that was opened by a key. I mean, a regular old *key*, for God's sake. That's plenty bad enough, but then? Then they gave out *seven* keys and didn't really pay attention to what happened to them. And as a clincher, they put a guy guarding it who liked to get totally blasted and wear the jewels around the place, like, *Hey, look at me! I'm the Queen of Ireland! Erin go bra-less!*

After that, it was pretty much what you'd expect. The jewels were "locked up" in June 1907. When somebody went to get them in July, they were gone. Over a hundred years later, they were still gone, and there'd never been a hint about who took them or how. There was an investigation, naturally, but the report from that vanished, too, suppressed by somebody for some reason that was probably incriminating. There were rumors that the Irish Republican Brotherhood had something to do with it, but I'm pretty sure nobody asked them about that. Those guys tended to be kind of tough to talk to, especially if you were British. And maybe it wasn't them. Nobody really knows. The jewels just disappeared.

A while back, I started hearing rumors that an insanely dangerous collector had them. He was known only by the nickname the Cobra, which I guess was supposed to make people go, *Oooh, scary, a Cobra, I'm staying away.* And to me, that's like hanging out a sign that reads, WELCOME, RILEY!

Nobody knew where the Cobra was, but there were a few whispers when mangled bodies turned up now and then, things like that. So I tracked the whispers until they became rumors, and I chased the rumors until they turned into leads. And I followed the leads until I finally found the Cobra's nest. And it wasn't just hard to find; it was pretty hard to get to. It was in Canada, of all places, in the middle of a huge wilderness area called the Algoma Highlands. And because that was way too easy to get to, it was also on an island, in the middle of a big lake. No roads led to it, not even game trails. You had to get there by float plane.

If you got there, and that's a good-sized "if," the place was surrounded by a tall electrified fence with razor wire on top. It was inhabited by a nasty group of mercenaries, and loaded with electronics that could find you and fry you before you could even blink.

I'd been ready for all that kind of lethal crap, and I'd found plenty—psychotic guards, deadly traps, all that stuff. But I had a perfect plan, it worked like clockwork, and I got around all the death traps without a bruise. I got the jewels, I got out, and I never even saw the Cobra. And like I said, it all seemed way too easy, which always makes me nervous. That's science, not superstition. Riley's Fifth Law clearly states: If you think it's easy, you missed something. And the amendment is, that overlooked something is on its way to bite you on the ass.

So I off-loaded the jewels as quickly as I could, to an Irish patriot who was also a fanatical collector. And then I laid low and watched my back trail.

After a couple of months, there was nothing coming after me, and I started to get bored. I figured it was time for the next chapter of Riley's Big Adventure. And this time I was looking for something that would be a little more of a challenge, because I kind of felt like I had to balance the scales and do something way harder to make up for the too-easy jewel heist. And anyway, that's how I roll. I have to do things that everybody else has given up on and called impossible. It's hard to explain; I just need to do things nobody else can do, and that's more important to me than the money. I mean, I love having money. But I love even more the feeling of pulling off something that leaves everybody gasping and saying *How the hell did he do that?*

So I needed something extra tough this time. I poked around a little, made a list of three impossible jobs, and settled on the one that seemed *most* impossible, which is probably a phrase that is, um, impossible? I picked one you've probably heard of: the Nazi gold train.

JEFF LINDSAY

If you haven't heard of it, it's an entire *trainload* of treasure. They call it "gold," and there was a couple of tons of actual gold in it—but there were also jewels, incredible artworks, all kinds of beautiful and valuable stuff. How valuable? Hard to say, because you could take one item at random and it might price out at a few billion dollars. And we're talking about an entire freaking *train* loaded with stuff just like it.

If you are a solid, law-abiding citizen with an IQ of at least ninety, you are probably asking how the holy hell somebody loses something like that, right? I mean, not just something that's worth enough to pay off the national debt of the whole G7, which is an amount to make anybody watchful. But hello—it's a *train*! You know, really big, lots of cars, has to be on a track; how do you lose that?

It's a fair question, but the answer is easy; some very devious and incredibly guilty people wanted it to get lost, and they were powerful enough to do things like move a train somewhere and kill everybody who saw them do it. And if it happened at all, that's what happened here.

The story goes that a bunch of high-ranking Nazis stole all this great stuff by murdering anybody who owned it, which was the way they rolled. When the Nazis all knew the war was ending, they realized it might be kind of awkward if they turned up wearing some old king's legendary crown. They also wanted to keep the stuff and use it to finance their retirement from being a Nazi. You know, Spanish lessons, learning the tango, that kind of thing. So they figured they'd hide their loot and come back for it later when things had cooled off.

According to the experts' favorite guess, they loaded up this whole freaking train with treasure and drove it into a tunnel in the side of a mountain. Then they sealed the tunnel, got rid of the tracks, and killed

6

everybody else who knew about it. But things never did cool off, because, duh, they were Nazis. Eventually, all of them who were in on it died. They must have told somebody, but all this time later, none of the missing items have turned up, and nobody has found the train. Sure as hell a lot of people have tried. Some of them even died searching. Not always from natural hazards, either. I mean, there are plenty of those. But there are also some very hard people who are either trying to find it or trying to keep it hidden.

That's the story. Some people say it's just that, a story. Urban legend, fairy tale, myth. Maybe it is—but if I really wanted to hide something, that's exactly the story I'd want going around. And a lot of people have gone to considerable trouble to put that story out there. On top of that, like I said—none of the missing items have turned up.

So I thought, *Okay. Maybe the Nazi gold doesn't even exist. If it does, it's dangerous, it's impossible to find, and when I do find it—it's an entire freaking train, which is impossible to steal and move somewhere safe. Perfect.*

I started doing the research. And the best place in the world for doing research on obscure historical junk is the British Museum in London. I knew right where that was—and even better, I speak the language. I packed a bag, changed into someone else, and went.

PART 1

London

CHAPTER

1

When she made the decision to go freelance, Alex knew it would not always be easy. Easy would have been to take one of the dozen prestigious job offers that came to her for graduating at the top of her class at Stanford. Prestige didn't interest her. Money did, and none of the available jobs came near to the amounts that got her attention.

But Alex had a plan, one she knew could catapult her into the seven- or eight-digit incomes she wanted. She made a very basic calculation, based on pure logic. People with the most money could pay the most. But *people*—not corporations; those had too many rules, too much oversight. There were plenty of people who had the money she wanted and didn't want the oversight. And many of these same people paid so well because they could not use ordinary sources when they had a tech problem.

Criminals. Drug lords, arms dealers, all the people who lived and worked in the shadows. And the ones who made it—the ones who lived—had the money. They also had a need, and Alex could fill it. Better, she could do it without the danger of getting killed at every step.

There were still big risks. That was inevitable. It went with the big paydays. But if it worked at all, the risks would be well worth it.

And it did; it worked. It took her a mere six months to make her reputation with the right people. Some of them were very scary people. But she made sure they understood that they needed her, and she learned to deal with them without fear. It was part of her job. It was a part she chose, because that was how she made her genius with computers pay exponentially better than anything her classmates at Stanford could earn. She worked the dark side, and she didn't regret it, either. The way money poured in made it worthwhile. And she always made the clients get the picture right away—they were much better off with Alex on their side. Harming her was actually harming themselves.

They got the idea, or Alex didn't work for them.

There was one client who still scared the hell out of her. Scared everybody, in fact. Alex knew that before first contact. Still, this particular client was pretty much the apex predator, and they paid twice what everybody else paid, so it was worth it.

Mostly. Alex still had to remind herself of the size of that payday before every job for this client. Even this one, which had been relatively simple. It had taken a long time, maybe longer than the client wanted, but Alex was pretty sure that nobody else in her business would have been able to do it all.

Still, that wasn't the hard part. It had been tedious, it took a lot of time, but it was mostly routine. No real skull sweat. The hard part came now. Delivering the results, which the client wanted in person, face-to-face. That made Alex's stomach churn. And it was a long trip, which didn't help. There was more time to worry, which she did. And now she was there, ready for the meeting, trying to brace herself for being in the same room with the scariest person she'd ever met. She swallowed hard, clutched her folder of results in suddenly sweaty hands, and opened the door.

"Sit."

Alex obeyed before she was even aware of doing so. There was just so much menace radiating from the head of the table that if she'd been told to strip naked and dance, she would have done it without thinking twice.

"Report."

Alex licked her very dry lips and opened her folder. "There's sort of a bulletin board on the dark web," she said. "I went through all the posts from three months ago and worked backward. It took some time, but I pulled seven posts that I thought might be something. Six didn't pan out." She lifted the top sheet of paper from the folder and slid it across the table. "This one did."

Those terrible eyes lit up with a cold fire. "The crown jewels."

"I believe so."

The eyes held her for a long and very uncomfortable moment. Then: "Go on."

"Right, so when I was sure, I traced that and found the guy who posted it?" She slid the second sheet across.

"And?"

Alex shrugged. "He's nobody, really. Just a business guy. But he had the money. And his family had strong ties to Ireland."

"Obviously. And on the other end?"

Alex swallowed. "We sort of knew who did it, like you said? And so I just confirmed it. He went into hiding after he delivered? And, uh—"

She could see her audience was impatient, so she jerked to a stop. "Where is he?"

Alex nodded and tried to push away the raw fear that was clawing its way up her spine. "Right, so—I found him," she said.

"Not enough. I need to *know* him, too."

Alex found that she couldn't swallow. She took a ragged breath. "Yes, I— So that's why, uh— I hacked into the FBI and found his file." She tapped the manila file folder she'd carried in. "There were *two* profiles on him, which—that's really unusual?"

She took a printout from the folder and slid it down the table.

"That's really all anyone knows about him, because, you know . . . But there are no known photographs of his face, but—the file had his birth name? I used that and found a picture from his seventh-grade yearbook."

Alex took out the top photograph and pushed it down the table with the printout. No reaction. Those terrible cold eyes never blinked and never left hers.

Alex found that her hand was trembling. She took a deep breath, willed the hand to stop shaking, and went on. "I used an AI program I developed to age that picture. You know—project what he'd look like now?" She raised a hand half-heartedly to stop an objection that never came. She let the hand flop down into her lap. "I know, there are lots of programs that do that. Mine is better. Much better."

"Go on."

"Yes. I'm sorry. Yes. So . . . Using the new picture"—she slipped the next photo out of her folder—"I began an expanding search pattern with my AI facial recognition system. There were a number of hits, possibles, of course. But all relatively low probability—until finally, it picked up a probable in New York. Kennedy airport."

Alex placed the next photo on the table.

"AI gave it an eighty-three percent positive. That was the highest percentage I'd gotten, so I followed. Subject used an American passport and flew first class."

"Destination?"

"Yes, of course. Heathrow. In London." She tapped the photo. "This is him."

Dead silence for what seemed like a horrible long time. Finally: "You're certain?"

"I am," Alex said. "Subsequent surveillance photos improved the AI rating to ninety-five percent. I programmed it for a certain amount of caution, so . . . That's pretty much totally sure."

More silence. Alex felt her whole body bathed in cold sweat. "He seems to have settled in one location, indicating he will most likely be there for a while? So . . ."

She slid out a single piece of paper. "The address is here, with a floor plan."

"Good. The name on the passport?"

Alex took out another photo, a screenshot of a passport, and slid it across the table. "Harry Metzger," she said.

CHAPTER

2

And there I was in London on a beautiful summer afternoon, one of those rare English days when you can actually see the sun, and even feel it on your face. But instead of frolicking on the green—and there really is a Green Park—I was slouched in a carrel at the library of the British Museum going through a stack of dusty intel reports from the last few months of WWII. I found stuff, of course—you can't help it. But nothing really important. Just lots of interesting factoids.

One of them snuck under my guard and turned into something I wanted to know more about. Maybe it was kind of a sidetrack, but I'd gotten interested in a treasure known as the Amber Room. It's a personal thing, but I totally love amber. It's very valuable, of course, but that's beside the point. It's *beautiful*. The good stuff seems to glow from inside, and it has a feeling to it that is pure sex. And this was a whole freaking *room* made of it.

If you've never heard of that, it's really an actual room—or anyway, it was. A whole room made mostly of amber. And if you're saying, *Gosh, I thought you said amber was sort of expensive*—then you are on the right page. At a guess, this room is worth a couple billion dollars. And nobody knows where it is.

You're way ahead of me now, right? Because wait a sec—it's a *room*. A room has to be in some kind of building, so . . . How did they lose it?

The first part is easy. The Nazis took the amber walls apart into neat sections and packed them into crates to protect them from bombs and wartime theft. Kind of ironic, because the biggest wartime thieves were the Nazis themselves. But anyway, they took the room apart, and then—this is where it gets kind of complicated. The story that is usually accepted is that the Nazis stuck all those crates into Konigsberg Castle in Germany. The Royal Air Force bombed the castle, and then that part of Germany turned into Soviet-controlled East Germany, which means nobody could go look for the crates. And then the Soviets knocked the rest of the castle down and said the Amber Room had been destroyed in the bombing.

Kind of hard to prove or disprove, right? A lot of people leave it right there and look for something else worth a few billion. And that's too bad, because if you keep chasing the Amber Room, the story gets even more interesting.

First, in 1945, as the war was ending, a bunch of people claimed they saw those exact crates loaded onto a German ship, the *Wilhelm Gustloff*. The *Gustloff* was a huge ship, and it had to be, because it was a big part of something the Nazis called Operation Hannibal. If that makes you wonder about elephants—it did for me—there weren't any. But there were lots and lots of Nazis. Because WWII was coming to a rapid conclusion, and not in a fun way for the Nazis. Operation

Hannibal was their plan to evacuate their key people from the Baltic area as the Soviets came charging in. And the Nazis were absolutely on fire to get away. If you don't know this part of history, the Nazis would do pretty much *anything* to get away from the Russians, who were the most brutal, heartless, cruel, and crushing people anybody had ever seen. Except maybe for the Nazis. Kind of a pattern, huh? And since everybody knew by this time that the Reds were sort of peeved at the Nazis, they had a pretty good idea what was waiting for them if the Reds caught them. Because, you know—it was stuff that they'd been doing to the Reds.

Anyway, there were a lot of anxious Nazis wanting to get out of the way. The *Gustloff*, huge as it was, couldn't take all of them, even though people were willing to sit on deck for the whole trip. Hell, some of them would have been glad to hold on to a rope and get towed behind the *Gustloff*.

So like I said, the *Gustloff* was packed full of important Nazis and left a lot of pals on the dock waving bye-bye. And one of these Nazis who didn't get on said they saw these crates.

It's the kind of story that's really hard to take seriously, unless you can back it up. So why didn't anybody check it with the people who went with the *Gustloff*? Great question!

The *Gustloff*, loaded with Nazis, and maybe a few crates of Amber Room, took off from Poland, managed to make a few good miles without tipping over—and ran into Soviet submarine S-13. The S-13 couldn't believe their luck, and I guess they got suspicious. They farted around for a few hours, circling the ship and looking for some kind of trap. But it really was a huge, fat, overloaded ship full of Nazis, and finally, S-13 fired four torpedoes. One of them stuck in the tube, but the other three did the job. A couple of the *Gustloff*'s lifeboats got away, but most of them were frozen in their davits, because, you know, winter in the Baltic. And twenty minutes later, still with most of the passengers on board, the *Gustloff* rolled over. Half an hour later, it went down.

Poetic justice, right? Nobody is really sure how many people went down with it. Best guess is around ten thousand people died. An accurate count wasn't possible because first, they were stampeding on at the dock, and second, they had some "unofficial" passengers—the kind of evil-in-the-flesh people who didn't want to be seen or put on any list. But like I said, it was winter in the Baltic. Anybody who went into the water was dead pretty quickly.

And in any case, it's the end of our story. Or this version of it. Amber Room sleeps with the fishes. . . .

Except a soldier going through the wreckage of Konigsberg Castle said he found some pieces of the Amber Room. Which would imply it was never on the *Gustloff* at all, because why leave just a few pieces behind? So maybe it did get left behind in the castle.

Of course, if that's true, if it had been in the castle the whole time, they want you to believe that the bombing destroyed the entire Amber Room. *Nothing to see here, folks—it's all gone, sorry. Nothing left.*

Okay, sure. Except—if you think for a minute, does it really make sense that a couple of bombs would wipe out all traces of the room? And if this guy really found a piece—it was only a few pieces, and where's the rest of it? And it's worth a couple billion dollars. Is anybody really going to say, *Oh, the castle is just a pile of rubble. Too bad about the Amber Room?*

No, of course not. If it was in there when the bombs hit, it would almost certainly have been in the basement. Or if it makes you happier, the dungeon. And when the smoke cleared, somebody would try to dig down and find what was left. Since this area was now a part of the

USSR, it would have to be somebody with government approval. And things being what they were in the Workers' Paradise, something that valuable would probably be snatched by somebody important—smart money on Stalin himself.

And for one more left turn? The Soviets put out word that they'd made a full-size copy of the thing. And if you are paying attention, that is now either three separate rooms—one on a ship, one in the dungeon, and one stellar replica—or a whole fistful of liars. The only definite conclusion anybody could possibly come up with is that it was destroyed, except that it wasn't because it sank on the *Gustloff*, until later when it didn't. And anybody with a nasty suspicious mind—me—has to think about the Soviets' copy and wonder if it was really the real thing with a cover story.

It's a twisty, wicked story, with a high body count and no way to know what really happened. In other words, exactly my kind of problem. Or, since I was in London, maybe I should say my dish of tea. So I'd been working it back and forth, following different threads that would pop up and then vanish as soon as I found the right dusty file. Every now and then I'd catch a glimpse of the sun and clear sky out the window and think, *Damn, a beautiful day in London. Not sure I've seen that before.*

And finally, I'd flipped too many dusty pages, sneezed too many times, and looked out the window once too often, and it was all just too much. I quit for the day and went outside.

For a while I just walked, not really going anywhere specific. Just enjoying the air, the look of the old buildings, the frosty focus of the other pedestrians. After an hour or so, I realized that I'd wandered into Hyde Park. Hyde Park has a real green, but I didn't frolic on it.

Instead, I remembered that the park was right next to the area that holds most of the art galleries in London.

And yeah, I know, the whole idea was to get outside and enjoy the day. What is so rare as a day in June and all that, right? Well, as it happens, there is something a lot more rare. Great art. And there was a ton of it right over *there*.

I went over there. And for once I wasn't checking it out for a heist. I was just looking. I do that sometimes, because I love really good paintings. Not just because I love stealing them; I love the paintings and the artists who made them. Maybe I'm so enthusiastic about art because I found out about it late. Maybe because I'd once fallen for an artist. I don't know, that's for the shrinks. I just know I love it.

I moseyed through a gallery featuring contemporary stuff. It all seemed like it was trying too hard. I went on to another with a terrific exhibit of traditional sub-Saharan African art. There were a couple of masks that made my hair stand up and some carved wooden figures that were breathtaking. And then the real showstopper: some Benin bronzes. I gawked for almost an hour and then moved on.

The next place was a gallery I'd been to before, several times, the Ardmore-Blackfinn. They had a really great bunch of German Expressionist paintings. If you've never seen it or heard of it, German Expressionism was a thing that happened in the early twentieth century in, you guessed it, Germany. It's a style that exaggerates lines, and light and dark, to make you feel more immediately what the painting's about. Sometimes it can have an almost cartoon look to it, except that there's usually not much funny about the subject matter. The artists painted through a filter of emotions, so instead of just seeing a face, you see an exaggerated, distorted expression of what the artist *felt* about that face, kind of like the true hidden face of the subject. And what those guys were feeling was nothing cartoony.

Because Expressionism really took off between the two world wars, and hot damn, did Germans have stuff to be emotional about. The things they'd seen and done in WWI changed their world forever. I mean, if you don't know much about WWI, it was pretty much a couple of years of hiding in the mud with heaps of rotting corpses piled up around you, with lots of shooting and shelling and every now and then poison gas coming at you. It was the first war with machine guns, tanks, airplanes—and the generals were still fighting those battles with cavalry charges, infantry in line marching forward into the enemy's fire, all the cool old stuff that worked so well for Napoleon. And as a predictable result of that, the piles of decomposing corpses just kept getting higher, and both sides stayed in pretty much the same damn spot the whole time, so you could get real familiar with all the rotting faces.

An experience like that changes your perspective forever. You go back to life after the war and try to find Normal again. Except now you're seeing the bare bones sticking out of the flesh—because you just spent three years looking at faces around you rotting until the bones were showing. And this becomes the New Normal. So it was understandable that a sense of horror took over the paintings—but horror pretending to be normal. The paintings start to look like a really good cartoonist took LSD, watched zombie movies all night, took a few more hits, and then started painting. The sense of normalized, extreme horror comes at you right off the canvas, and it maybe hits harder because it's super grotesque but still feels sort of realistic.

So it's not really the kind of thing most collectors want to hang over the dining table. And if you have a couch that goes with the colors in these paintings, you've got big problems—and a really horrible couch. For some reason, a lot of people object to hanging up paintings of animated rotting corpses, scary-looking naked women, heaps of grinning dead bodies, that kind of thing. All this means it's maybe not the most popular kind of painting—which is probably one reason I like it so much.

One of my favorites of these painters is a guy named Otto Dix. You've probably never heard of him, because, like I just said. Not really popular. World War I changed him forever. He had recurring nightmares afterward, and definitely had PTSD, even though that wasn't a thing yet. His paintings show it; they tend to be little tours of Nightmare World, images that rip into your head and give you bad dreams, too.

This exhibition had a bunch of Otto Dix paintings, and some I'd never seen before, so I went on in and checked them out. Gorgeous. I mean, maybe not within the ordinary definition of "gorgeous," because, you know. Not many people find rotting flesh and so on gorgeous. But I couldn't peel my eyeballs off them. And after fifteen minutes I came to one I'd never seen before, not in person or in picture, and it really hit me. It was titled *Good-bye to the Good Times*, and it depicted two badly maimed and scarred soldiers waving farewell to a pile of corpses.

I was putting my eyes onto every inch of the picture when I heard a soft female voice behind me. "You could fall right in, couldn't you?"

I jumped, I admit it. It's not easy to sneak up on me, because I know there are plenty of people who would like to do that, and with bad intentions. I whipped around to see who it was.

The woman was about thirty, five foot six with a slim figure and skin so pale it probably glowed in the dark. She was grinning at me from under short red hair, green eyes lit up with the fun of it. "Aw now, did I put the fright up you?" She spoke with the lilt of an Irish accent.

"Of course not. I don't know the meaning of the word."

She snorted. "Yes, I thought you'd jumped like a rabbit out of good manners."

It might have been insulting, but for some weird reason it made me like her. I played along. "Not at all. It's just in my DNA. You wouldn't have a carrot, would you?"

She shook her head. "Left them all in my other jacket," she said, and we both went back to looking at the painting. I really liked it, and it looked pretty good to me, so I asked the obvious question. "You don't much like it, do you?"

She shrugged. "I'm not a big fan of zombie apocalypse movies, either."

"Yeah, I'm not, either," I said. "But something about this artist's paintings really grabs me."

She shuddered. "I shouldn't much care to be grabbed by anything this man might dream up."

"Maybe not. But . . ."

"Oh, dear God, you find it beautiful, don't you?" she said, and she looked properly horrified.

I shrugged. "I guess so," I said. "In a weird kind of way, it reveals a sort of truth, and, uh—truth is beauty."

"And beauty is truth. That is all you know in this world," she said softly.

"And all you need to know," I said, finishing the quote.

She looked at me with a new, slightly appraising expression. "Well," she said. "An American who likes weird art *and* knows his Keats."

"Can't help it," I said. "Besides the lightning reflexes, I have an amazing IQ, too."

She cocked her head to one side and studied me for a moment. "You wouldn't be the illegitimate grandson of Albert Einstein, would you?"

"No, Alan Turing," I said.

She nodded. "That's very illegitimate indeed," she said. She stuck out her hand. "Caitlin O'Brian," she said.

I took her hand. It was warm and soft. "I'm Harry," I said. "Harry Metzger." Because right now, that's who I was, according to my passport. To be completely honest, Harry Metzger, PhD, Associate Professor, History, East Arkansas State University.

I didn't even tell her the "Dr." part, and she still frowned and cocked her head to one side. "Are you, though?" she said. "Metzger? That doesn't quite fit you somehow."

A herd of tiny and very cold feet ran up my spine, because I hadn't done a huge makeover to turn into Harry Metzger, and for a second I thought she had somehow seen through to who I really was. But that wasn't possible, so I just shrugged.

"That's what my passport says," I said. "But I was adopted, so . . ." I shrugged again.

"Ah, well, that would explain it," she said. But she didn't look completely convinced.

"So," I said, figuring it was a good idea to move on. "Are you a fan of German expressionists?"

"Not yet," she said, shaking her head. "But I heard about this exhibit and thought I'd pop in to have a peek." She raised an eyebrow at me. "And you? Do you fancy this sort of thing?"

"I do," I said. "I mean, it probably hints at a very bad character, but I really do like it."

"Well, then," she said, with a very serious face, "convince me."

CHAPTER

3

That's how it started. I don't even know if I convinced her, but by the time we left the gallery together it didn't matter.

There's always a kind of awkwardness when two people are together for the first time. Especially in a case like this, when one of them is an incredibly hot woman and the other one is a man who has been on his own too long. There's a long, uncertain probing process that happens, with the guy trying to figure out if she's interested and if she's worth it. And at the same time she's probing back, trying to figure out what kind of asshole he is—because they always are—and whether it's maybe a kind she can put up with or even get to like. So he's watching to see how she takes what he says, and where her eyes go, and she's trying to figure out what the hell he meant by *that* and is it time to fish out the pepper spray. Until, finally, either the two of them get on the same page or one of them decides absolutely not.

For some reason, that didn't happen with me and Caitlin. Almost from the first moment in the gallery, standing in front of that horrible-wonderful Otto Dix, we just clicked. By the time we stepped into the street, there was no hint of any kind of awkwardness. We walked along, talking, laughing, and snarking at the Londoners we passed like we'd known each other for twenty years. We slid into an easy, happy connection we didn't have to work at, without worrying about what happened next. We went into one more gallery—some way-too-pious etchings from Edwardian country life—and then agreed enough was too much, and anyway, wasn't it time to eat something?

It was, so we decided we would. But since it was a little too late for lunch and a little too early for a real dinner, we decided a drink first would be a grand idea.

"Happy hour," I said.

She cocked her head to one side and looked at me, like a robin deciding if the worm was any good. "I'm sure it is," she said. "But—"

"It's an American thing," I said. "What the bars call cocktail time."

"In the first place," she said sternly, "I think you mean *pubs*. And in the second—we don't really have a formal name. It's just, *Hello, let's pop down to the pub for a pint*. And in any case—*happy hour*? Really? Is it actually happy?"

"Not remotely. And it's usually two hours. But it's also kind of early, and the drinks are usually half price, so mostly the people who show up are tragic alcoholics, if you know what I mean."

"God's sake, man—I'm Irish. Of course I know."

"Well, so you look in on happy hour in most places, and it's just about the least happy thing you can see without wanting to rend your garments."

"Not my garments, thank you, they're rather pricey."

"What you see is a handful of shabby people slouched over their drinks and staring into space. They look like they're all coming from a funeral."

"You've never been to an Irish wake, have you?"

"And it's dead quiet, unless some idiot puts money in the jukebox. And then everybody turns and glares at them until they slink away."

"All that being said, why on earth would you suggest we should have a happy hour?"

"I was afraid we were having too much fun," I said without thinking. And as I said it, it hit me that—*shit*—I actually was having *fun*. Which is something I don't do. Fun is a distraction; it keeps you from paying attention to the important stuff, like staying alive. And while you're giggling, somebody else, whose idea of fun is to see how much blood you have inside you, is probably sneaking up behind you with an assegai.

Just to be sure, I looked behind me. No assegais in sight. Not even a nakiri knife. I looked back at Caitlin, who was watching me with one eyebrow raised. "Sorry," I said. "Somebody walking on my grave."

"Well, it could be worse," she said. "You might be in it."

I looked around again and saw just as much nothing as I had seen the first time. I felt her hand on my arm.

"Come on," she said. "Let's find our tragic happy hour."

She led me down an alley, across what might have been Grosvenor Square, through a twist of small streets and then, triumphantly, up to the door of a battered and dingy old place with a sign that read, BRENDAN'S.

"A word of advice?" Caitlin said. "Order a Guinness?"

"But I don't like—"

"Hush," she said, placing a finger on my lips. "Don't even think that here. Much safer to insult St. Patrick." She nodded solemnly and pushed open the worn wooden door.

Immediately, a multimedia blast hit me in the face, a cloud of acrid tobacco smoke carried by a cool wind, a bright burst of singing in a room much darker than the street outside. I paused for a moment, blinking to adjust to the dimness and trying to take it all in. Caitlin took my arm and pulled me in, and the door swung shut behind us.

Off to my left, a man and a woman concentrated fiercely on a vicious game of darts. On the right, a wooden bar ran the length of the room, with a great tier of shelves behind it, holding dozens of bottles in all the many shapes and flavors of whiskey, gin, brandy, cognac, even American exotics like bourbon. And behind the bar, a stout, red-haired woman held a glass under a gleaming bronze tap, frowning angrily at the glass as the level of the light brown foam slowly rose up its side. A dozen men and women lined the bar, facing the back of the room and singing.

And back at the far end of the room, the green, white, and orange flag of the Irish Republic hung on the wall. In front of it a slender young woman stood on a raised wooden platform, about a foot off the floor. She sang in a pure, unpolished alto voice, leading the crowd through the chorus of a song about love and small free birds. As I followed Caitlin across the floor, the chorus ended and the throng of drinkers fell silent as the young woman sang the verse.

Caitlin paused at the bar and called, "A pair of pints, please!"

The barkeep looked up, nodded, went back to frowning at the glass, and Caitlin led us across the floor to an empty booth with a great view of the dart game. A frost was growing visibly between the two dart players. The man threw and clearly scored; he said something unpleasant to the woman and picked up his drink—not a Guinness but a tall and chilly glass with a wedge of lime on the rim.

Caitlin and I settled into our booth, facing each other across a table that looked like people had been carving things onto it for at least three hundred years. I looked back at the barkeep. She now held two mugs and was glaring at each of them alternately. I looked back at Caitlin. She was scanning the room, maybe looking for familiar faces. I cleared my throat, and she looked back at me.

"You didn't say pints of what," I pointed out.

Caitlin snorted. "You did notice, did you not, that you are in an Irish establishment?"

"Oh," I said. "That would explain the flag."

"And the name, Brendan's," she said. "And the fact that people are happy, singing, and every one of them clutching a pint of Guinness." She frowned. "Except that cheeky wee fucker at the dartboard with a gin and tonic. Probably a British spy." She glared at the man, then nodded. "Well, and no doubt there will be a nice bit of gelignite waiting for him when he leaves, the vile manky wanker."

"I thought the Troubles were all over," I said.

"It's Ireland. It never ends. It just changes shape." She looked down at the tabletop and ran a finger across a deeply carved word I couldn't read.

The mood had gone dark so quickly it had taken me by surprise. It felt like we had fallen into one of those conversational tiger traps. You know; you're having a great time going on about the weather and you say something about lightning. And the person you're talking with so happily all of a sudden falls silent—because there was no way you could have known it, but it turns out their mother was killed by lightning. Snap! You have stepped on the innocent-looking branches covering a deep dark hole lined with spikes, and you fall through the camouflage and into the tiger pit, and the good times are over. And since you don't know what caused it, you don't know how to climb out.

She was still silent when the song ended and the crowd applauded, yelling and whistling, and the girl on the platform made a small curtsy and hopped down. But across from me, Caitlin was still staring moodily at the table. I figured it was my duty to try to pull us out of the trap and back into the fun part. I cleared my throat and said, "Manky wanker is good."

Caitlin looked up and raised an eyebrow. "Is it the sentiment or the poetry of it you like?"

"The poetry," I said. "Insulting someone is a neglected art. Ever since Cyrano died."

"Ah, that poor bastard," she said. "He had the way of an insult."

"He did," I said. "But tragically, it turns out he was French."

"Nobody's perfect," she said. "At least he wasn't English."

Just in time, I stopped myself from asking—are you really that pissed off at the English? I mean, anybody could be. They have that snotty attitude, and they drive on the wrong side of the road. But it obviously went a lot deeper with Caitlin. Just making a wild guess, based on little things like the whole evening so far, I would have to say it might have something to do with being Irish. So I closed my mouth before anything stupid came out. I mean, I didn't want to step in another tiger trap.

But Caitlin noticed that I had been about to say something and then didn't. "What?" she said. "Out with it."

"I, uh, I'm getting thirsty," I said. "And I was wondering if it always takes that long to pour a glass of beer."

She shook her head as if that was a truly stupid question, but she should have expected it from a manky wanker like me.

"In the first place, it's not beer, it's Guinness," she said. "In the second, you don't pour a pint of Guinness—you *build* it. And for third, yes, it always takes that long, and if it doesn't, you're getting cheated."

"I think the American way is easier," I said. "You just open the can."

"Oh, truly, the American way," she said. "Throw out everything good, substitute whatever is *easy*, and before you know it you all weigh one hundred and fifty kilos and you're permanently banjaxed and half asleep in your comfy chair watching *Real Housewives*."

"Wow," I said. "That sounds like paradise."

There was a piercing whistle from the bar, and the barkeep held up two large mugs and nodded at us. I started to stand to go get them, but Caitlin waved me down.

"I'm buying," she said. And before I could object, she was up and away to the bar.

I watched her walk, and I enjoyed it. She didn't sway seductively or anything like that. She walked with grace and purpose, moving like a really good athlete, but at the same time, completely feminine. And as I thought that, I realized it was exactly the kind of thing a fatheaded guy would think watching a woman he was starting to like a little too much.

Caitlin said something to the barkeep, and the two of them looked toward the dart players and shook their heads. Then she picked up the two mugs and brought them back, setting them carefully on the table as if she was scared she might break a bubble in the foamy head.

"There now," she said. "Try to pretend that you like it."

I sipped. As a rule, I don't much like thick brown beer. But this was a lot better than I'd thought it would be, so pretending wasn't that hard. We drank our pints and talked, and I managed not to say anything to break the mood again. And when the pints were gone and my stomach was sloshing and growling, it was definitely time to eat.

"And this time," I told Caitlin as we stepped out of Brendan's and into a pleasant London evening, "it's on me."

We walked out of the alley to the main street, and happily for my gurgling stomach, a black cab was just cruising by. I stuck out my hand, and he swerved to the curb to pick us up.

"Twenty-Eight Berkeley Square," I told the driver.

"Yes, sir. Morton's it is," he said, and we were off.

Caitlin looked at me with both eyebrows up. "Morton's?" she said. "And I've left my tiara at home."

"We can ask them to lend you one."

"Seriously, Harry," she said. "They're known to be a bit stuffy about dress, aren't they?"

"I'll reason with them," I said.

She gave me a very odd look but said no more.

In truth, I didn't think it would take a whole lot of reasoning. When I came to London as Harry Metzger, I had wanted a quick and easy way to show the natives I was credible. Dealing with the staff at the British Museum, and anywhere else my research might take me, I wanted something that said I was one of the "Right People," even for an American. Morton's did that in one. And if you thought Morton's was an American steak chain, you are exactly the kind of low-class riffraff they're trying to keep out. This one was a members-only exclusive, upper-crust London club that said everything without saying it. Besides, it was supposed to have the best wine cellar in London, and a new chef, who everybody said was a genius. And since all it took to join was a big chunk of cash, and I still had a few hundred million lying around, I was in.

The chef lived up to his advance notice, and so did the wine list, so I'd been going there frequently. I got to know the staff, because I make it a practice always to get to know them, wherever I go. You never know when you might need a special favor—you know, a little help hiding a body or something. And honestly? They're usually a lot nicer than the guests they have to put up with. So I built up a relationship with the staff at Morton's, and they'd come to know me as a cheerful American with too much money and not enough sense, the kind of guy who would forget his blazer but happily slip the doorman an impressive amount of currency to be led inside to a private room where my unblazered appearance wouldn't frighten anyone. And to be totally honest, I was kind of hoping to impress Caitlin. I mean, membership at Morton's is kind of an eyebrow raiser. And when I took it to the next level with the whole they-know-me-here thing, done with the right dash of casual confidence, I thought it might score me a few points.

Luckily for me, the man on the door was someone who had shown me before that he had a true aficionado's appreciation for cash. He opened the door of the cab with a formal flourish and then saw my face.

He assumed a scolding tone and said, "Dr. Metzger! You have forgot your jacket again!"

"Hello, Hamza. Yeah, I'm sorry." I lowered my voice confidentially. "I kind of wanted to impress my date, so . . . Is that private room available tonight?"

He looked appropriately doubtful. "I don't know. I will see . . ."

"Thanks, I would really appreciate it, Hamza." I shook his hand—and, of course, there were four fifty-pound notes folded up in the handshake.

Hamza didn't even look. He didn't need to—a good doorman is

a master of money counting by touch, and his eyes widened slightly. "But for you, Dr. Metzger, I am sure we can find something. Please, come in."

Hamza led us inside and around the perimeter of the main room, presumably so as many diners as possible would be spared the sight of us, me with no jacket and her without her tiara. Then, with a knowing wink, he handed us off to Clive, a waiter I already knew. Clive bowed and took us up the stairs to a small private room at the back. It is not well-known, since part of the purpose of going to a club is to socialize, and most people hang out where they can see and be seen. But I'd had dinner in there a few times when I "forgot my jacket," meaning I just wanted to be alone. Clive held the chair for Caitlin, and I thanked him with a fifty-pound handshake.

The dinner was excellent because, you know—Morton's, new chef, all that. Caitlin started with pumpkin soup, with a main of Black Angus filet. Was pumpkin and beef a sly tribute to dining with an American? If so, I returned the favor by having Cornish crab with cucumber jelly and a main of roast Guinea fowl.

It was very good—but of course it raised a serious problem. Black Angus called for a robust, full-bodied red wine, while Guinea fowl clearly required a hearty white. I solved the problem neatly by getting a bottle of each; Château Lafite for her and a Louis Latour Montrachet for me.

That created a new problem; with wine that good, it always seems kind of sinful not to finish the bottle. And since the dinner went on for a couple of hours, with a great deal of lighthearted banter, we managed admirably. By the time we finished, both bottles were empty and the world seemed like a very happy place. Caitlin held on to my arm as we headed down the stairs and out, whether because she needed my support to navigate a whirling room or just because she wanted to, I couldn't say.

And then we were on the sidewalk in front of the club and we were at That Moment. You know, that sudden time at the end of a date when you abruptly realize that there is a next phase and you're at it. And if you've had a really good time and liked your date, I don't have to spell out what you're hoping that next phase might be. I had had a great time, in fact, and I definitely wanted it to continue. But before I could come up with a smooth way to suggest it, Caitlin flagged down a cab and hopped in—and closed the door behind her.

I knew I had to say something, anything, to stop her from taking off. But it had happened so fast, and yeah, I was so full of amazing wine that, for a long moment, I just blinked.

Just before the cab pulled away, something to say battered its way into my liquid brain.

"Hey!" I called.

Caitlin rolled down the window and looked at me.

"Can I see you again?" I asked.

She looked at me for a long moment. "I think so," she said at last. She gave me a half smile, tapped the driver's shoulder, and the cab was gone into the night, before I could ask anything silly like, *What's your phone number? Where do you live? How the hell do I get in touch with you?*

But somehow, I might get to see her again. That's all I knew. It seemed like a very good thing.

CHAPTER

4

The next few days were weird. I tried to push myself back into my routine; breakfast, go to my carrel, work until my eyes hurt, go to dinner. But it's hard enough to concentrate on dusty old papers at the best of times. And since I couldn't help thinking about Caitlin every time I flipped a page, it started to get impossible. Even worse, I got stuck in a kind of fugue, a time loop of nothing but I-shoulda-said. Like, if I'd tossed off exactly the right line, I might have spent the night with Caitlin. Or, you know—at least got her phone number?

Instead, all I had was that half smile and her even more cryptic good-bye line: "I think so." What the hell did that mean? I mean, I knew what all the words meant. I even knew what they meant when they were strung together into that particular sentence. But seriously— what the hell did they mean when someone just asked if they could see you again?

I went over the whole evening in my head, dozens of times. Every time, it came out the same way; Caitlin had been having a good time with me and showed every sign that she liked me. That had to mean that "I think so," meant yes, she wanted to see me again.

Except that right after she said it, she drove away without giving me any clue about when she could see me again or even *how*. And that obviously meant . . . um . . . what exactly?

It was driving me totally wacky. It was bad enough that I was obsessed with somebody—that's really a lethal distraction for somebody like me—but even worse, there was absolutely nothing I could do about it. Smart money said forget her, walk away. And to be fair to me, I've always been smart money about these things. You don't get to be king of this particular hill if you let yourself form attachments to people. They will always be used against you. Always.

So yeah, absolutely, I knew I should just walk away. And I couldn't. I mean, something about the way she'd left me, with a smile and a maybe, set the hook in deep. It was like it had been designed by somebody who knew me—crafted to keep me, and only me, on a string. And it worked. I flogged myself in all directions. Half the time I was ready to pack a bag and leave London, maybe do the Smithsonian instead. And the other half of the time I was trying to figure how to find her. I went back to the Irish pub, but they claimed they had no idea who I meant, which I should've known they would say. I mean, the Irish and informer phobia.

After a week of this mental merry-go-round, I couldn't take it anymore. After all, there were other birds in the sky. London is like most big cities; it's easy to find somebody for some quick, no-strings sex. But this had somehow turned into a whole lot more. I was acting like a high school kid scheming to get a date with the hot girl. And not even a high school senior. More like a sophomore, somebody who hadn't figured out how to talk to girls yet. That didn't stop me from acting that way, but it was nice to have a label for it. It also made me decide that, things being what they were, I would just hang around London until either I heard from Caitlin, or so much time had passed that it was obvious even to me that I wasn't going to.

Meanwhile I would go back to finding the Nazi treasure train. There was plenty of research to keep me busy.

Except there wasn't. After another week, I hit a dead end. I had followed a series of clues down a faint trail that finally led to one man who had probably been in charge of securing the treasure train, a Gestapo lout named Obersturmbannführer Otto Schleisser. There was no record of his death or capture—he just vanished. But I had one of those lightning bolts of *I wonder if*, and I listened to it. I knew there had been a whole bunch of different ways that Nazis escaped, even as Berlin was falling. Some of them were pretty well documented, easy to check.

So I did. Sure enough, Otto disappeared at about the same time a series of transport planes had left Berlin for Spain. Spain, I knew, was the site of a big Nazi submarine base. And from that base, several U-boats had slipped away, heading for South America, loaded with high-ranking scumbags running for their scumbag lives.

As an obersturmbannführer, or lieutenant colonel, Schleisser would be high-ranking enough, especially if he had something worth saving. Something really valuable, for instance. Like, let's say, the whereabouts of one of the biggest treasures in history, loaded with enough loot to finance a comfy retirement *and* help launch the Fourth Reich—because, yeah, they were already planning for that. They probably still are, if the recent news is any indication.

So it was a decent guess that Schleisser had made it to South America. If he was still alive, he would be 114 years old. Didn't seem too likely—but he might well have left either verbal or written clues. A lot of the Nazis who escaped to South America found a very welcoming new home, prepared in advance and inhabited by sympathetic people. Otto might have married, had children, and told them about the train. Or he could have just bragged about it to his pals after a couple of schnapps. Either way, there was a chance I could find something.

But only if I went to South America. And that meant leaving any chance of hooking up with Caitlin.

I have a pretty definite code. Riley's First Law very clearly states, The work comes first. That obviously meant I should say, *Oh well, this thing with Caitlin could have turned into something, but I'm off to New Deutschland*, and in the background you can hear the male chorus humming something about Duty Calls, farewell. That's what I had to do, my job, go to South America and chase the train. There was no wiggle room; Riley's Laws are strict.

And yet . . . It had been a really long time since I'd been so strongly attracted to a woman. And yeah, I know that part of the attraction was the way she left me with a definite maybe. That was a challenge, and I've never met a challenge I didn't want to beat. Knowing it made no difference. I still wanted to find her.

So there it was. On the one hand, I had to forget Caitlin and go. And on the other hand, I really wanted to stay and *not* forget Caitlin. An impossible contradiction, right?

Right—but if you know me at all, you know the words I live by. *There's always a way.* So I finally did what I always do; I found a third hand.

Not right away. These things take time. You have to spend a while pondering. But happily, I was in one of the best pondering spots on earth—the British Museum. There's nothing like wandering through one of the greatest museums ever to unleash a really good ponder.

I spent a day strolling through the museum. Then another day. It's easy to do. If you have any tiny little scrap of brain and soul, the place has endless things to make them both go aha, or ooh, depending on whether it's your brain or your soul talking. It's room after room of real, tangible history and beautiful objects, things you can look at and feel connected to, stuff you've only read about before.

And if you're a little short on gray cells and depth, fine. The museum has lots and lots of big shiny things that are worth more money than you could spend in a lifetime at Tiffany's. Since I have brain and soul, but I also love loot, the British Museum felt like a place specially designed to keep me happy.

Which it did, for two whole days. And then it made me even happier. Because as I was rambling through the early Roman room, marveling at the goodies, it suddenly came to me. It wasn't the lightning bolt of inspiration I get when I have a truly spectacular idea. Instead, it was the snarky little voice in the back of my head that tells me just how truly fucking stupid I am sometimes.

I was standing in front of the case that held the Portland Vase, which is a real eyepopper of a thing from first-century Rome. It's a vase made of dark blue glass, and it's covered with raised white glass pictures of naked people with heroic figures, cupids, all kinds of stuff like that. It's been restored and repaired a bunch of times, but you can't see any signs of that without getting closer than they let you get.

I was leaning in to look at the reclining nude woman—and just as a fan of art, because seriously, no woman who ever lived had breasts like that. And as I did, the snarky little voice in my head cleared its throat and said, *Gosh, Riley. There sure are a lot of really nice things here. Valuable things, right?*

And I told it to shut up, I was looking at art.

It didn't shut up. It said, *But gee whiz, Riley—weren't you looking for something to do so you could hang around London? And doesn't "something to do" usually mean steal something?*

This time, I listened. Because yeah, that is what it meant. And yeah, come to think of it, I really needed to steal something, and it had to be something impossible. I stood up straight and looked around me. And, of course, the snarky voice wasn't done with me yet. *Gosh, Riley,* it said. *Look at all the cool stuff to steal! Right here in front of your nose!*

I told it to shut up, because, yeah, all very nice items. But most of the stuff in this room was relatively portable. Just smash and grab, no real challenge, and that part of a job is more important to me than the price tag. But there were lots of other rooms. I figured if I worked my way through the museum, I would find something that felt right.

So I went down to the first floor, thinking I should do it methodically. I went through the first three rooms—all beautiful things, but nothing that really hit me. And then I went into Room 4, and it did. It hit me really hard, and I stood and looked at it and smiled and thought, *Okay, this is it.*

I would steal the Rosetta Stone.

CHAPTER

5

I f you are one of those blissfully ignorant numb-nuts who don't know what the Rosetta Stone is—first of all, shame on you, because it's important. Why, anyone with a seventh-grade education ought to know that it's a granodiorite stela inscribed with a mixture of alphabetic, determinative, and syllabic elements in hieroglyphic, demotic, and Greek. That's kind of basic, right? But if you had a public-school education in the US, I'll translate.

The Rosetta Stone is a big gray rock. There's a proclamation carved on it in three ancient languages, and it says the same thing in all three. When the French army found it in 1799, nobody could understand two of the three. The Brits grabbed it from the French and immediately slapped it into—ta-da!—the British Museum. Scholars worked on it for twenty years and finally figured out what it said. The message was the same in all three scripts, which was a big help, because ancient Greek was mostly known. Character by character they deciphered the demotic and Egyptian, and that's how we can read Egyptian hiero-glyphics nowadays.

Just as a side note, because it's funny: The Stone was found in Egypt, which technically means it belonged to Egypt. The French stole the Stone from the Egyptians. Then the Brits stole it from the French. And when Egypt finally got around to asking to have it back, we have one of the truly inspiring acts of international generosity in modern history. Did the Brits give the Rosetta Stone back to Egypt? Of course not! Instead, they made a full-scale fiberglass replica and presented that to Egypt! Real authentic top-quality fiberglass! Doesn't that warm your heart?

It's kind of typical of the British Empire's way of doing things—but then again, it also gave me a really self-righteous feeling about stealing it—*How does it feel, huh? Serves you right!*

It was going to be tough to pull off, too, and like I said, that's important to me. If you're only in it for the money, there are millions of things you can steal, no matter how clumsy and stupid you might be. That's not for me. I didn't get to be the very best thief ever by shoplifting, purse snatching, or grabbing stuff from art galleries with primitive security. For me, the cash payoff is secondary. I mean, don't get me wrong, I love having money. But what I love more, what I absolutely *need*, is to take something that everybody else agrees is absolutely impossible to steal. And if I grab it from the snotty overprivileged .1 percent of entitled born-into-it asshats who are holding it in a hereditary death grip—that makes it even sweeter, because I hate those trust fund shit bags. And to be perfectly fair, the Brits made the mold for that kind of self-loving born-rich butthead.

On top of that, it was important that nobody would ever waste two seconds wondering if somebody might steal the Rosetta Stone. Because nobody ever would. Nobody but me.

There were good reasons for that. For starters, there was the Stone itself. It's a pretty tough thing to push out the door. It weighs almost a ton, and if you figure a way to get it up on wheels, someone is bound to object. Because the Stone is pretty distinctive-looking, and they don't sell full-size souvenir replicas in the gift shop.

And, of course, there are a lot of security measures like CCTV—cameras everywhere, and they record what they see. Because I'd just been looking for the fun of it, I hadn't made a full catalog of all the ways it was protected, but as a professional I couldn't help noticing little things like wireless motion detectors and some things that looked suspiciously like pressure sensors.

None of that worried me. I had gotten around all that stuff and more, dozens of times. I was pretty sure I could do it again, any time I wanted to. Because I don't just snip wires or spray-paint cameras. What I like to do is make all that stuff irrelevant. So everybody is like, *Hey, no alarms went off and none of the cameras show anything weird—but holy crap, the jewels are gone.* So it's more like a magic trick than a straight heist.

I took one more trip around the room, looking at the Stone from all angles and snapping a few casual photos. Then I got to work.

CHAPTER

6

She owned the Irish crown jewels.

Jessica Trahan still had trouble believing it. But there they were, the star and badge, missing for a hundred years—and now sitting right there in front of her, perched on dark green velvet atop a plinth in her home's basement vault. For the last three months, Jessica had spent a very large part of her waking hours here in the vault, just looking at them. She still couldn't quite believe it was true. There was just too much history attached—and not just Irish national history, either.

Her great-grandfather Cormac Fitzgerald had begun searching for the jewels some eighty years ago, when it was clear to him that the authorities were either too incompetent to find them or else somehow complicit in their disappearance. As a true Irish patriot, he felt it was his duty to find the jewels, and he took a holy vow that he would find them and return them to their proper place, in Dublin Castle. He had died without finding them, as had his son, Bernard.

Bernard's only surviving child had been Fiona, Jessica's mother. She had failed to find the jewels, too. But the bedtime stories she had told young Jessica had all been Irish tales, and perhaps because of the history of family sleuthing, the search for the jewels had been central to many of the stories.

Jessica grew up, of course, and the stories stopped. But they had made a very deep impression on her, along with the notion that it was somehow a family duty to search for them. And a year and a half after her mother's death, Jessica began to feel the pull of that responsibility.

And so the quest passed down to Jessica. At first it was mostly a hobby. After all, how could she even begin? It just didn't seem real to her, especially against the backdrop of her opulent life here in the Maryland countryside, in what was basically an estate. Her father, William, had inherited a great deal of money, and he had grown it exponentially. Jessica had grown up with horses and expensive cars and ski trips to Switzerland. Somehow, an ancient family quest for some missing jewelry seemed kind of fantastic.

But she would still flip through the several volumes of research compiled by her forebears now and then, all the documents, rumors, photographs, and articles that three generations of her family had hoped might shed some small light on where the jewels had gone. Mostly she just looked at the pictures, enjoying the sense of connection to her family's past.

And one day, her father, Bill Trahan, caught her with the final volume, the one her mother had been working on when she died. He took the book from her, flipped through a few pages, and then simply held the book silently. The page that had stopped him held a picture of her mother. And to Jessica's surprise, she saw a tear roll down her father's cheek.

"Dad . . . ?" she said hesitantly.

"This meant so much to your mother," her father said, tapping the book.

"I know," Jessica said. "And her father and her grandfather—"

"But not to you?" he said.

It sounded to Jessica like an accusation, and it caught her off guard. "I—I don't know," she stammered. "It never seemed, like—totally real?" She shrugged. "And, you know. I'm not any kind of detective? And it's been so long, I just—where would I start? And how?"

Her father frowned and didn't say anything for a moment. Then he abruptly closed the book. "My family has a tradition, too," he said. "When you hit a problem you can't handle, throw money at it." He looked up at her, his eyes bright. "That's one thing your mother's family never tried. But we can. Let's do this, Jess. We have plenty of money. We'll hire somebody, the best somebody, to find the jewels." He laid the book gently on the table. "For your mother."

And so they had. Through a series of shadowy business connections her father had gathered over the years, they had found a man for the job. He was supposed to be the best—he even said so. Very expensive, but he did it. He found the crown jewels and delivered them to the Trahans. Somehow, the last part of the quest, returning them to Dublin, had been overlooked, and the crown jewels stayed right here in the Trahans' Maryland basement.

Jessica thought about returning them, but she was getting too much pleasure out of looking at them, touching them, savoring the historical importance to her family. And, of course, the hypnotic gleam of the gems. She leaned closer, looking at the play of lights on the badge. Beautiful. And it was hers now. She could just look all day, and—

There was a noise behind her, a muffled scuffling sound, and Jessica turned to look. Her father stood in the door of the vault, strangely blank-eyed and unmoving. "Dad . . . ?" Jessica said. "What's wrong?"

Bill didn't answer. Instead, he toppled forward, slowly at first, and then falling to the floor face-first with an awful wet thud.

And as much as she wanted to rush to her father and see if he was all right, Jessica did not. First, because she was fairly certain he was *not* all right. No one could be with that large knife sticking out of their back.

But the more important reason was that someone stood in the doorway where her father had been a moment before. They had a second knife, just as large, and its tip was pointed at her. And behind the knife, the coldest eyes Jessica had ever seen. Focused on her, just like the knife.

"They're *mine*." The voice was a venomous hiss, but the eyes . . .

The eyes told her everything. Jessica wanted to scream, to throw something to run. She didn't. The most she managed was a whimper.

That was the last sound she made.

CHAPTER

7

No matter what the New Agers tell you about self-actualizing, deciding to steal something like the Rosetta Stone is not quite the same thing as actually doing it. I had to have a plan, and it had to be spectacular. It was a little harder than usual to get going because, after all, I was just killing time until I hooked up with Caitlin. And anyway, I'd been sitting around reading for weeks, and I needed something to jump-start my creative process.

So I did what I always do when I need to think. I grabbed my MP3 player and headed out for some fresh air. It's kind of hard to find in London, but I figured air pollution is heavy, so the more elevation I had, the fresher the air would be. I waited until it got dark and the museum closed for the day, and then I strolled back to Bloomsbury, clipped in my earbuds, and fired up the tunes.

I don't stream other people's crappy playlists. They're usually based on what's popular, which means a lot of people with no taste had decided it was good. Screw that. I had a playlist I'd built over the course of my whole life, based on what was actually *good*. Tonight, I started out with Rockpile "Play That Fast Thing." It gets you moving, and I needed that, because I hadn't done any parkour recently, and I was a little rusty. I cranked the volume and went to the side of the museum, en route to the roof.

The museum is neoclassical, which means there were lots of things to hold on to on the way up, and in about thirty seconds I was sitting on the tessellating glass roof of the central court.

I let Rockpile play out and went on to something contemplative—Boccherini Cello Concerto #9—and I took a deep breath. It was still the same old dirty London air, but the view was a whole lot better. You can't have everything. And then I thought about it.

The big problem was taking away something that weighed almost a ton. You can't really slip it under your shirt and stroll for the door, whistling a happy tune. In the past, I'd snagged even bigger, heavier things, usually using a Chinook helicopter with a pilot I trust. That wasn't an option this time. The only possible way in for a chopper was right here, via the huge glass roof I was sitting on. But I didn't even think about trying that. I mean, yeah, sure, it's glass—but it's over three thousand separate panels of the stuff, held together by four miles of steel, and it weighs something like eight hundred tons. So, okay, I did think about it, just long enough to look up the specs and make sure it was not an option. It would take a couple of days to break enough of the glass to get through, and it's too heavy to move. So I wasn't up there looking for a way in. I just wanted a place to sit and get inspired, close to the thing I was going to steal.

It should have been a perfect spark. But I spent like five minutes admiring the view, and then I was mooning about Caitlin again. I mentally slapped myself. Maybe it was the music—Boccherini is kind of romantic. I skipped ahead and played Miles Davis's "In a Silent Way," instead. Kind of stoned and trancey. Much better. . . .

I let my brain drift. But still nothing came to me. Probably because I wasn't organized enough. "Enough"? Hell—I wasn't organized at all. I'd just jumped into this on a whim. I hadn't even thought about where or how to start. So I thought about that. If I ever teach a class on how to heist, I'd probably have it structured with three basic approaches. First, and simplest, grab and go. No subtlety, just take it and run to a prearranged getaway. And the getaway is where you get creative with this approach. Like, do something unexpected; a hang glider, or a submarine or something. Anything that will leave the pursuit just gaping after you and going, *Oh, shit. Didn't see that coming.*

That was not going to work here. Like I said, the Stone is a bit hefty for that. So the second technique: shock and awe. That usually means violence, or the threat of it, and I freaking *hate* it. In the first place, it mostly requires a couple of nasty-looking helpers, which almost certainly ends up with one of them turning on you. In the second place, violence as a means of acquisition sucks. Where's the fun in it? Seriously—gimme that or I smash your head with a rock? Boring. It also makes cops a lot more interested in getting you, and they won't do it gently.

My favorite is number three: Watch this hand! If you've ever seen a good magician work and wondered, *How did they do that? I was watching the whole time!* Yeah, you were, but you were watching in the wrong place. The magician makes sure your eyes are on their right hand—and they're doing the trick with their left.

That's how I like to work. I make you expect to see something—no, I make you really *see* it—and then I do something that can't possibly fit into that picture. That's the kind of thing I needed to come up with now. But I'd been spending all my time in the reading room, rubbing dust out of my eyes. I needed to get my groove back, and the best way to do that was doing the sort of reconnaissance where I walk around the target from every possible angle, and a couple that are not really possible.

A lot simpler, right? Sure it is. Except the details are kind of important, like what's the distraction and what's the trick. Which is why there aren't that many really good magicians. Also why there's only one Riley Wolfe. I always find a way. Always. And it's never what anyone expects—not what anyone else can even imagine. I would find that this time, too.

Just probably not tonight. I let Miles Davis play to the end. I didn't come up with anything, except that Caitlin would probably like the view from up here, too. That didn't seem really productive, but at least it was better than just thinking that I couldn't come up with anything. I gave up, put on Jobim—"O Boto"—and climbed down. If you don't know the tune, it's the kind of music that's easy to get lost in. Lots of cool changes in volume, orchestration, everything. And, of course, it's Jobim, so a great melody and rhythm. I like it a lot. That's probably why I wasn't paying attention.

So when I hopped over the fence and my feet hit the pavement, I didn't see anything at all until the hand came down on my shoulder and the voice said, "Right—you're nicked."

CHAPTER

8

've been living on the dark side of the street my whole life. Living in a place where shadows hide enemies, the stranger approaching you is never a friend, and something is always just about to jump out at you. "Eternal vigilance is the price of freedom" was written for people like me, because if we nod off even for a second, we're going to find ourselves with a really good close-up view of a set of steel bars.

Living with that kind of constant threat gives you truly great reflexes when something unexpected happens. So when I felt that hand, I had a lifetime of training to draw on.

I froze anyway.

Just stood there like a total chump.

Totally off my game.

"Now, then, let's have a look at you," the voice went on. The hand pushed me around and shined a flashlight in my face. I blinked and turned my head, and after a moment the light clicked off.

"Right. No trouble now, we'll have a car round to take you in."

I'd been near blinded by the flashlight, but my sight came back enough to see who had me. It was a middle-aged man in the uniform of a London cop, which I kind of expected, but with a couple of differences. First, he was wearing a helmet; not the kind you're thinking of, the "bobby" helmet you see in all the old pictures. It was a bicycle helmet. And to round off his ensemble, he was wearing a pair of shorts.

My humiliation was complete. It was bad enough to get caught like that. But to get caught by a cop wearing shorts—a *bicycle* cop!—no. It was too much. My pride might never recover.

That was probably what woke me up, the sight of those shorts. As he reached for his radio, I yelled out, "*Ils ne passeront pas!*" in my perfect French accent, pulled the helmet down over his eyes, and sprinted across the street.

I'd hopped the museum's fence near a dumpster, on Montague Street, and the far side of the street was a line of row houses. The front of each house had one of those fake balconies, just big enough for a flower box and surrounded by a short wrought-iron fence. I figured if I could get one hand on that balcony, I'd be up on the rooftop and away before the cop could follow.

The helmet over the eyes was an obvious move, and it would gain me maybe a second of run time. The French battle cry had two purposes. First, it startled the cop, and that gave me another second while he tried to figure out what it meant. But it would also confuse things a little because, like I said, my French is perfect, so they'd be looking for somebody from France and not an American professor.

I used those two seconds and really legged it. He almost caught me anyway. I guess the whole bicycle thing kept him in good shape, because I barely made it to the ornamental fence in front of the row house and he was reaching for me. I leaped for the balcony, with his fingers brushing my foot. But he didn't get a grip on me, and I was up the front wall, onto the roof, and away.

I went across to the back side, down on Bedford Place, and up again on the other side. I turned right and ran across the rooftops all the way down to the end of the block, and then down into Bloomsbury Square. I cut across the garden and over to Russell Square, where there was a Tube station, and rode the train home. And for the whole ride, I sat there replaying the truly stupid thing I had just done, and I had only one thought.

What the hell was wrong with me?

I t was very late by the time I got back to my little flat, but I didn't go to bed. First, because the cops got a good look at me, I needed to change my appearance. But I also needed to be recognizable for if—when!—Caitlin got back in touch. I shaved my mustache. I'd grow out my beard, too. It wasn't a lot, but I thought it would be enough. What the hell, the cop hadn't taken any photos.

Next, I put on some thinking music—Schubert's D Minor String Quartet—and opened a bottle of Cognac Frapin Château Fontpinot XO. I poured a big slug into a snifter and sat at my desk, swirling the liquor and letting my hand warm it. And I asked myself again: *What the hell is wrong with me?*

The first dose of cognac didn't take me any further than Caitlin. I was thinking about her and not about the job. But the second glass opened something up. Of course I wasn't thinking about the job. I had been thinking about Caitlin.

So now I had a new question: *Did I really want to do this?*

I didn't know. Not a clue. I put my mind in neutral while I sipped and tried to shut out everything except the music. Nice bit of cello there. Sip. I finished the cognac as the quartet finished. The first light of dawn was leaking in through the window. I stood up and went to the window. On the street below, the first few people were hurrying along, clutching briefcases, purses, cups of coffee or tea. Morning in the former heavyweight champion of the world city.

It was really a stupid idea, stealing the Rosetta Stone. Doing it just because I was bored. Did I really want to do something that senseless? I felt an enormous yawn stretch my whole face out of shape and turned from the window. But just before my head hit the pillow and I conked out, I had one last thought.

Yeah. I really wanted to do it. Because that's who I am. And if I was only doing it because I had to do *something*, fine. All the more reason to do it. Idle hands are the devil's workshop, as Mom used to say. I never really figured out how that was supposed to work, but Mom was usually right. So I probably should do something. Why not this?

Okay. I would find a way, and I would do it. Next: What had changed as a result of me being so freaking stupid tonight? On the downside, they would have my description now, because the cop had gotten a really good look at my face. On the plus side, they'd think I was French. Even plus-ier—*Hey! It's me! Riley Wolfe, master of disguise.* I don't have to look anything like me—like Harry Metzger me. I can do recon looking like anybody I want.

In the words of the philosopher James Carrey—all righty, then.

CHAPTER

9

Nigel Blount loved his job. That's rare enough in today's world. But the reason he loved it was even more uncommon. Whatever perverse reason or childhood trauma made him this way, Nigel loved people, and he loved talking to them and, if possible, helping them. It made him happy. And his job gave him hundreds of opportunities to meet and help every single day, because Nigel was a security guard at the British Museum.

Today he was having a nice chat with a lady from the States. She'd asked where the Greek vases were, and he'd explained that she was in Egypt, Room 4, and she wanted Room four-*teen*, which was out that door over there and left and then just across the way, and where was she from anyway? Iowa, she said, which Nigel thought was somewhere in the west but he asked to be sure, and then they were just chatting away like old chums. By the time she left to go see her Greek vases, Nigel had given her a long list of other wonders that she just had to see while she was here, and she seemed grateful, which made Nigel happy.

That's when he noticed the older gentleman, leaning on the plexiglass case around the Rosetta Stone. He looked quite stout, eighteen or nineteen stone, his face red, but he had both hands on the case. This was strictly forbidden, and Nigel hurried over.

"Excuse me, sir," Nigel called as he approached. "Please don't touch the— Oh! Are you all right?"

For the old gent was gasping for breath.

The man looked up; he was sweating heavily, and his mouth was open in the middle of his round red face. "Oh my," he said. "Oh Lordy, I'm afraid I went and lost my breath there for a minute." And he gasped again, as if he couldn't quite get enough air in.

Nigel almost smiled, because the old man had a rich American Southern accent, and that was something Nigel loved to hear. But he said, "Shall I call for a doctor? You're quite red in the face, sir."

"A doctor? Oh, no; no, I don't need a doctor," the man said with a half smile. "All this walking, and the excitement! No, I'm just old and fat, and this is what I get for letting myself get in this kind of shape."

"Let me see you to a bench, then," Nigel said. "Just you sit down and you'll be right as rain in two minutes."

"Oh, I'm fine now, really I am," the man said, straightening up. "And I don't want to lose a single minute with this wonderful thing. Why, I've waited my whole life to see the Rosetta Stone in person, and now I'm here? I just don't want to leave."

"Understandable, sir," Nigel said. "It's a true wonder of the world, and no lie."

"I'm sorry if I put a little smudge on the glass," he said, and he took out a handkerchief. "I'll just wipe that down—"

"No, sir, please don't," Nigel said.

The man looked up, clearly puzzled.

"You might set off an alarm," Nigel said. "Can't have that, can we, sir?"

"An alarm? Oh Lordy, no, I wouldn't want to—but is it really necessary to put an alarm on this great big ole thing? Why, it must weigh a ton!"

"Yes, sir, three quarters of a ton, near enough," Nigel said, wiping the case carefully with his own handkerchief. "Or, if you like, 120 stone, as we measure it in the UK."

"Well, that's just it," the old gent said. "Now, for the life of me, I can't imagine anybody trying to steal a thing like that—and you say there's an alarm on it? On the Rosetta Stone?"

"Yes, sir, more than one, actually," Nigel said.

"Well, that really is just the oddest thing," the old gent said.

He seemed to have caught his breath now, Nigel was pleased to see.

"But for the life of me—" He bent his head, chins wobbling, and looked at Nigel's name tag. "Is it Mr. Blount? Rhymes with 'count'?"

Nigel smiled encouragingly. "Yes, sir. But we say it 'Blunt.' But please, just call me Nigel, sir."

The old fellow smiled back. "Well, now I will be glad to do so—if you'll stop calling me 'sir.' Just plain old Cady is fine. Cady Archambeau." He held out his hand, and Nigel shook it. "I'm right pleased to make your acquaintance, Nigel."

"Likewise, Cady," Nigel said.

"Now, what was I on about? Back there a minute ago?"

"The alarms, sir—I mean, Cady."

Cady clapped his hands together. "Yes! That was it, right enough. Now why on earth do you all need more than one alarm on a big old thing, near a ton, that nobody on God's green earth is ever going to be able to move?"

Because the gentleman seemed genuinely interested, and he was a nice old codger, Nigel explained that there were different kinds of sensors, all designed to detect some different form of malfeasance. And watching the gent's eyes widen with surprise and curiosity, he pointed out where all the sensors were located on the case, and then on the Stone itself.

Cady had more questions, lots of them, and Nigel answered them all happily. When the old fellow finally left, it probably should have occurred to Nigel that most of the questions had to do with security. But he was so pleased that he had been helpful it never crossed his mind.

The man was clearly lost. He had that befuddled, hopeful expression that goes with being in unknown territory without any idea of how you got there. Natalie Prentiss thought he looked a bit foreign, too, which didn't make her terribly happy. She'd come out to the loading dock to be alone for five minutes, have a smoke, try to rewind her patience before she went back to her job in the gift shop.

All day she'd been dealing with clueless people. Rude, too, most of them. And this foreign gent looked to be cut from the same cloth. Wrinkled old suit, greasy hair, and good Lord that mustache. He looked like a Marseille pimp coming home from a bender.

And aside from the fact that he was ruining Natalie's break and putting fresh strain on her frayed patience, he definitely had no business being back here on the loading dock. This area was closed to the public.

With a surge of fresh irritation, Natalie ground out her cigarette and turned on the man. "Sir! You can't be back here! This area is off-limits!"

The man gaped at her, mouth moving soundlessly. Going with her assumption that anybody this thick must be French, she said, "*Interdit! Zone fermee!*"

Immediate comprehension flooded across the man's face, and he let out a torrent of gabble. Natalie caught perhaps one word in six, but she nodded. French right enough.

When the man finally wound down, Natalie used just about the last of her French vocabulary. "*Je nes comprens*," she said.

"*Ah! Oui—ou est le toilet, s'il vous plaît?*"

The toilet. It figured. "That way, sir," she said, pointing back down the near hallway. "Down there, on the left. *La gauche!*"

"*Oui, gauche, merci,*" he said.

He added another incomprehensible paragraph, gave her a small bow, and wandered away down the hall—the correct one at least, Natalie thought. She glanced at her watch.

"Shite," she muttered. Time to get back.

The man came striding through security as if he were leading a parade. He had a bushy, ragged beard and a shaved head and looked to be in his thirties, and he wore the kind of high-priced sloppy clothing that tried so hard to be casual that it absolutely screamed, "I am an American with money!" He breezed through the scanner at the front door and then put on a helmet festooned with a microphone that hung in front of his face. A GoPro video camera was mounted on top. The man ostentatiously turned it on and then began to walk rapidly into the museum, talking in a loud voice with a harsh, nasal accent.

"The British Museum is, like, the most amazing museum anywhere. Like, in the whole freaking *world*! They got stuff like you wouldn't believe from all over the damn world. Hard to believe now, but the British used to practically *own* the whole damn world! That's how they got all this incredible stuff! Stole it from countries they took over! Some of it—it's thousands and thousands of years old and it would blow your mind! Kaboom!" He made a gesture of a mind being blown and continued his rapid progress in. "And here I am, right there, in the goddamned museum, and I'm taking you with me."

One of the guards at the door looked after him, but there was such a large queue waiting to clear security that he simply shook his head and went back to checking bags.

The annoying American moved quickly and steadily down the perimeter of the Great Court, chattering in his loud and grating voice, punctuating his prattle with frequent obscenities and current street slang. He turned left into the Egyptian room, announcing, "And *dude*! This is like two light-years past awesome! It's stuff that fucking *Cleopatra* hung out with! Wait'll you see—"

He meandered down the long room, slowing his pace now and then, stopping at some of the gaudier and less significant treasures— but never stopping his persistently irksome monologue.

One of the guards at last politely asked him to lower his voice in consideration of the other visitors to the museum, and the man exploded into an angry tirade; his podcast was *viral*! Over 350,000 subscribers! What about consideration for them! And so on until it was clear to the guard that he could either call for help and escort the man out of the museum, or walk away and hope the fellow left soon of his own accord.

He chose to walk away, and the monologue continued for another half hour, until finally, mercifully, the front door closed once again behind the massively irritating podcaster.

CHAPTER

10

When I'm working on a scheme, I go at it full speed. I put all my concentration on it, to the point that I forget to eat. And when I finally remember, it's just quick takeout, and throw the containers somewhere out of the way. So my little flat looked like a gang of grad students cranked up on meth had had a study session that got way out of hand. The walls were covered with pictures of the Stone from all angles, maps of the museum and its exits, stuff like that. Every flat surface was stacked a foot high with books and papers, half-eaten takeout meals, and empty bottles and cans.

I was deep into an idea that involved taking the Stone after clearing the museum with a biological weapon scare, and I had music turned up to an appropriate level for thinking about biohazards—*Metal Machine Music* by Lou Reed. If you've never heard it, my advice is to stay away from it unless you want a serious headache, and probably a hefty dental bill from grinding your teeth. Or unless, you know. You're planning a biohazard?

I say this with great respect to Lou Reed, who was a true artist. And the album itself is brilliant. But there's a big but; it's not actually music by most popular standards. The story I heard was that he went into the studio, turned everything on, turned it all up to its highest settings, and then turned on the tape recorders and walked away. So what you hear is a couple of hours of agonizing feedback—squeals and shrieks and roars of, you know; metal machine music.

The weirdest thing about it is what happens when you listen to it. For the first ten minutes or so, like I said—headache and teeth grinding. But in case you haven't noticed, your brain is a very bizarre thing, and maybe the most peculiar thing about it is, it likes you! It really, really likes you! Which is truly weird, considering it knows all your dark secrets and horrible habits. But yeah, it cares. So when you are being subjected to an awful experience, it tries to change your perception of it to make things a little less painful. Like, if you ever broke your leg, you notice that you kind of get used to the pain after a while.

With *Metal Machine Music*, about ten minutes into listening to it and thinking about poking sharp objects into your ears, all of a sudden the sound changes. I mean, really? *It* doesn't change—*you* do. Your friendly neighborhood brain makes the change. And all of a sudden you hear real, actual *music*. The painful noise you'd been hearing actually gets melodic, even soothing, in a jagged kind of way. And that made it the perfect soundtrack for planning a biohazard. And then to realize, what the f was I thinking?

Because I wasn't. The music was just right, but something wasn't clicking. First, I didn't have a team, and the idea of a solo biohazard response was not going to fly. And even if it did, then what? Carry the

Stone out on a gurney, claiming it was contaminated? That seemed like a pretty tough sell.

I put that idea aside and pondered other options. I could deface the Stone and then come in as the clean-up expert, sneak it away under cover of restoring it. But I'd used that before. That always takes the sparkle off an idea.

For a few minutes I played with the idea of doing a David Blaine. You know, big press conference, and then say, "I can make the Rosetta Stone disappear!" And then I would. Of course, when it came time to bring it back, I would somehow forget how. It sounded fun, and it had a dramatic flair to it I really liked. But the problem with it was coming up with the actual trick. And if I could do that, I didn't need to do it as a fake magician—I could just do it and take the Stone.

Lots of ideas. But when I really looked hard at them, none of them was worth a rusty possum fart.

Pondering turned to stewing, which required half a bottle of Black Bull forty-year Scotch. So I wasn't really thinking clearly when I heard the pounding on my door. I mean, really loud, actual *pounding*, which it had to be or I wouldn't have heard it over the music. I was pretty sure it was a neighbor wanting me to turn down that bloody noise, *if you'd be so kind*. But whoever it was, I just wanted them to go away quickly, so I could get back to work. I opened the door.

I didn't say anything for a long time. I couldn't. Because it was Caitlin.

"Am I interrupting something?" she said.

I just shook my head.

"Well, then, perhaps you'd consider inviting me inside?"

I still couldn't think of anything to say. I just held the door open, and she brushed past me into the flat.

Two steps in she whirled around to face me and said, "And for the love of God, can you stifle that hideous cacophony?!"

I didn't tell her it takes ten or fifteen minutes and then she might like the music. I just switched it off and turned back to see her surveying the mess I'd made of what had never been more than a rather modest apartment. She shook her head dubiously.

"Well, your flat has a certain rustic charm, but I expected rather better from a member at Morton's," she said, looking around with a raised eyebrow. "And would there be a chair at all?"

There would be. It was under a stack of file folders. I moved them to the floor, brushed off the chair's seat, and waved Caitlin into it. I settled into my desk chair and swiveled to face her.

"I like the beard," she said.

"Oh, yes. Uh, good."

"Well," she said, looking around at the heinous mess. "Keeping busy, are you?"

"Oh yes, I, uh—" It hit me that there were an awful lot of papers and pictures scattered around that showed an unhealthy interest in the Rosetta Stone. And I was so completely boggled by her being here that my brain was not working. But I had to say something, so I blurted out, "The, uh—my sabbatical leave will be ending soon, so I, uh. Have to finish my research . . . ?"

"With pictures and floor plans?"

"I, uh—I find it helps to visualize it," I said.

"But you said history—isn't this archaeology?"

"What's that?" For some reason I had no idea what she meant. Like I said, boggled.

"You're a history teacher, aren't you?"

"Yes, that's right," I said. And my cover story came back to me, and I began to babble. "Certain aspects of Ptolemy the Fifth's reign are poorly researched, and I thought, uh—"

I trickled to a halt—first, because I didn't really know a whole lot about any aspects of Ptolemy V's reign. But maybe more important, also because she was giving me the "manky wanker" look again. So I took a deep breath and grabbed at Riley's Fourteenth Law: When in doubt, go on the offensive. "But hey, how did you even find me?"

She shook her head. "The wonder of it is that I didn't see you sooner. My flat is just across the street."

"What? But that's—unbelievable."

"Yes it is—but there it is. Straight across, one window up and two over." She tilted her head toward the window.

"That's—I mean, I wasn't sure I would see you again."

"Nor was I," she said. "But since I'd have to move to avoid it, I thought I should just get it done." She said it so completely deadpan that I wasn't sure if she was kidding.

"Well, I'm glad you did," I said, and I reflexively reached for my glass. "Oh—would you like a drink?"

"I would, actually," she said.

I poured her a generous slug of Black Bull, and she lifted her glass. "Slainte," she said. She sipped, raised an eyebrow. "This is quite good."

"I like it," I said.

She took a larger drink and looked slowly around the room. "So," she said thoughtfully. "Associate professor at a small state university, which I understand means rather financially limited." She sipped again. "And yet—here you are, living it up in one of the more expensive cities in the world, with a membership at an expensive private club, and guzzling whiskey that I will guess costs around a thousand pounds for a bottle . . . ?" She looked at me. "What is wrong with this picture, Harry?"

There's a funny thing that happens to you when you're caught in the spotlight with your pants down. Your whole body goes cold, but you break out in sweat all over. Actors call it flop sweat. That's what happened to me. Because I hate stupid, and I work hard to avoid it, but here I was caught in a really stupid lie. To be fair to me, I hadn't expected to make any social connections here in London, so I hadn't put a whole lot of work into my cover identity. I grew out my hair and dyed it, grew a mustache, but that was about it. Pure sloppiness, and I knew it. When the cover is for a job, I craft it like a Fabergé egg; perfect in every tiny detail, even under a microscope. But now, for Harry Metzger? Not so much. Enough to get me in and out of a foreign country and into the British Museum. But if anybody were to start to close in on me and look too carefully, there were holes. And Caitlin had spotted a couple of big ones.

It seemed like I just sat and sweated for a very long time. It probably wasn't really all that long, but it was enough for Caitlin to notice it.

"What, can't think of a good one? Shouldn't be that hard. Come on, Harry, give it a lash. Where did all this money come from?" she said. "I'm in suspense here—will it be an inheritance, or shrewd investments?"

Of course those were the first two things I'd thought of saying. And now? I had nothing.

"Right," she said. "I'll be going, then." She stood up, started to put down her glass, and paused. "Be a shame to waste this." She drained the glass, made a small *aahh* sound, and put it down.

"Cheers, Harry," she said, and took a step toward the door.

I was in a kind of pain I didn't know anything about. I really didn't want her to leave—but I was out of lies. My mouth went dry, my brain whirled, and I came up with the same nothing.

And then, from somewhere far away, I saw my mouth open. I had no idea what would come out—but the last thing I expected was what actually did come out. "I stole it," I said.

Caitlin paused in mid-step, one foot in the air. Then she put it down and turned to me. "I thought as much," she said.

CHAPTER

11

t turns out this was a day for surprises. Because if I was amazed by what came out of my mouth, I was totally gobsmacked by Caitlin's response.

She looked at me very seriously for a few seconds; not really frowning. More like appraising something before you buy it. And every microsecond of that time I was dead certain she would say something caustic, call me a few foul names, and then stalk out.

Nope. Nothing like. Instead, she nodded and said, "Good, glad that's settled. Could I have a wee small bit more of this lovely whiskey?" And she sat back down and held her glass out to me.

I couldn't think of anything to say, so I filled her glass. I filled mine, too, and took a big gulp as I sat.

"Aren't you going to ask me anything?" I said. "Like, where I stole it, or how or why or . . . anything?"

She shook her head. "You've no reason to trust me with that," she said.

I thought my head was spinning before. Now it was about to whirl off my neck and out the window. Her answer was straight from the Thieves' Code, and it was obviously crazy to think of her with even one foot in my world. Aside from that, I could only think of one plausible reason for her to answer like that.

"Is that—are you saying that because of, um, you know. Growing up with Irish politics?"

Her eyes narrowed. She sipped, and slowly the forehead lines disappeared.

"Yes," she said. "My father was—involved in, as you so nicely put it, Irish politics. And I was raised to believe that nothing is worse than an informer." She shrugged. "You don't tell, and you don't ask, unless you need to know." She sipped her whiskey and then said, "I admit I'm curious, but I don't have the need, do I?"

"Well," I said, which was just about the smartest thing I'd said so far.

I tried again, with "I'm really glad you came to see me."

"Since I got some truth out of you, I'm glad, too," she said. She raised her glass. "And this whiskey is worth the trip even if I wasn't glad."

And with that, there was nothing I could do but help her finish the bottle. Somewhere along the way, something opened up between us. We went back to the easy talk we'd had the night of our dinner at Morton's. Just talk—not really about anything special. Art, since we both liked it, and some history, since I do actually know some, and so did she. Nothing personal from either of us, which was no surprise on my part, since I had no intention of letting her know who I really am. She didn't offer a whole lot, either, which I was okay with. I mean, I had already figured out that she had grown up in a family that was neck-deep in the Troubles, and it had clearly put its mark on her.

After a while we went out for something to eat. Not Morton's this time, just a Jamaican jerk place that was an easy walk from my flat. Some jerk chicken, rice and beans, washed down with Red Stripe beer, and more easy talk. We left the restaurant full and happy and strolled back.

Caitlin stopped abruptly and looked around, blinking. She was swaying slightly; not surprising after a great deal of whiskey and two Red Stripes. "How did that happen?" she said.

I didn't see anything that had happened. "How did what happen?"

"Are you blind? Look!" she said, pointing vaguely upward. "It's gone all nightish!"

I nodded. "So it has," I said. "Should we do anything about that?"

She laughed. It was the first time I'd heard her do that. It was a full throaty sound, and I liked it. "I believe we're doing it," she said.

We walked on, taking our time, but even so, we were at her door much too soon. We paused there on the sidewalk. "Well," she said, and then went silent.

"I guess so," I said.

I looked at her. She looked back.

And then somehow we were kissing, and after that?

I'll just say it was worth the wait.

CHAPTER

12

Autumn was on its way in. But somebody forgot to tell the weather, because Washington, DC, was still firmly wedged into one of the hottest summers on record. It was so hot that people had died from the heat, and there was no end in sight. Anyone who could afford it left the city and headed for higher elevations where the temperatures were a little more reasonable. The majority of the population could not afford it, of course, so they stayed in the city and suffered through the endless summer. The only people who enjoyed the sweltering heat were the movie theater owners, because everyone who couldn't afford air-conditioning of their own was flocking to the theaters. It was well worth $14 to sit in the cool dark theater for a few hours, even if the movie was bad.

As always, there were a few who didn't mind the heat—didn't even seem to notice it. Most of them came from places where days this hot and humid were normal. Places like equatorial Africa and Southeast Asia.

And, of course, Miami, the city that Special Agent Frank Delgado called home. He'd grown up spending all his daylight hours outside in a climate that matched this one, and so the high temperatures and humidity were no novelty for him. He was not immune from its effects, of course. It was only eight o'clock in the morning, and already his shirt under his gray tropical-weight jacket was plastered to his back by the inevitable flow of sweat.

Delgado barely noticed. His focus was on the summons he'd received from the executive assistant director of the Crime Division, the branch of the Bureau in which he'd spent most of his career. The call had come last night, and there had been no hint as to the reason, no clues about the subject, and Delgado was a little anxious. Any call from the EAD was rare enough to cause a trace of anxiety. Not that he had anything to worry about, as far as he knew. Delgado's record of success was enviable. But he had not always adhered to all of the Bureau's rules. Never any serious violation, but an impartial observer would have to admit that he did not always play well with others. His appearance, too, was somewhat outside the accepted standard. His tie was often looser than Hoover would have liked, and his hair was a trifle shaggy for a special agent.

Still, he had achieved near-legendary status with fellow agents for his virtually unblemished record of success. Time after time Delgado had gone after the most difficult and dangerous criminals, and he brought them in almost every time. Almost. Except for some very notable failures, all with the same criminal.

A homicidal thief named Riley Wolfe.

Catching Wolfe had become an obsession for Delgado, a preoccupation that had nearly derailed his career. But not lately; Delgado had been far too busy with postings in far-flung foreign lands. He'd only been back home for a little more than a week, and he was technically on a brief vacation—a mandatory holiday, since he hadn't taken any for several years, as was required, and his vacation days had accumulated to an alarming number.

Which made the EAD's summons even odder, and Delgado a little more anxious. So he walked into the Hoover building fifteen minutes early, in spite of the heinous DC traffic, with its plethora of drivers who had diplomatic immunity and therefore felt they were above the law. He had figured he could sit for a few minutes, allowing the sweat to dry and his nerves to return to neutral. But the secretary waved him right in with a perfunctory, "The EAD is waiting for you," and Delgado had time for only one deep calming breath before he was through the door and into the unknown.

The man behind the desk was not a stranger. Frank Delgado had known him for many years. Robert Buxbaum was almost everything Delgado was not—a neat and careful dresser, a stickler for protocol, and a born administrator. They'd worked together a few times, and although they'd never become friends, there was a mutual respect between them.

"Sit down, Frank," Buxbaum said.

Delgado sat.

"I'm sorry for interrupting your vacation," he said. "Something has come up, and it's time-sensitive."

Delgado nodded but said nothing.

"We've had a request for your assistance, from our friends across the pond."

Delgado raised an eyebrow. "Across the pond" usually meant Britain. He couldn't think of anything urgent over there that only he could assist with. "They asked for me? By name?"

Buxbaum nodded. "That's right, and only you will do. Apparently it's something that you are the sole acknowledged expert on."

"Where did the request come from?"

"The NCA," Buxbaum said.

Delgado nodded; at least that made sense. The National Crime Agency performed many of the same crime-fighting functions as the FBI, the same sort of criminality Delgado had spent his career on.

"All right," he said. "What exactly is their problem?"

"They've received a tip, about what they consider a credible threat." Buxbaum pushed a folder across the desk. "Somebody is supposedly planning to steal a national treasure."

Delgado flipped open the folder. "Do they have any idea who this guy is?"

Buxbaum nodded. "They do. That's why they asked for you."

Delgado looked up.

"It's a guy named Riley Wolfe," Buxbaum said.

CHAPTER

13

The next two weeks were pure vacation. I mean, based on what I've heard, because I've never actually had a vacation myself. But whatever you want to call it, it was all Caitlin and no work. And that was a completely new experience for me. Not just Caitlin—the part about nothing but vacation. I'd never taken time off like that, and I'd never wrapped myself in just one person who truly reciprocated, except a few times when I was play-acting it as part of a heist. This time it was real. I was just totally involved in being with her. Not scouting a job, not maneuvering to make a move, nothing but hanging with somebody I really liked.

And if it was risky as hell to feel that way about somebody, and way too soon to feel it . . . Well, too bad. I was having a good time with it. Me, Riley Wolfe, Sultan of Swipe, having fun—and fun caused by being with somebody! Aside from being kind of weird, I knew it was definitely wrong. It's stupid to get so lost in another person that you forget who you are. If you're me, that is. If you don't have people with an active interest in ending your freedom or your life, go ahead, have fun. But for me, it was dangerous—absolutely stupid dangerous. Because the entire who's who of crime and law enforcement would just love to find me.

But what the hell, it was a really good time, and I've always figured you've got to ride the pony while it has its wind, so that's what I did. And if the pony gave out and it all ended up as no more than a time-out, at least I could enjoy it while it lasted, right?

So I hung out with Caitlin. There's plenty of good stuff to do in London, in case you were wondering. We went to some really good theater, and we even did all the dumb tourist stuff: watched the classic changing of the guard at Buckingham Palace (I didn't see Alice), took a river cruise through the city, did the tour of the Tower of London, and we even rode the Eye, which is maybe kind of a goofy thing for grown people, but what the hell. We did it—twice—and it was fun.

We went to art galleries and museums, too, which was great—except Caitlin kept pushing for the British Museum, and I was trying to avoid it, for a bunch of reasons. But it got to the point that I couldn't dodge any more without making a scene of it, so we went. I just hoped my new beard would be enough to fool anybody still looking for the French guy who climbed onto their roof. And as much as I tried to steer us to the upper floors and away from the Egyptian room, Caitlin finally pulled me into it.

And, of course, she went right to the Rosetta Stone. She walked around it slowly, then stood and just looked at it, with long side-glances at me, while I stood there sweating and shifting from one foot to the other. Finally, she shook her head. "I don't get it," she said. I braced myself for evasive maneuvers, but she just turned and walked away.

The rest of that day didn't match the kind of fun I'd been having with her. In fact, it was like everything had turned gray. And I know, we were in London, so things were mostly gray anyway, but it hadn't seemed like it for the past two weeks. Now it did. I kept waiting for Caitlin to ask me why I was really interested in the Stone, but she didn't. She didn't ask me anything. She was mostly silent, and her face seemed stuck in a kind of thinking-it-over frown. I tried to break her out of it, but she ignored all my inane tries at cheerful talk and kept stewing. And even though I couldn't say specifically what Caitlin had gone all grim about, I knew it was about me and the Rosetta Stone and how that just might make her rethink our relationship.

She didn't even want to have dinner together, just said she had to go. And even though she said she'd see me later, she said that word, "later," like it might mean tomorrow or it might mean ten years from now.

Two days went by, and "later" didn't happen. I called her, texted her, and knocked on the door of her flat, and it was all nothing. Like she had changed her phone number and moved to some faraway country.

And then day three came, and I was about to write off the whole thing when a knock came on the door. Caitlin. She was smiling again, and holding a flat wrapped package about the size of an elementary school desktop. She breezed in through the door and whipped around to face me as I closed it, and before I could say anything, she handed me the package and said, "I know you don't actually trust me, and there is no reason you should, in fact, except that I would rather you did, right? So I thought about this an awful lot and here's what I came up with." She nodded at the package. "Go on, then. Open it."

I looked at her, trying to figure out what was happening, but she shook her head and said, "Open it, Harry, for all love, it isn't a bomb."

So I opened it. For a minute I could only blink, not really sure if I was seeing what I was looking at, because it appeared to be a painting. A painting by Otto Dix. The one called *Good-bye to the Good Times*.

I didn't believe it. I mean, would you? I looked at Caitlin. She was beaming.

"That's— I don't even— Is this a copy?"

"Bite your tongue!" she said, looking horribly indignant. "Am I such a heathen as that?"

"But that's . . . I mean, it must have cost—"

"It cost exactly nothing, put away your Protestant guilt."

"Then how—"

Her smile got even bigger. "I stole it," she said.

There are times in life when no matter how hard you scrabble and grab for words, there just aren't any. This was definitely one of those times.

"I know you're up to something ridiculous, something that somehow involves the Rosetta Stone," she said. "I wanted to know what, but as long as you didn't trust me enough to let on, I knew you wouldn't. So I thought of a way to make you believe that you can, in fact, trust me." She showed all her teeth and nodded at the painting. "I stole that for you."

I looked at the painting, but I'd seen it before. So I looked at this brand-new Caitlin. The one who had stolen a painting for me.

Caitlin the crook.

A thief like me.

For a long time I couldn't say anything, and finally she broke the silence for me.

"Well?" she said.

There was really only one option. I hugged her and kissed her and liked her a whole lot more than I had before. Because she had just opened up a whole new world of possibilities.

And just when I was ready to move on from the hugging and kissing and maybe progress to something a little more horizontal, she pushed away from me.

"Yes, lovely, but come on, Harry. Time to tell all."

I looked at her, and I liked what I saw. But trusting somebody is hard for me. It never works out. Maybe I thought about it too long, because Caitlin said, "Harry. Shall I take the picture back?"

So I told her.

When I was done, she looked a little doubtful. "You want to steal it. Steal the Rosetta Stone."

"I do."

"For the love of God, why, Harry?"

"Because it can't be done."

"The thing has to weigh a ton," she said.

"One thousand six hundred eighty pounds," I said. "Not quite a ton."

"Oh, well, then, that's a relief, should be a bloody walk in the park."

"It's kind of my specialty," I said. "Doing stuff that nobody else could do."

"Ah, brilliant—so you have a plan?"

"Not yet," I admitted. "But listen, that doesn't really matter. I don't need to do this now. I was just doing it to kill time. While I waited, uh . . ." Kind of funny. It was hard to say. I mean, I don't have a lot of experience showing that kind of weakness to somebody. Not when I really mean it, anyway.

"I, uh—I was killing time until I found you again," I said. I could feel heat rising in my face, but what the hell, at least I said it.

Caitlin opened her mouth, then closed it and looked thoughtful. "Well, lovely, but you've found me. What happens now?"

"We could take a trip, maybe someplace with a beach," I said. "Whatever you like."

Caitlin shook her head, looked around my room, and then walked over and stared at one of the pictures of the Stone. She looked at it for a long time. And then she turned to me and smiled again, a big bright smile.

"Let's give it a lash, Harry," she said. "You and me together. It'll be cracking."

CHAPTER

14

Delgado's plane landed almost four hours late, and he hadn't slept much on the flight from Dulles. He'd closed his eyes and tried to sleep, but the thought of another run-in with Riley Wolfe kept elbowing into his mind, with a mixture of excitement and anxiety. Would he finally put the cuffs on Wolfe? He'd tried, and failed, many times. And that was when he had full control of the case. Now it would all depend on the competence and intelligence of the NCA officer in charge. The organization's reputation was good, but so was the FBI's, and Delgado had known agents he wouldn't trust to hold a ballpoint pen without hurting themselves.

And even if it all went perfectly, it wouldn't even be his arrest. Officially, any credit would go to the NCA—and likely enough, all the blame would fall on the foreigner, the FBI fellow who couldn't quite measure up. Delgado knew he did, in fact, measure up. Given half a chance and decent cooperation, they *could* catch Wolfe. But it all depended on the NCA and its case officer.

Delgado half expected someone from the NCA to be waiting to shepherd him through customs, but when there was no one, it wasn't any sort of problem. He had been to London before, and Heathrow held no mysteries for him. He got through the lines and stepped out of the terminal, looking for a cab, and an official NCA car was there waiting for him. He'd hoped the case officer might be there to give him an introductory briefing. But there was only the driver, which was a little disappointing.

The driver said nothing more than that he was to deliver Delgado to NCA headquarters in southeast London, just across the Thames from Vauxhall. His driver made the trip without speaking and handed him over to a young woman in an NCA uniform, who whisked him rapidly to a conference room, where he was greeted by a roomful of higher-ups from the NCA, the London Metropolitan Police, and the British Museum. They peppered him with questions about Riley Wolfe, intelligent and quite serious, but friendly enough. Delgado had answered them all with equal openness and good cheer.

But the bonhomie ended abruptly. When a slight pause came, Delgado said, "Thank you for your welcome. I'm very glad to have this opportunity. As you know, I've had several encounters with Riley Wolfe."

"None of them at all successful, were they?"

Delgado blinked, somewhat shocked by the sudden rudeness. He looked at the speaker, a thin man of about forty, sitting across the table.

The woman sitting at the head of the table, the deputy director, Emma Pullings, cleared her throat, clearly embarrassed. "Ah, Special Agent Delgado, may I introduce you to Investigator Michael West? You'll be working with him in an advisory capacity."

West looked at him without expression. "Pleased to meet you," Delgado said, and received a brief nod in return.

"Do try to behave, Michael," Pullings said. She gave Delgado a weary smile. "Michael is feeling a bit protective," she said. "The tip came from one of his confidential informants. And to bring over a cowboy cop from the colony, as he so poetically put it, he feels is a waste of his time and the agency's money."

"I'm Cuban," Delgado said mildly. "Not really a cowboy." He'd been hoping his joking response might provoke some slight letup in the hostility, but it didn't happen. West simply turned his head away.

It didn't get any better.

Delgado tried to engage West with a few standard questions and was met with a short, cold, distant response. And when he asked about the reliability of the source of their tip and if West were sure that it was, in fact, Wolfe, West would say only that yes of course he was sure, but it was a confidential informant and he really couldn't risk revealing any information on the subject.

One of the main characteristics of good cops everywhere is patience in the face of hostility. Delgado was a very good cop, so he simply ignored the attitude and turned back to the assembled officials gathered around the table. Pullings seemed somewhat sympathetic, and she smiled encouragingly at Delgado and asked, "Assuming this is Wolfe, what can we expect in the immediate future?"

"Most decent thieves will explore their target ahead of time," Delgado said. He looked around at the group in the conference room. "That's elementary."

They seemed to be following politely.

"Riley Wolfe does it with a thoroughness that might seem obsessive. But that's one reason he's so successful." He let them absorb that for a moment before continuing. "If the Rosetta Stone is really his target—"

"Of course it is. This is bollocks," West muttered.

Delgado ignored the interruption. "If that's his target, he'll want to explore every possible approach and every escape route. And almost certainly a few of them will be what we might think of as *im*possible. So I'm fairly confident that he's been in, around, and even *on* the museum several times already."

"What do you mean by 'on'?" Pullings asked.

"The parkour," West said.

"Yes, very good," Delgado said patronizingly, just to show West he could play, too. As he had hoped, West took it as a dig, frowning slightly.

Suck on that, West, he thought.

"Wolfe is a master of parkour. He will use that skill to get him up on the roof of the museum."

"He won't get the Rosetta Stone out that way," the museum's security chief said, and he was rewarded with a few smiles from the others.

"Probably not," Delgado said. "But he won't neglect it anyway. As I said, he's very thorough."

"Ah, actually?" The representative of the Metropolitan Police, a chief superintendent, raised his hand. "When I read your file I did a bit of checking, you know, anything unusual in the area? And it seems one of our bicycle patrol officers had a run-in with a fellow? The officer says the man appeared to be coming down from the roof of the museum. But the fellow made off over the adjacent rooftops."

"Any sort of description?" Deputy Director Pullings asked.

"Yes, our man got quite a good look. I'll have the description sent round. But I do recall that he seemed to be French—shouted out something in French."

"I'm going to go out on a limb and say that was probably Wolfe," Delgado said.

He was met with raised eyebrows.

"He speaks French like a native. And Italian, and possibly other languages."

"He can speak all the bloody French he likes," the museum security chief said. "He won't get the Stone talking foreign."

"You'd be surprised," Delgado said. "Wolfe doesn't just put on a disguise. He *becomes* his characters." He gave them a very brief smile. "Recently, he turned himself into a French national and infiltrated a target the major intel agencies—Russian, Chinese, US, probably others—had been failing to penetrate for several years. And I don't need to say, he was convincing enough to get out alive."

"In this case, I'm afraid I don't see how he can do anything of the sort," Pullings said.

Delgado nodded. "Riley Wolfe will see a way," he said. "He always finds a way."

There were a few more questions and a few more grumpy, mumbled comments from West.

And then, mercifully, the deputy director said, "All right." She looked around the table. "I know most of you regard it as improbable. I'm asking you to accept Special Agent Delgado's assurances that it is *not*." She looked around the table, then nodded. "Right. You know what we're up against. And I don't need to tell you how important this matter is. The Rosetta Stone is the number one attraction at the museum." She looked at Reggie Maugham, the museum's head of security.

Maugham nodded. "Quite right," he said.

"But beyond that," Pullings continued, "it's a rather important token of national pride, hm? So it simply wouldn't do to have it pinched. Particularly from our wonderful national museum." She slapped the table with a hand. "Investigator West will head the task force. Please give him all possible cooperation. That's all, gentlemen."

CHAPTER

15

S top!"

NCA investigator Michael West slapped the keyboard, and the picture froze. "Yes?" he said.

Frank Delgado leaned closer to the monitor. The picture was a little bit fuzzy—security cameras don't generally give the very best image, and he didn't want to make a mistake. He studied the figure on the screen carefully; a very fat elderly man, leaning on the Rosetta Stone's case as he gasped for breath. It didn't take long before Delgado was sure.

"That's him," he said.

"Is it? Dead cert?" West asked, one eyebrow raised.

Delgado nodded. "Positive," he said. "He's used that disguise before. That's who he was when I met him face-to-face."

West frowned and looked at the figure on the monitor. "Rather sloppy, wouldn't you say? To put on a face that's known to your agency? Or is he that bloody confident?"

"He is that confident," Delgado said. "Partly because he never makes mistakes like this. It doesn't make sense."

And it didn't. Delgado had pursued Wolfe for years. He knew the thief and his habits better than anyone else alive, and as he knew all too well, Riley Wolfe was supernaturally careful. Always. For him to repeat a known disguise, knowing full well that he was within range of the security cameras, was completely uncharacteristic. Delgado rubbed his nose with a forefinger and thought about it.

Knowing Wolfe as he did, he had to consider the possibility that he meant to be spotted and identified, in order to further some subtle piece of his plan. Was there some advantage in alerting the museum and the police? It could only benefit Wolfe as a distraction if his actual target was somewhere else. Possible . . . But stealing the Rosetta Stone was absurd, so completely impossible, that it was exactly the sort of thing Wolfe would want to do. So what was the point?

Wheels within wheels, he thought. Any time you thought you saw Wolfe's plan, it was because he wanted you to, so you would concentrate on what you saw. In the meantime, Wolfe would be busy executing his *real* plan somewhere else.

Since hard experience had proved that to be true, and since Wolfe knew very well that Delgado had seen him in the fat-man guise, wouldn't it make sense that he did it deliberately, knowing he would be seen and identified?

But wait: Delgado shook his head. The thief could not possibly know that the Brits would call him in, and he was the only one who could make a positive ID on that disguise. There had to be some other explanation.

But what?

And if it really was exactly what it seemed to be—Wolfe surveilling in a known disguise—the first question remained: Was it possible that Wolfe was really doing something this careless?

He shook his head. "It doesn't make sense," Delgado said again.

"And yet, there it is," West said.

"Let's watch it to the end," Delgado said, and West started the video again.

They watched as the fat Riley chatted with the museum guard. For quite a while, too. That was consistent with the character he was playing, a talkative old man. But nothing else offered a hint of what Wolfe was really up to.

Still, Delgado had been in London for three days now, and this was the first confirmation he'd had that it was, in fact, Riley Wolfe he was dealing with. Until now he'd learned only that a confidential source had assured the NCA it was Wolfe and he really was going to steal the Rosetta Stone.

Delgado couldn't get any specific information out of West about the informant. Cops everywhere guard their informants' identities with extreme care, but it would have been nice to have a few details. Especially since they'd brought him all the way over from the US for this. So while it was not completely unexpected that West had refused him with an aloof, almost sneering attitude, it rankled more than it should have.

And it was not the only source of irritation Delgado was feeling. He admitted to himself that he had never been really good at working with others, but apparently West had the same problem. He remained just as standoffish, even unfriendly, as he had been at their first meeting, giving Delgado no more than the absolute minimum of cooperation. And he used his upper-crust British accent as a tool to keep the foreigner in his place.

It was irritating, but Delgado was a pro. He'd worked with assholes before and was sure he would again. And he'd been ordered to give full cooperation and hold nothing back. So that's what he was going to do. It was what he had done since his arrival. Not just because it was his job, though.

He would have put up with a hell of a lot more for another shot at Riley Wolfe.

"Fast-forward," Delgado said. "Let's look at the following day."

CHAPTER

16

Planning a job with somebody else is hard enough. I mean, I almost always work alone, and I am what my mother called "set in my ways." I have my own way of doing things, looking at things, and parsing things. And I know from a whole lot of experience that my ways work. So I don't really want to try somebody else's ways, because I don't know if they will work.

So sure, there's all that. But naturally, *they* usually are set in *their* ways, too, either because it's worked for them or because they just can't see my way. To be fair, not many people can see my way. That's why it's *my way.*

So if you really have to work with somebody, which is almost always a bad idea, at some point you have to find a place in the middle where you can both go at the same puzzle at the same time. And that's hard. Turns out, it's even harder when the somebody else you're planning with is somebody that, every time you look at them, you just want to move the planning session over to the bed.

That's kind of a roundabout way of saying that planning with Caitlin was slow going. On the plus side, every now and then we actually did move the session over to the bed, and then the slow pace didn't seem to matter quite as much.

But there's a point when you realize that you haven't made a whole hell of a lot of progress, and if you're actually going to, you know, really *do* this thing, you need to pull on your pants and figure out how.

Caitlin and I had reached that point around noon, and it was now five o'clock, and we still hadn't gotten very far. I was pacing around the cluttered flat. She was standing at the window, looking out at the rain. That beautiful sunny summer was over and autumn weather had already laid siege to London, and it was raining a lot. It didn't seem to help our creativity.

"Right," I said, talking mostly to myself. "Taking it after closing is totally out, okay? When you're the only thing moving, you're way too conspicuous. And, anyway, it's no fun. What we want to do is take it when they're watching us. Because we made them see the picture we want them to see, something else completely."

Caitlin didn't say anything. I mean, why should she? She knew I was just blathering.

"So what we want is to find that picture, and then—"

"How often do they set up a new exhibit?" Caitlin said.

"Huh?" I said, because I am a great conversationalist.

Caitlin turned to face me. Something in her face was new and different. I wouldn't say her eyes were shining, because I'm sorry, eyes just don't. But that was the idea. And whatever her eyes were doing, I knew what it meant. She had found something.

"I said, how often do they set up a new exhibit? Or even change what's on display? You know, at the British Museum? The place we were talking about?"

And yeah, she'd found something. She really had. And I got it.

"Damn . . . ," I said. "That's it . . . !" And I couldn't help it—I ran over and grabbed her. "God damn it, girl, you got it!"

She looked up at me from inside my hug. "I think I might have done," she said.

There's this man named Babcock," Caitlin said.

"Yeah, there would have to be," I said.

It was two days later, and we were still trying to find a few specific pieces to fit our plan.

"Dr. Charles Weston Babcock," she went on. "Renowned Egyptologist, brilliant collector, and filthy-rich member of the old aristo class. Third son of an earl, I don't remember which, and the family have pots of money."

"Oh?" I said.

She had my attention now, because I thought I knew where she was going. It sounded like someplace I wanted to go.

"He has some rather famous pieces, several from the Ptolemy the Fifth era." She cocked an eyebrow at me. "He's essentially an aristo grave robber."

I hated him already. "Are any of the pieces kind of big?" I asked, trying to sound innocent.

Caitlin matched my naive expression. "Odd question! But as a matter of fact, since you ask, there is a rumor—about his collection? It is whispered in certain circles that he has in his vile money-grubbing hands an enormous head from a statue of Horus."

"Money-grubbing?" I asked.

Caitlin shrugged. "In this case, perhaps it's more accurate to say, illicit Egyptian-antiquity-grubbing?"

"Because the head should not be in his hands, no matter what they grub." I frowned. "That didn't sound quite right."

"We shall overlook that comment for now," she said. "Other than that, yes, exactly. The head was not legally obtained. Babcock's grandfather the Old Earl, as he was known, was also a collector, and he stole the bloody thing. Right out of a dig in the Valley of the Kings. To get it into Britain he just flashed his peer of the realm card and threw around some cash, and that was it. He tucked it away at his ancestral manse, and that was the end of it. But as it was never officially discovered, there's no official record. So the bloody thing is thought to be no more than a rumor."

"But it isn't a rumor?"

"Oh, no, absolutely not," she said. "It is as real as the national debt."

"And how do you know this?" I asked. "The part about the head of Horus, not the national debt."

Caitlin nodded. "A fair question." She smiled. "Babcock's father had an Irish cleaning woman." Her smile grew. "My cousin's aunt, actually. So I know it's there."

I was almost salivating, because this little side trip had just turned into the kind of thing I live for—taking cool stuff from the overprivileged overentitled .1 percent. People born into money and power who use it to get all the good toys and keep them away from everybody else. That is absolutely the very best kind of job for me. And if one of these spoiled-rotten asshats gets in the way of my work, I don't mind tipping them over the edge into the long dark.

"It's perfect," I said.

"Assuming we can get our hands on the thing—"

"Of course we can," I said.

"But, ah—" Caitlin looked away, an uncomfortable expression on her face. "It's rather awkward, but . . ." She looked at me quickly, then away again. "Babcock really loves the thing . . . ?"

"Oh!" I said. "You think he won't be willing to part with it?"

"That was actually a thought I had, yes," she said.

"But the museum can't really accept it without a clear provenance," I said. "So we need *him* to offer it to the museum."

Caitlin nodded. "Yes, exactly. And they know him, of course. I mean, he's rather private, but he's at the museum enough for them to know him when they see him."

"So it has to be Babcock, in person, who offers the head," I said. "But he is highly unlikely to want to do that."

"Highly unlikely."

"Can he be persuaded in some way?"

Caitlin shook her head. "Also unlikely," she said. "He's a total loner. No friends, no family, no known vices."

"Except his somewhat illicit collection."

"And particularly this head of Horus," she said.

I thought about it for a few seconds. "We don't actually have to deliver the head," I said. "We just need to make them *think* we did."

"Yes, but that's not the real problem. What about the real Babcock? He could show up at the same time and we're fecked. So unless—" She started to say something, stopped, looked away. "We need to keep him out of the way long enough to do this, and I don't know how."

"I do," I said.

Maybe it was something in my voice. But Caitlin's head whipped around to face me. Her eyes were huge, and her mouth was hanging half-open and for a long moment she didn't say anything. "Oh," she said at last.

"Yes," I said.

She finally blinked. And then she gave a single nod. "All right," she said.

CHAPTER

17

D r. Charles Weston Babcock seldom went into town. He very much disliked the dirt, the crowds, and, most of all, the great flock of foreigners, with their odd accents and dreadful cooking smells. Furthermore, the flock seemed to increase exponentially every time the doctor went into London. The creatures were everywhere, and every breath Babcock took seemed laden with the stench of foreign cooking and unwashed riffraff. It had been quite overwhelming, and if there hadn't been urgent business with his barrister, Babcock would certainly have stayed home. It would take days to wash off the accumulated odors.

Besides, he had always much rather be at home, Hedgemont Hall in Buckinghamshire. It was a lovely old Georgian estate with a splendid garden that was quite beautiful on those rare occasions when the weather allowed. It was clean and quiet. He had no household staff; Babcock couldn't really tolerate the notion of someone else lurking about day and night. He paid a gardener, and a crew came in on Wednesdays to tidy up. Otherwise, he was quite alone, and he preferred it that way.

Of course, he had his collection. He had inherited most of it, but he had added to it whenever possible, and it took up an entire wing of the old manse. There was so much to do, just to curate it properly. Especially since it had been ignored for so long. Father had not been terribly keen on what he called that great useless lot of dusty old rocks, and he'd neglected it frightfully. Charles, however, spent most of his boyhood with the collection. He felt a connection to the wonderful ancient objects that he simply didn't experience with living human beings. He'd been an awkward child, and although he got top marks at Harrow, he had formed no friendships. But he hadn't really minded. All he'd wanted was for the term to end so he could get home to Hedgemont Hall and the collection.

None of this changed at Oxford. Once again he got top marks, and once again he had no real friends and picked up no distracting hobbies. And there were certainly never any romantic entanglements. The idea of intimacy was, quite frankly, disturbing, embarrassing, unthinkable. In any case, he never felt the need. The collection was all that and more to Charles: friend, hobby, and paramour.

His particular love was his glorious great head of Horus. In Charles's opinion—and his opinion on these matters was widely praised—there was nothing like it anywhere else. The finely chiseled lines of the face, the decorative work around the hood, were unparalleled. Babcock could stand in front of the head for hours, sometimes running his hand over the beak, closing his eyes and feeling things he couldn't really acknowledge, much less explain.

All told he was rather pleased to return home after this particular trip into London. He was quite nearly aching for a cup of tea—his tea, made his way, and not the vile brew his barrister tried to foist off on him. So it was with a sense of relief mixed with anticipation that he slid his Bentley Continental into its stall in the old stable house that served as a car park for Hedgemont. He switched off the motor, sighed quite loudly, and stepped out of the car. He closed the door, turned to leave the garage, and stopped dead in utter shock.

There was a man standing in the garage doorway. It was the postman, the same man who had been delivering the mail to Hedgemont Hall for more than twenty years. But the fact that he was here, at the garage? Highly unusual and utterly distasteful. Babcock detested unnecessary human contact. He shunned it when he could, and he had carefully arranged his life to avoid it whenever possible. And yet here was this fellow standing there, plain as day, when he had given the fellow very clear instructions to leave the mail and go, without pestering Dr. Babcock with attempts at fellowship or meaningless chatter.

For a moment Babcock simply stood and let his outrage wash over him. Then he mastered himself and snapped, "Well? What is it?"

"Sorry, sir," the postman said. "I've a letter for you here—"

"Of course you do; that's your job, isn't it?"

"Yes, sir. But this one requires your signature. Sorry, sir." He held out a clipboard and a pen. "If you'll just sign it, I'll be on my way."

Babcock took the clipboard, which was unavoidable. But he declined the pen, which was certainly greasy and completely festooned with the germs of dozens of grubby hands. He scrawled his name with the pen he always carried inside his jacket pocket and handed back the clipboard.

"Right," the postman said. "And here's the letter. Sorry to intrude, sir. I'm off now."

Babcock took the letter gingerly. He glanced at it, then did a double take. It was from the Ministry of Tourism and Antiquities in Zamalek, Cairo, Egypt, and that was extremely interesting. He slipped the letter into his attaché case and waited impatiently for the postman to vanish before leaving the garage and striding up the path to the house. The path was lined with roses, in full bloom now, but he barely noticed. Instead, he hurried into the house and headed for the kitchen.

From beneath the sink he took a container of disinfecting wipes and thoroughly cleaned the envelope. He washed his hands just as carefully and then opened and read the letter.

When he was done, he placed the letter on the counter and washed his hands again. Then he stood for a moment, looking down at the letter.

"Well, well," he said at last. It was very gratifying. His due, of course, but even so. Something like this would provide excellent opportunities to add to his collection—carefully, of course, since it would be technically theft. But again, a small and illicit sample from this pristine grave was really rather his due. He thought about the possibilities. And for just a few seconds he actually smiled.

CHAPTER 18

Have a peek at this," Caitlin said. She slid a magazine across the table. It was the new edition of *Egyptian Archaeology*. It was an important publication for anyone in Babcock's field, Egyptology, and we'd been studying up on the subject for a few days now, just so we could talk smart about it once we shifted into different people.

I had also been studying all the photographs and the few videos I could find of Babcock himself. Luckily, he'd done a lecture series at Oxford a few years back and it had all been recorded. So I had a good start on what he looked and talked like.

Caitlin had been working up a disguise of her own, which she wouldn't tell me about. She said she wanted to surprise me. "Go on, have a gawk," she said, nudging the magazine.

I picked up the magazine. It was opened to a small article toward the back of the issue. The headline read, "Pristine Pyramid Unearthed." It detailed the discovery of a previously unknown pyramid south of the Valley of the Kings. Apparently it was untouched, which meant unlooted, and was now under heavy guard as a team of Egyptologists began the exciting work of examining it and cataloging its contents.

All very interesting—but it didn't really grab my attention until the bottom of the third paragraph, where it said, "Dr. Charles Weston Babcock has been named to direct the excavation."

Which meant, of course, that Dr. Charles Weston Babcock was not in England but in Egypt. And that put a large lump in our grand plan.

"Shit," I said. I threw down the magazine.

Caitlin nodded. "I would have said *shite*, but otherwise I agree."

"Why can't there be pyramids here? Maybe in Worcester or something?"

"That would be lovely," Caitlin said. "But unfortunately, they all seem to be in Egypt lately."

"If he's known to be there, and I show up being him here—"

"Yes, of course, it's a kick in the bollocks, I got that part on my own," she said. She raised one eyebrow at me. "So?"

I sighed and looked out the window. It was raining. I mean, of course it was. We were in London. I was starting to miss warm weather, sunshine—why hadn't I tried harder to talk her into going someplace warm and with a beach? I could almost feel a warm breeze, and the hot sand under my feet. If only . . .

"Oh," I said.

Caitlin looked quizzical. "Yes?" she said. "You've got a thought?"

"I get them now and then," I said.

"Well, what is it?"

"Elementary," I said. "Pack a bag."

CHAPTER

19

"Dr. Babcock! Come at once!"

The call came from far down the corridor. Babcock was only about forty feet into the interior. There was a wonderfully intricate panel of hieroglyphics there, and he was working on a translation. The voice came from deep enough into the pyramid that it was somewhat faint, but it was female, American. The young doctoral candidate from that provincial university in the States. Duke, it was called. As if conferring a noble title on it might make it the equal of a real institution like Oxford. The Americans were truly— But in any case, she was here to help, and if nothing else, she was eager and willing to do menial jobs. He'd sent her down to the sarcophagus, which sat in a chamber at the far end of the corridor. She was supposed to be carefully photographing and cataloging the funerary items piled in the chamber. As with every pharaoh's tomb, the pile was large, rich, and varied. A meticulous record of every piece was essential, and not merely for a better understanding of the pharaoh and his life. Many of the items were gold, bejeweled, exquisitely crafted, and therefore of great value. And because of that, two armed guards were posted outside, at the entrance to the pyramid. Once the items were photographed lying as they were found, and cataloged carefully, they could be removed to a place of safety, so no one could walk off with anything.

Or almost no one, Babcock thought smugly.

"Dr. Babcock!"

Her call came again, more urgently this time, and Babcock sighed.

"Coming!" he called. She was the only other team member on site right now, so of course she would call on him. But he had to wonder what the problem might be. Her task was an uncomplicated one, because he did not really trust her, nor her bucolic university. Still, she hadn't ruined anything yet, and the urgency in her voice was undeniable. He tucked his notes into a pocket and headed toward the far end of the corridor.

It was not terribly rapid going. He had to use a flashlight and step carefully down rather small stairs. And the passage was narrow—this was not, after all, a major tomb. It had been built for an obscure pharaoh, one who had reigned for a very short term before succumbing to illness. But a recent quirk of climate change had revealed the tip, careful excavation had uncovered the rest, and an expert team had been assembled to explore it. Babcock was certainly well qualified to be a member of that team—but so were many other men and women. Unfortunately for them, they did not have Babcock's great wealth. A few carefully placed gifts, bequests, and outright bribes, and he was not merely on the team; he was leading it.

This had put him in the perfect position to pursue his only real passion—adding to his collection. This pyramid, unknown until now, was untouched by thieves, tourists, and primitive archaeologists without a proper sense of how to proceed in these matters. And Babcock, very properly as team leader, decreed that he alone had the necessary expertise to avoid any booby traps, and therefore he would perform the initial examination of the king's chamber and the accompanying funerary gifts. In this position he had found a wonderful piece, practically unique. It was a *wesekh*, the wide necklace worn by pharaohs. But he had never seen one like this, and he did not know of one anywhere in existence with this exceptional design.

It was solid gold, which was not unusual. There were fourteen golden spikes radiating from the center and pointing outward. Fourteen was a sacred number, of course, representing seven for Upper Egypt and seven for Lower. Each point had been set with a ruby, and a spray of scarabs adorned the part above the points.

The work was exquisite, but none of it was particularly unique. What really made this *wesekh* one of a kind was that there was, wrapped around the neckhole and twining itself upward, a golden cobra, encrusted with jewels. It was designed so that, when the *wesekh* was worn, the head of the cobra would rise up over the top of the pharaoh's head and menace anyone in the royal presence. The scales and other details were stunningly rendered. It was gorgeous. Far and away the most beautiful one Babcock had ever seen. And since there were four *wesekhs* in the chamber, no one would miss this one. Since he wouldn't be cataloging it, no one would even notice its absence. Babcock had slipped it into his pack. It would look lovely in a glass case set in his collection, perhaps next to Horus.

"Dr. Babcock! Please, hurry!"

There was outright panic in the girl's voice now, and Babcock paused for a moment. Was it a serpent? If so, he was certainly not going to risk himself trying to protect this girl. A saw-toothed viper was no laughing matter, far less a cobra.

But if it was not—if it was some minor problem, or perhaps an unexpected treasure—he really ought to have a look. From the door of the king's chamber he would be able to see what was bedeviling the girl and act appropriately without exposing himself to danger.

Another minute and he was there, at the chamber. And so was the young woman, standing just outside the chamber itself. Babcock shone the beam of his light around her and saw nothing alarming.

"What is it?" he said.

She shook her head, her eyes wide. "I don't—it's not possible, but— the sarcophagus is— Dr. Babcock, it's been opened!"

She was right. It was not possible. They hadn't yet pried the lid off the great stone sarcophagus. These things had to be done very slowly, with exquisite care and guided by an experienced hand, such as his own. So many things could go disastrously wrong if one rushed head-long into a sarcophagus for a mummy.

Truthfully, though, the mummy of a nonentity pharaoh was one of the least important items to him in the entire pyramid. The hiero-glyphics, the gifts, and the pharaoh's possessions gathered around the sarcophagus were far more beautiful and informative. And no one was down here other than Babcock and this girl. The lid was most defi-nitely in place—the girl was obviously hallucinating.

"You must be mistaken," he said.

"No, it's true—see for yourself!" she said, pointing a trembling finger into the chamber.

Babcock paused. Of course it was impossible; but what if some-how, someone—or something—had managed to . . . ?

No. Ridiculous. There was no other living human in the pyramid, and the idea that some nonliving—after all, there were all the stories of curses, and Babcock knew well that misfortune so often followed the men who opened the tombs. Was it at least possible that—

No, of course not. Bollocks. He would certainly not entertain any ignorant superstitious notions. The girl was clearly mistaken. He nodded his head firmly to her, said, "Very well. I shall look," and stepped into the chamber. Three steps in and he stopped, shone his light on the sarcophagus . . . and felt the hair rise on his neck. Because somehow, impossibly—

The sarcophagus was open.

Someone, somehow, had rotated the stone lid and now a great dark opening gaped at the head.

For a long moment Babcock neither moved nor breathed. But then he shook himself, took a breath, and told himself quite firmly that there was some simple explanation. He marched forward again, up to the very sarcophagus itself, and peered in. It was much too dark to see, so he shone the light inside.

Time stopped.

The sarcophagus was not empty. But the figure lying inside was not a mummy. It appeared to be a living man. That was shocking enough. But what froze Babcock's blood and slapped him into utter immobility was that as he peered inside . . .

The figure moved.

Stretched out its hands, and began to sit up.

And as it did, any chance Babcock might have had to move, to run, even to gurgle a choked call for help—it all drained out of him and left him standing beside the sarcophagus completely paralyzed, mentally as well as physically. Because as the figure in the coffin rose up out of

the shadows inside, its face became visible. And that face . . . It was a
face that Dr. Charles Babcock knew very well.

His own.

*A nd there he stood. The waiting was over. Mouth gaping open, eyes wide,
multiple chins trembling. The snotty, born-rich prig with his eternally
privileged lifestyle and his endless unearned inherited wealth. Even with that
shocked expression on his face, he didn't look scared. Only offended that
someone had slipped through the protective screen of his money and privi-
lege. He was exactly all that I detested. Practically the avatar of the asshat .1
percent. Just looking at him flipped the switch, and I felt myself slide into the
Darkness. The place I stand when there are dark deeds to do. I don't go away;
I just step behind a screen, a smoked-glass window onto the world that lets
me watch what's being done without really feeling connected to doing it.*

*And it had to be done now, before he recovered from the shock. The
Darkness wrapped around me, and I lunged up and grabbed him by the
neck while the doughy snot heap was still gaping, and before he could understand what was happening to him it had already happened.*

I t took a good half hour, but like Mom always said, "A job worth doing
is worth doing well." And when I stepped back and looked, it was
worth it. Time well spent. "It's perfect," I said.

Caitlin leaned forward beside me and frowned critically, and then
nodded. "It will have to do," she said.

I looked it over again, head to foot. All the wrapping from the original mummy, carefully wrapped around Babcock. It looked like the

real thing. We'd taken a great deal of care to get every detail exactly right. The only real difference was that Babcock was a lot chubbier than the Pharaoh had been. But since no one had seen the original mummy yet, no one would know.

"I think it will do nicely," I said. I kissed her. "We do good work."

"Don't we, though?" she said. She took my hand. "Let's go home, yes?"

"Absolutely," I said. I rotated the stone lid so the sarcophagus was once again closed, and joined Caitlin by the chamber door. We started out of the burial chamber, pausing only to pick up a small pack Caitlin had filled with some of the more valuable funerary gifts.

Just before we passed through into the corridor, Caitlin paused and looked back at the sarcophagus. "How long will it be, do you think, before someone opens the thing and finds him?"

"Oh, weeks, even months," I said. "They'll have to miss him, which won't be until we finish in London. Then they search for a while, declare him dead or missing, then replace him here, then—no, it'll be many months, I'm sure."

"Hmph," she said. "Well, I hope the poor sod doesn't wake up too soon."

"That would be tragic," I said. "Shall we?"

CHAPTER

20

D r. Baahir El-Shenaway was having a great deal of trouble containing his excitement. Only a few years out of his doctoral program, he had been selected to work with the famous British archaeologist Dr. Babcock. And Dr. Babcock had asked for him by name! Apparently his doctoral thesis, on the contextual hieroglyphic symbolism of Horus iconography, had caught the great man's eye. Now here he was, arriving at last at this untouched pyramid, to assist in the translation of what were said to be some remarkable hieroglyphs.

Another thrilling element of this wonderful experience! To be one of the first into an untouched pyramid, to work on hieroglyphs unseen for more than two thousand years! Only a very few got such a chance. For him to be one of those fortunates—and at the start of his career— it made him want to laugh aloud from pure joy. All the hardship and hard work of growing up poor, grinding through school, university, postgraduate work, all while working at his uncle's restaurant, just so he could afford to live. And now, with this one magical opportunity, it was worth it. It had all paid off.

Baahir paused in his trek across the sand and wiped the sweat from his forehead with a handkerchief. He looked ahead at the looming shape of the pyramid—*his* pyramid!—and he actually did laugh aloud. Just two short syllables, but still, it wouldn't do. It wasn't consistent with the dignity of his new station. He took a deep breath, wiped his forehead again, and continued walking forward.

It was a very hot day, of course, to be expected out here in this sandy desert wasteland. He could feel the heat in the sand as he kicked through it to the pyramid. The sweat popped out of his pores and seemed to evaporate instantly. Baahir was a city boy, and he didn't like the blazing sun on his face. He much preferred the cool shade of a library—or better yet, the inside of a pyramid, such as the one he was headed for now.

He felt his pulse quicken. *His pyramid.* And guaranteed to be a huge step up for his career. He was making a very sudden rise in his chosen profession, and knew very well that it would be considered *too* sudden in the eyes of his peers. Well, let them stew. He had earned this, and he would prove to everyone that he deserved it. At the same time, Baahir was only human, and he was rather more nervous than perhaps he should have been. He felt—what was it? There was a word he had learned at university, a Jewish word, that one of his fellow students had used.

Shpilkes, that was it. He had *shpilkes*. He chuckled a little at the word, a Jewish word here at an Egyptian pyramid. It actually had several layers of irony. He chuckled again, and that helped steady him a little. *Shpilkes.* Very well, then.

Just ahead was the entrance to the pyramid, and Baahir quickened his pace. But before he could go inside, two people came out, a woman and a man. The guards at the entrance stood up straighter, obviously reacting to someone they considered important. The two began to walk briskly away, and Baahir recognized the man at once. Dr. Babcock!

His heart in his mouth, Baahir hurried forward and held out his hand. "Dr. Babcock! I am Dr. Baahir El-Shenaway."

For a long awkward moment, Dr. Babcock just stared at him. Baahir flushed and wondered what was wrong. Had he been too forward, too pompous, to introduce himself as "Doctor"? Or was it even possible that Babcock did not know his name? As the uncomfortable tableau remained frozen, all of Baahir's doubts and insecurities flooded through him. Perhaps he should—

"Sorry, you're who?" Dr. Babcock said, frowning.

"Dr. El-Shenaway, sir," he said again, feeling the heat rise in his face. "You liked my dissertation on Horus iconography and you hired me? Sir?"

"Ah. Ah, yes," Babcock said at last. "Well, then, you're here. Good, excellent. Well, get started, then." And he turned to go.

"Dr. Babcock!" Baahir called, and Babcock turned.

"Yes?"

"Get started on what?"

"Everything," the doctor said, waving at the pyramid. "I, ah—I've been called back to London. Urgent business I'm afraid. You're in charge now. Carry on."

"Should I start with the hieroglyphs?" Baahir called.

Babcock waved an arm and disappeared around the far side of the pyramid.

Baahir watched him go blankly. He realized he was still holding out his hand for a handshake that was never going to come, and he dropped the hand to his side. What on earth had just happened? Had Babcock really said— No, ridiculous. There had to be some sort of awful misunderstanding. He was barely out of his doctoral program, and this was his first important work in the field. To be put in charge, no, impossible.

But hadn't Babcock just said so?

Baahir stood for an endless moment of doubt and indecision. He looked all around and saw no one but the guards, no one else to aid him, and no one else to take charge or tell him what to do. And his eyes came to rest on the pyramid; the completely unknown pyramid. It was right there—and so was he.

Baahir took a deep breath, and he felt it surge through him and fill him with excited energy. *I am here*, he told himself. *I have a job to do, and I will do it.* And he stepped forward with determination and went into the pyramid.

Consciousness came back slowly. Even then, it took time to realize that it was, in fact, consciousness. The total darkness, the complete lack of sound, were not all that different from being unconscious. And on top of that there was the nightmarish inability to move, so familiar from old terror dreams.

It was the smell that finally persuaded Babcock that he was awake; a nasty odor that wrapped around every breath, a musty smell of moldy, desiccated ancient rot. The scent shoved into him when he inhaled, from something that was wrapped tightly around his nose and mouth and he could not move to push it away.

But you can't dream odors. Babcock knew he was awake. And that meant something was terribly wrong. Why couldn't he move? How could it be so completely, totally dark, with not the faintest hint of light anywhere? And it was just as silent as if he were deaf—no sound of faint voices, shovels, nothing. It made no sense.

And worst of all the smell—what was the fetid cloth bound so tightly around his nose and mouth? It was awful, nearly choking him with every breath. It smelled almost as though—

Yes, that was it. He knew the smell, had smelled it before, many times. And the darkness, the soundlessness? Of course that went with this particular odor in its native state. Add in the fact that he could not move, and yes, it added up perfectly. Suddenly it all made sense. Babcock knew exactly where he was.

That's when he began to scream. But of course, no one could hear him.

CHAPTER

21

don't see how you can be so bloody certain," West said for the third or fourth time.

Delgado took a deep breath, something he'd been doing a lot lately. To cover his frustration, he took a sip from a cup of something they'd told him was coffee. It was almost the right color, but that was where the resemblance ended. Of course the others drank tea. Delgado was certain it was much better than the dubious brown liquid in his cup, but he was Cuban, and he was from Miami. He had asked for coffee, and carried it as he followed the other two men into this small conference room in the office area of the British Museum.

Besides West, they were joined by Reggie Maugham, the museum's director of security. A retired Royal Marine master sergeant, Maugham appeared to be a bit more open and friendly than West, but Delgado was certain he hadn't really bought into Delgado's brief on Riley Wolfe, either. Even so, his attitude was far better than West's.

West was not even being merely unhelpful. His attitude verged on obstructive. Delgado hadn't expected to develop a lasting friendship, but he had expected cooperation. He wasn't getting it. At every step, West offered reluctance and objections instead of cooperation. But there was a job to do, and doing it well meant a chance at collaring Riley Wolfe.

So Delgado let the breath out and merely said, "The tip came from your informant."

"Yes, and it stands to reason, don't you think, that my informant will let me know when this Wolfe creature will strike," West said. "If he does."

"West," Delgado said. "It's your informant's word that he will. You obviously believe it. Believe that Wolfe is going to do this. So what's the problem?"

"The problem is a bloody FBI agent trying to make it seem like we're battling a fucking supervillain. Riley Wolfe isn't Thanos."

"Maybe not," Delgado said. "But he's very damn good. And I know how he works."

"And my informant will know when!" West said, clearly growing angrier. "I'll be ready for him. It should be my case!"

Aha, Delgado thought. Now it was starting to make sense. "As far as I've been told, it is your case," he said. "I'm just here to provide technical support."

"Fucking waste of time," West hissed.

"I'm sorry you think so," Delgado said. He looked across the table at Maugham, who gave him a sympathetic look but said nothing.

"West, I don't really want to be here any more than you do," he said, which was only a very mild lie. "I was called back from vacation for this." He had hoped he might raise a small tinge of sympathy for this remark. After all, West couldn't know he hated to take vacations. The last time he'd taken one, in fact, he'd used it to track Riley Wolfe.

Of course it didn't work on West. "That's bloody grim for you," he said. "Shouldn't be for me, too." And he stood up and stalked out of the room.

Delgado glanced at Maugham.

"He'll be back," Maugham said. "Just gone for a mug of tea, I expect."

Delgado looked down at his "coffee" and sighed again.

"Can we roll out the museum floor plan again?" Delgado asked. It had been spread on the table the day before, but British official neatness decreed that it be rolled up and put away at the end of the day.

Maugham obligingly rolled it out, and they bent over it together. "This great archway here," Maugham said, pointing to a spot on the map. "It leads to the loading dock, which I'd guess is his best exit. The other exits are all blocked, guarded, or too small. He'll almost have to go this way." He cleared his throat. "If, you know. He actually gets the Stone somehow."

Delgado ignored that and quizzed Maugham about other points on the map. While they were talking, West came back in, with his mug of tea, and sat again.

"Perhaps we should simply step down to Room Four and look the area over in person," Maugham suggested.

Delgado shook his head. "There is a decent chance that Wolfe will be doing the same thing. If he sees any police activity around the Rosetta Stone, he'll know something is up. And anyway, he knows me."

"And since you know him, you'd see him, wouldn't you?" West said archly. "And perhaps we could arrest him and have done with all this bloody clown show."

Delgado's patience was wearing thin. He leaned forward on the table and looked at West, hard. "Maybe you should reread the file," he said. "Especially the part about his talent for disguise."

"Oh, yes, of course, disguise," West said. "But perhaps on this side of the pond we might do a slightly better job noticing the makeup?"

"If it was makeup, I'm sure you could spot it," Delgado said. "It's a bit more complex than that. You may not be familiar with it on this side of the pond. Especially not with his degree of skill."

"I'm sure we can acknowledge your expertise with this, Special Agent," Maugham said, clearly trying to halt an escalation of unpleasant remarks.

Delgado glanced at Maugham and bit back the remark he knew he'd regret. Instead, he leaned back. "He's *good*, West. So good he could actually be one of us in this room and we wouldn't know it."

"And it may well be that our side have underestimated his ability," Maugham said, still speaking in a soothing tone. "So what exactly would you suggest at this point?"

Delgado turned to Maugham, grateful for his intervention. "I'd like to have one of your men hide a small GPS tracker on the Rosetta Stone."

Maugham frowned. "Yes, well, we do have all sorts of security on the thing, you know."

Delgado nodded. "I'm sure you do. And I'm sure that Wolfe will know you do as well. He's done a thorough recon—"

"Fifteen minutes in a fat suit talking to one guard," West said sarcastically. "If indeed that was him."

"It was," Delgado said. "And I guarantee that wasn't his only scouting trip."

"Yes, but, you do know," Maugham said doubtfully, "the bloody thing is quite heavy after all."

"One thousand six hundred eighty pounds," Delgado said. He allowed himself a tiny smile. "Seven hundred sixty-two kilograms, if you prefer metric."

"Yes, well, that's the thing," Maugham said. "Bit of a lift, isn't it?"

West snorted, and Delgado took another deep breath.

"Have you read the file?" Delgado asked.

"Of course, but . . . It seems a bit much, doesn't it?" Maugham said.

"It is a bit much," Delgado said. "So is Riley Wolfe. That's what I'm trying to make you understand."

They both still looked unconvinced.

"Look," Delgado said. "He stole a statue once, at its dedication ceremony. There was a crowd—police, VIPs, the mayor. He stole it as they watched."

"Perhaps so, but—"

"That statue weighed twelve tons," Delgado said, riding over Maugham's objection.

West rolled his eyes, but Maugham raised an eyebrow. For a former Royal Marine sergeant, it was the equivalent of yelling "Holy shit!"

Delgado plowed on. "This is what he does. What he needs to do—things that seem impossible. For Riley Wolfe, that part is more important than the money."

"What, ah—aside from the GPS tracker, what are you proposing we should do?" Maugham asked.

Delgado allowed himself a small smile. "Catch him," he said. "And can we get some good maps of the area around the museum, too?"

CHAPTER

22

f you've ever pulled off a very cool heist, you already know that one of the best parts is when you're in the clear with the swag. If you are one of those rare people who's never stolen something major, you'll just have to take my word for it. You slip the last trap, dodge the final bullet, and you're home with the prize. And then you feel great in a way that nothing else can match. All of a sudden all the risky moves, near misses, and broken bones are worth it, and you are filled up with this giddy, bubbly happiness that makes everything you say or do better than it ever was before.

Ninety-nine percent of the time, I got that rush all by myself. Because like I've said, I work alone. That's a pretty good feeling. But this time I did it with Caitlin, and that made it even better. Not just because I had somebody to share the high with, but mostly because I was sharing it with *her*. I'd finally found somebody who liked to do certain things I liked to do—which is a lot harder than you might think, if your likes include stealing impossible things and wrapping rich ass-hats up like a mummy.

So when we got back from Egypt and up into my flat, we didn't even need champagne. I mean, we had some, of course. But we were feeling the buzz before I opened the bottle. And on top of everything else, the loot we had was *bonus* swag, stuff that we hadn't planned on. We'd just picked it up from the burial chamber along the way to setting up the real job.

It was gorgeous stuff, too. Those pharaohs knew how to live, and they usually died even better. So the swag was always eyepopping, and it was this time. I laid it all out on the table by the window, very care-fully, because even a small scratch might knock the price down. I got it all neatly arranged, and we both stood there looking and grinning like idiots. It was stunning.

"Oh!" I said. "I just remembered something."

Caitlin cocked her head to one side. "Do share it, Harry."

I went over and picked up Babcock's pack, which I'd grabbed on the way out—part of the disguise and no more, I thought. But when I looked inside, it turned out to be more than that. A lot more.

I carried the case over to the table and gently cleared a space in the middle. Then I reached into it and pulled out the surprise I'd found in it. "*Pièce de résistance*," I said, with a really good French accent. I put it down. "Good old Dr. Babcock had light fingers," I said. "And really good taste."

I stepped back with a flourish, and said, "Ta-da!" It was a *wesekh*, one of those weird neck things that you see on pictures of pharaohs, and it was solid gold, totally covered with jewels, and had a gold cobra that rose up and was probably supposed to stick up behind the pharaoh's head. Cobras were special for the pharaohs, a sacred symbol of supreme power, and this one was beautiful and scary, just like you want your monarch to be. And just as I stepped back and pointed at the *wesekh*, a shaft of sunlight came in through the window and lit the damn thing up. It absolutely glowed, like it was filled with divine fire or something. It was magical. I heard Caitlin gasp, but I could only look at this amazing thing glowing on the table.

We both held our breath and just stared for what seemed like a really long time. And then Caitlin took a step forward. She had a look on her face like she was hypnotized. She didn't say anything at all; she just walked slowly forward to the table and picked up the *wesekh*. She lifted it up to eye level and then, like she couldn't help herself, she slid it on around her neck and turned to me.

The jewels gleamed, and the gold cobra sure enough rose up behind Caitlin's head like it would kill anybody who dared to approach her, its ruby eyes burning with light. And the sunlight from the window was behind her and made a kind of corona around her, and she looked like an ancient goddess come to life, and I did the only thing that made sense under the circumstances. I dropped to one knee and bowed my head.

Caitlin held it for a minute. Then she glided to me and put a hand on my head. "You may rise," she said.

I did, and I was suddenly nose to nose with a goddess. I looked into the greenest eyes I had ever seen, and somewhere deep inside them I swear I saw the same fire that was in the gold cobra's eyes, and I felt that fire come into me, and then we were burning together.

The champagne went flat, but we didn't mind.

I opened my eyes to a dark flat, which meant that a lot of time had passed. That was fine with me. It had passed in a way that's hard to beat. I sat up and looked at Caitlin lying next to me. She had the palest skin I've ever seen, so pale it looked like she had a faint fluorescent light under the surface. I ran a hand over her, and she opened an eye.

"What?" she said.

"I've never had sex with a goddess before," I said.

"You have proved worthy," she said, and she pulled me back down.

I woke up again when I felt Caitlin slide out of the bed. She padded over to the table where the loot was laid out and picked up the *wesekh*. She held it up to the light coming in through the window and ran a hand reverently over it. I sat up, and she glanced at me.

"I love this so much," she said. "Lustfully, sinfully, obsessively."

I got up and went to her side. "We don't have to sell it," I said.

"Oh, no, we can't sell it; I could never part with it," she said, holding the *wesekh* tighter. "It's mine. I will never, ever part with it. It is *mine* and I want it forever."

Nothing I could say to that. She looked incredibly possessive and fierce in a way that promised supernatural wrath. You don't argue with a goddess. I put my arms around her.

"All right," I said. She leaned back against me, and for a while we just stood there like that, Caitlin holding the *wesekh* and me holding her. It felt good; doing nothing but just holding her. And it occurred to me that it was a "good" that was a whole lot better than most goods I could remember. Maybe even good enough for—

For what exactly? What weird and twisty path was my brain trying to follow, and where was it trying to take me? Because I wasn't sure I wanted to go there. But maybe it was time I figured that out. After this was all over and we had the Rosetta Stone, maybe the two of us could go someplace warm and private and spend a couple of weeks figuring it out together.

A new thought poked in, and I listened to it for a minute, thinking about it until Caitlin interrupted.

"I can hear the gears turning," she said. "What is it, Harry?"

"I was just thinking," I said.

"Yes, I got that part," she said.

"I was thinking. We got some great stuff from the tomb. We don't really need to do the Rosetta Stone, too."

Caitlin was quiet. Then she pulled away from me and put the *we-sekh* back on the table. She looked at the whole gleaming, beautiful pile of treasure.

"It's true," she said. "And actually, we never really needed the Stone. It was just something to do." She turned around. "We've had a good bit of fun, haven't we? But I don't want it to end. I still want to do this, Harry. I want to do something great with you. Something impossible."

She came back to me and took both my hands. "I want to do this," she said.

I looked at her, standing there backlit by the light from the window and wearing nothing but the fire in her eyes, and there was no way in hell I could argue with her.

"All right," I said.

CHAPTER
23

A re you sure about this?" I said over my shoulder, in the direction of where Caitlin was getting ready. And I wasn't at all sure I liked what she was getting ready for. She was turning into somebody else and going in first, alone, setting up the whole job. She'd have to be believable, become a completely different person and never drop character, and that isn't as easy as it sounds. When you're doing it for the kind of reason we were doing it, one mistake can kill you or get you thrown in jail. It's how I always work, and it's always risky, sure, but I'm used to it. I don't mind the risk for myself—but the idea of Caitlin in danger wasn't a happy thought.

Maybe I was being overprotective. After all, she'd done a good job in Egypt, turning herself into an American PhD candidate. She'd probably do just as good with this—but it was much higher stakes, and I was nervous about it. Hell, about her—*for* her.

"We can do it a different way, you know," I called.

"What the bloody hell are you doing here?!"

A voice I'd never heard before came from behind me, a voice that was totally Oxford upper crust, and I jumped and landed facing the speaker—an ultrafashionable woman of about forty, tanned, dark hair, and wearing a designer women's business suit. Whoever it was, she was glaring at me. But before I could either jump out the window or attack the intruder, the severe and fashionable glare cracked wide open, and she began to laugh. And I knew the laugh.

It was Caitlin.

"Oy, the feckin' look of you!" she chortled.

I didn't.

"Ah, now don't go all grumpy on me. It was just a bit of fun."

"Hilarious," I said. And I admit I sounded grumpy.

Caitlin clearly thought so, too. She shook her head and said, "Ah, for the love of—don't be a melter, man."

"Is a melter worse than a manky wanker?"

"Infinitely worse," she said. "I'm sorry I put the fright in you—but you have to admit that if I can fool you, I can fool any gobshite at the museum." She stepped up to me and took my hands. "Come on now, Harry. I can do this, and you know I can. Worry about your bit—you still can't say the 'O' sound like a proper Brit Twit."

"You're going in cold," I said. "And you're going alone."

"I can manage, Harry," she said. "Come on now, don't pout."

Well, okay. Maybe I was pouting a little. But seriously, why shouldn't I? I cared about her, and I wasn't used to that. And if that made me all grumpy-wanky-gobshite, sorry.

"I'm just worried," I said.

Caitlin smiled. "Of course you're worried, pet. I'd be rather put out if you weren't." She patted my cheek. "I'll be deadly, never fear."

"And I'll be worried," I said.

"Don't be," she said, and I gave her a tight hug.

After a moment, she pushed away. "Right, I'm off," she said. She gave me a quick kiss. "Don't fret, luv."

She walked to the door and turned around to face me, and once again she was the severe fashionista who'd startled me.

"And work on the bloody 'O' sound," she said. And then she was gone.

It was suddenly deathly quiet. You know how that can happen sometimes? Just all of a sudden, no sound, like somebody flipped a switch. It can even happen in the middle of a city, in broad daylight. Like it had just happened here. No sounds in the apartment, or anywhere in the building. No squeal of bus brakes outside, no faint voice—nothing. Just silence . . . dead silence.

And because I was worrying about Caitlin, the silence hit hard. It was like a supernatural warning that something terrible was about to happen—to her, to me, to the whole world. She'd be unmasked and taken by the cops. They would question her, and they would scare the shit out of her. They were really good at that. And Caitlin was new to this stuff, she wouldn't last ten minutes before they had her spilling her guts. And they'd come for me—

Then a taxi's horn blasted in the street outside, somebody yelled, a hairdryer started upstairs, and everything was back to normal. The paranormal paranoia faded, turned into grumpy worry again. That was something I could deal with. Just keep busy and that kind of crap fades away.

I sat and began to practice my "O" sound. I said "O." It still didn't sound right. I said it twice more. Then I started to think about Caitlin. And that made me think about why I was thinking about her so much.

Okay, I cared about her. Big whoopy shit. Did that really mean I had to let her invade my whole brain and make me all googly-eyed? It absolutely did not. I had cared about plenty of women. And the caring always ends. This wouldn't be any different. Where the hell did I think this was going, anyway? Someplace permanent?

Sure, why not. Just picture it, Riley. Me and Caitlin settle down in a nice cottage. On weekends we slip into the city together and steal things. After a while we have a couple of kids. We start them out small, train them as pickpockets. And if they show any real aptitude—someday, son, all this will be yours. Riley and Son, Unlicensed Thieves, Ltd.

Stupid. It could never happen. Way beyond stupid. I wasn't going to give up my freedom. Not for anybody. Sure, Caitlin was great now, and we'd have a few more laughs before it ended. But it would end. It always ends. Sooner or later the roses wilt and the radio starts to play Wayne Newton singing "Danke Schoen." Always.

So why worry? Just concentrate on doing this job. Then we can take a vacation somewhere warm and float away on strong drinks with fruit in them. Okay? Good. Now, the "O" sound.

I said it fourteen more times. It still didn't sound right. But what the hell. After all, I was a manky wanky melter.

131

CHAPTER

24

Helmut Schmeisser couldn't believe his luck. "Incredible," he murmured, walking around the enormous stone head for the fourth time. "Absolutely incredible . . . !" He had been, he now admitted, somewhat skeptical that this marvelous piece really existed at all. So many times, an enthusiastic amateur had gushed about the wonderful thing they owned and it turned out to be a copy at best. Or at worst—he had once driven out to Cardiff to see what a woman assured him was "*The Blue Boy*—dead cert, the real article!" The woman led him into the garden and waved proudly at a concrete statue of a young man. Covered with bright blue paint, of course.

But Dr. Babcock was no amateur. He had an impeccable reputation as a scholar and an Egyptologist. And so Schmeisser had made the long drive out to Babcock's home in Buckinghamshire.

He was very glad he had done so. This piece was magnificent. With difficulty, he ran a hand through his thinning hair and gained control of himself. He stood at the front of the head, gazing up at the stone features with wonder. "This was thought to be merely a rumor," he said. "Or at very best, lost—for almost a century." He turned to the woman standing behind him and raised an eyebrow.

The woman smiled, an elegant and perhaps somewhat condescending show of perfect teeth. "As you can see, it was neither. It was merely . . . shall we say, out of circulation?"

"Yes, of course," Schmeisser said. He studied the woman carefully. Beautifully coifed dark hair, a designer business suit, and a simple but very expensive brooch on her breast. Clearly a woman of class and breeding. But of course she would have to be, to be an executive assistant to someone like this. He cleared his throat. "Forgive me if I am blunt, Miss Farnsworth, but what does Mr. Babcock want for this beautiful object?"

"Dr. Babcock," she corrected.

"Of course! I beg your pardon! I'm an idiot."

"I certainly hope not," she said. "That would make this conversation rather a waste of time, wouldn't it?"

"Yes, but in this case—of course I'm very aware of Dr. Babcock's reputation in the field. Which includes, ah . . ." He paused, well aware that this was not the time for his usual bluntness.

"It is said," he said carefully, "that Dr. Babcock is passionately devoted to his extraordinary collection. And forgive me, Miss Farnsworth, but I must ask why he would wish to part with this magnificent piece."

"Dr. Babcock wants only to correct a great wrong perpetrated by his grandfather Sir Hubert," Miss Farnsworth said. "He has come to believe that a treasure like this one ought to be accessible to the public.

And so, Dr. Babcock would like the British Museum to have the head of Horus."

Schmeisser took a deep breath. Everything about this woman, everything she said about the glorious head, sounded expensive. And the British Museum did, after all, have a rather tight acquisitions budget. Schmeisser braced himself for an answer he couldn't afford and asked, "And what is his price, if you please?"

Miss Farnsworth frowned and turned her elegant head slightly to one side. "Oh, dear, did I not make myself clear? This is a matter of conscience, Herr Schmeisser. Dr. Babcock wishes to *donate* the head to the museum. Free of charge."

She smiled again, a larger smile with a bit more condescension in it. "Absolutely free," she said again.

"Of course, fantastic!" Schmeisser said. "Naturally a man like Dr. Babcock—that is, how wonderful! Very generous."

"He has only two very minor conditions," Miss Farnsworth said.

Schmeisser smiled and said, "Of course," but on the inside he was thinking, *And here it comes. God save me from "minor."*

The woman gave Schmeisser a smile he could only see as predatory, and he fought to keep his own smile on his face. "First," she said, "Dr. Babcock would like to keep this absolutely secret. No word of it must leak out until just before the grand unveiling. And so no one must see it until then. No one at all. Yes?" She raised an elegant eyebrow. "This will of course include turning off all the cameras, hm?"

Schmeisser felt a small trickle of relief. "I think we can do that, yes. Certainly." He gave her what he hoped was a polite and unconcerned lift of an eyebrow. "And the second condition?"

"Dr. Babcock will supervise the installation personally," she said.

"And the head is to be displayed in the Egyptian Room. As close as possible to the only item that can compare to it."

"Yes, certainly," Schmeisser said. "That would be, ah, perhaps the Amenhotep the Third? Or the Ramesses the Second?"

"Not at all," Miss Farnsworth said, this time with undisguised condescension. "Naturally that would be the Rosetta Stone."

Schmeisser paused, trying to picture the layout of the room; what was in the near vicinity of the Stone? Could it be moved in such a way that—but then his eye fell again on the fantastic head. That magnificent head of Horus. To have that piece—for him to acquire it for the museum—that would set a true crown on his career. Whatever it might take, it was worth it.

He raised his eyes to Miss Farnsworth, and now Schmeisser's smile was large and genuine. "I think that can be arranged," he said.

CHAPTER

25

I t was time.

Time to get ready to do this impossible thing. That meant it was time for my preparation routine.

I always do it, and I always do it the same way. That isn't negotiable. Because I have always done it before, and always the same way, and every time it worked. To change anything about it might be to set myself up to fail. So I never change it. I sit in front of the mirror, study my face. And then I make it into a different face. Same music playing, same everything until Riley is gone and a new face looks back at me from the mirror. The result was always the same magic. It worked.

This time, I had skipped it for the dress rehearsal in Egypt, because I would only be seen; I didn't have to *be* Babcock, just look like him. And okay, that went well, and it should have given me a little confidence in my New Look. That wasn't enough to break my routine when

I did it for real, though. I was back in London now, and I might be dealing with people who had met Babcock.

In fact, there had been a lot of things different this time, with this job. And the whole thing was—I don't know. Odd? Slightly off? I mean, I was way off my usual routine, and that always makes me uneasy. But this time? It didn't. Like I said, the whole thing was not normal—but because I was doing it with Caitlin, that was okay. It was something new and different, having fun in a brand-new way because I was doing it with her. We were growing a new piece of a new relationship, and that's always a little bit like exploring unknown territory. So if there was a tiny little alarm bell ringing somewhere deep down in my cranium, it was easy enough to shut it down. Because, come on, this was all new and different and with Caitlin, and that's a *good* thing, right?

I have to admit that I would have been a little embarrassed to do the whole transformation ritual with her there. Not that there's anything weird or stupid about it. Just, I don't know. It's private? I would have felt awkward if she were watching. That's another reason I hadn't done it for the quick out-of-town tryout.

But now, the dress rehearsal was over and the show was about to begin. Caitlin was already out and at work. And I really would feel better about things in general if I sat in front of the mirror and did what I always do. Maybe it is superstitious. It's also scientific—because research has shown that every time I do it, I'm successful.

So I sat down in front of the big mirror and did it.

It's exactly the same every time. Same music in the same order. I do the same things the same way. Every time, without fail. And when I'm done, Riley Wolfe is gone, off on vacation, while some new person rents his face.

I started the music.

PART 2

———————

THE HEIST

CHAPTER

26

I'm going to quit, absolutely, Natalie Prentiss thought, snarling at the rumpled packet of Player's cigarettes she held in her hand. *For certain this time . . .* But she added, *Not today—but very soon,* and lit the cigarette, gratefully pulling the smoke into her lungs and then letting it trickle out. There'd been rather a crowd in the gift shop today, quite a queue at her register, and this was only her second break for a smoke all day. *Aaahhh.* She closed her eyes as the effect of the smoke flooded her. It was wonderful. This was why it was so bloody hard to quit, this euphoric rush that came when you took that first puff after going without for a bit too long. The rest of the time it was just habit, but that first smoke after a long time without? Pure bliss. *If it always felt this good I'd never quit,* she thought.

A sound came from down the alley. She stepped farther out on the loading dock for a look. As she did, a large lorry rumbled in, backing up to the concrete platform where she stood. Natalie stepped back against the wall to be out of the way and watched as a big, rough-looking man jumped down from the lorry's cab. He had a big belly and a shaved head, and an air of cheerful, blue-collar confidence. A moment later a smaller man, thin and with ragged brown hair, climbed out of the other side of the lorry's cab. Both wore stained and battered light green coveralls with a company patch on the breast.

The large man carried a clipboard. He grinned and swaggered to the edge of the platform nearest Natalie. He looked up at her and said, "Hallo, luv. Got a delivery. But we're to wait here and not unload it, right?"

Natalie took a drag and cocked her head. "Well," she said, blowing out the smoke, "you can't simply park there like that."

The big man shrugged. "Afraid we've got to, luv." He held up the clipboard. "It's on the fucking order sheet."

"But you're blocking the entire area," she said.

"Sorry," the man said, grinning, and holding up the clipboard with the order form.

"Oh, right, sorry," he said. He looked at his clipboard, frowned, flipped to the second page.

"Yeah, right, here it is," he said. "We're to notify a Mr. Skm-eye . . . Bloody hell, it's German." Concentrating fiercely, he sounded it out. "Shim-eye—Shmy—Is it Schmeisser?"

"We've got one of those," Natalie admitted.

"Right, brilliant. He's to come down for this in person, all right?"

Natalie sighed and took one more puff. Then she dropped the cigarette and ground it out with the toe of her shoe. "I'll fetch him," she said.

Helmut Schmeisser hurried down the hall, his heart pounding. He had been waiting anxiously, and now it was here! He felt like a small child on Christmas.

He stepped out onto the loading dock. Two men waited, obviously laborers, making the delivery. The smaller was sitting on the edge of the dock, and the large man leaned against the lorry.

"Hello!" Schmeisser said. "I am Helmut Schmeisser."

"Brilliant," the big man said. But he didn't move.

Helmut frowned. "I should like to see the delivery, please."

The big man shook his head. "Sorry, mate," he said. "Our orders are, inform you, then wait for the doctor. We don't open the truck till he says so, in person."

"But that's—but this was to be delivered to me—to the museum! And I must see it to make certain—"

"Not happening," the big man said. "Not wifout the doctor's say-so."

"The doctor—is that Dr. Babcock?"

"That's him," the man said. "Dr. Babcock."

Schmeisser fumbled desperately for something to say, some argument that would allow him at least a quick peek, but the man just folded his arms, shook his head, and leaned against the back of his lorry, and nothing Schmeisser said had any effect on him. He felt his temper slipping, knew himself to be on the verge of losing it and shouting threats. But luckily, just before his anger erupted, there were footsteps behind him.

Schmeisser turned, to see Miss Farnsworth emerge onto the

platform—and right behind her, Dr. Babcock himself. Before he could speak, Babcock stalked up to him and said, "Schmeisser? Good. Whatever you need to do to clear things away so we can begin without anyone observing, please do it. Hm?" And without waiting for a reply, he turned to the two men at the lorry. "You're Bonden, hm?"

The big man straightened up. "Yes, sir. Arthur Bonden, Dr. Babcock," he said.

"Right," the doctor said. "Let's get started."

Schmeisser made a few quick calls on his cell phone to have Room 4 cleared of visitors and then blocked to prevent anyone more entering, and then turned his attention back to the men at the lorry. He watched as they unloaded a large crate—the head of Horus!—and trundled it onto the platform with a forklift. He led them all down the hall and into Room 4. And he followed in, eager to see at last the wonderful head in its new setting.

But Dr. Babcock put out a hand and stopped him. "Our agreement was that no one was to see it until the unveiling," Babcock said. "No one."

"But that's—surely, Dr. Babcock," he said.

"No," Babcock said.

Feeling completely deflated, Schmeisser turned away and headed back to his office. But he told himself that at least the head was here, and soon it would be unveiled. And he would damn well be in the front row when it was.

CHAPTER
27

Anyone with any true knowledge of the military will tell you that it is never generals who win battles. They don't actually control and operate their commands, either. Nor do the colonels, majors, and captains under them. No, any decent military organization will win or lose, prosper or founder, based on the quality and performance of its sergeants. This basic truth is at least as old as the Roman legions.

Sergeants run armies. They are the interface between order and action, strategy and tactics, and how they perform is the thin red line between victory and defeat.

Reggie Maugham had spent thirty years in the Royal Marines, and the last fifteen had been as a sergeant major. In his career he had learned two very important lessons about leadership. First, check everything—twice. And second, don't make it obvious that you check everything; trust subordinates to do things right without breathing down their necks.

He had taken these lessons with him to his postretirement job as head of security at the British Museum. He delegated tasks, he trusted his people to do them properly, and he always checked to make sure they'd done so. But he never made his scrutiny obvious. He always had some kind of clear "reason" for passing by and looking in. Something like, I'm getting lunch, do you want anything?

And now, as he did a careful perimeter check of the first floor, he was simply strolling down to "get a packet of Rothmans." He managed a word with each of his guards as he passed, nothing much. Just hello, bit of a crowd today, hm? That sort of thing.

He wasn't anticipating anything different when he stopped to speak with Nigel Blount, just outside of Room 4. He hadn't even planned to break stride; just a quick hello and on, because Nigel was a bit of a talker, tended to go on about nothing at all. Maugham generally felt it best to say hello and move on quickly. It didn't quite turn out that way this time. First, because Nigel saw him coming and strode down the hall to intercept him.

"Chief, hoy, what's all this?" he said, gesturing back toward the doorway to Room 4. "They won't say a word, and I'm told to stay out and stay mum."

"What's that?" Maugham said, puzzled.

"Look!" Nigel said, sounding quite indignant. "They've bloody well sealed the room!"

Maugham stepped around Nigel and toward the doorway, and stopped in his tracks, shocked. A floor-to-ceiling piece of plywood covered the entrance to the room.

"What on earth . . . ?" he said.

"What I said," Nigel said, nodding vigorously. And he took a breath to go on, but Maugham cut him off.

"No, you're quite right, something's off. I'll just have a look. You," he said, putting a hand to stop Nigel, who was already moving forward to accompany him, "you had best wait here. Until I see what's what."

Maugham pushed at one edge of the plywood. It gave way, just enough for him to slip past it and into Room 4.

He was no more than two steps in when his brain registered what he was seeing, and he stopped dead.

He had been in this room many times, and he was certain that the Rosetta Stone was right *there*. And there was *something* there, about the right size and shape. But it was covered by a large tent of canvas—as were all the items on display near it. And just beyond was another canvas, stretched over something taller—something that had not been there the last time Maugham had been in the room. A man and a woman stood beside it and looked up as Maugham entered.

"What the devil do you want?!" the man demanded angrily. He hurried toward Maugham, frowning. He was in his late forties, a bit plump, and spoke with a very upper-class accent, and the authority that went with it. "Well? Explain yourself—you shouldn't be here!"

"Actually I should," Maugham said mildly. "I'm director of security."

"I don't care what your little job is, no one is supposed to be in this room!" the man said indignantly.

"Part of my little job is knowing what's going on in the museum, including this little room," Maugham said. "And I'm afraid I don't know about you."

"Of course you don't," the man snapped. "I told them it stays a secret or I take my Horus home."

"Your—what?" Maugham said. He was sure he hadn't heard correctly.

"Hor-*us*," the man said. "This!" And he pointed with a flourish toward the tall canvas-draped something.

"Very nice," Maugham said. "But surely you told someone?"

The man frowned. "Bloody stupid man," he muttered. He turned his head and shouted, "Elizabeth!"

A young woman stepped into view from behind the head. "Yes, Dr. Babcock?"

"Please come deal with this," the man said, waving at Maugham. And then he spun away and went back to his head of Horus.

The young woman came over to Maugham with a cool expression. She raised one eyebrow and said, "Yes? Is there some sort of problem?"

"I'm afraid there seems to be, actually," Maugham said. "I'm Reggie Maugham, director of security." He held out his hand.

The woman took it, briefly. "Elizabeth Farnsworth," she said, dropping his hand. "I am Dr. Babcock's personal assistant."

"Ah, that's Dr. Babcock, is it?" Maugham said. He had of course heard the name, but he'd never run into the man in person. "Well, then, I'm sure there's no real problem—it's just that I haven't been told about all this."

"Yes, we asked Mr. Schmeisser to be sure it was kept secret," she said, with a very small smile. "But he may have gone a bit too far, hm?"

"I believe so," Maugham said. "Well, I'll just step up to his office and have a word, then. I'm sure this won't be any sort of problem."

"I certainly hope not," Miss Farnsworth said.

"Stay on the door, Nigel," Maugham told Blount. "Make sure no one gets in." He raised an eyebrow. "Or out, hm? I'll have a word with the gentleman upstairs and let you know if anything changes."

"Right you are, sir," Nigel said. "I just think it's totally irregular that they should—"

"Yes, you're quite right, but no worries, we'll get this sorted," Maugham said, cutting him off before the other gathered too much steam. He turned and hurried away.

My God, you didn't offend them, did you?" Schmeisser burst out.

"I couldn't say," Maugham said. "That was not my primary concern. I'd no idea who they were or what they were doing."

"Yes, but this head of Horus?" Schmeisser said. "Wait till you see it— It's utterly magnificent! Certainly worth a bit of inconvenience."

"Helmut, I rather think you're missing the point," Maugham said. "I should have been informed."

"Perhaps so," Schmeisser said. "But that was Dr. Babcock's only condition—that I tell no one until the head is ready to receive the public. And this head—it is a unique treasure, worth a small break in routine procedure, yes?"

"Not quite so small as this," Maugham said, and he leaned in and spoke rather emphatically. "I need to know these things, Helmut."

"Yes, I suppose you're right, I'm sorry, Reggie," Schmeisser said. "If there is ever a next time I promise I'll tell you." He smiled to show that the idea of a next time was ludicrous.

"All right, then," Maugham said. He stood up to leave.

"Oh!" Schmeisser said. "Please, Reggie, don't tell anyone else? As I said, the gift is conditional on it staying secret."

"I'll not tell," he said, and left the office.

He headed back down to continue his interrupted trip to get

cigarettes. It was a bit annoying to be left out of the loop on something like this, but all right. What's done is done. At least there was a simple explanation.

Still, though, he couldn't help thinking. *Whole thing is bloody odd, isn't it?*

CHAPTER

28

He knew it was a problem. More than that, it was an addiction, an actual sickness. That's what they were saying nowadays, all the experts, that compulsive gambling was a disease. And it felt like one, especially now. It made his stomach boil with acid and turned his bones to jelly, and he felt like he might faint, or vomit, or both—but he gambled anyway. He couldn't help it. He had to put down a bet—on a horse, or a football match, or even an election. It didn't matter what he bet on. He just had to bet. So he did. Several times every week he made his bet.

And every week, he lost.

More and more losses. Very few wins, certainly not enough to put a dent in the monstrous debt he had run up—was continuing to run up. He'd run out of money long ago. But they let him bet anyway, giving him credit he didn't deserve, because he was a high-ranking cop. They knew that sooner or later, they could ask for a favor. And when they did he knew he couldn't refuse. If word got out about his gambling, and about the enormous amount he owed, his career was over anyway. As much as he owed, he would have to say yes, no matter what the ask was. Sooner or later, all debts come due, and he would have to pay.

When the call came at last, he was ready. And he had braced himself to do whatever horrible, unforgivable, illegal task they demanded of him. It didn't matter how filthy it was, he was ready to do it if it wiped out his debt.

The call finally came. And now he was, in fact, doing it. But he hated it. He hated it worse than he'd ever hated anything in his life, hated it like the fires of hell. And he hated himself for doing it. But he did it. There was no way around it. He was in a trap—a trap he'd made himself, as he'd told himself a thousand times. His own fault, and this was the only way out. It went against everything he believed, everything he'd worked for his whole career, and he'd no one to blame but himself.

Several times already he'd received instructions, and he'd done exactly what was asked of him. Now it was time to report, and receive his new orders. The acid in his stomach was halfway up his throat, but it didn't matter. He slipped away from all possible prying eyes, took out a burner phone, and made the call. It rang three times before there was an answer. Then he heard the voice say, "What." Not a question; a flat statement, even a demand. That same awful voice; unnaturally deep, gravelly, and it felt evil somehow, a basso growl from the pit of hell. He knew it was just a normal human voice somewhere using a simple app that made the voice sound like that, the kind of thing kids downloaded to make prank calls. But it still scared him. His mouth was dry and his hands were wet with sweat, but whatever else he was—whatever else he had turned himself into—he was not a coward. He took a breath and said, *"Beithir-nimh."* His password. He'd looked it up; it meant "venomous serpent" in Gaelic.

There was a short pause. Then: "Go on."

He described everything they were preparing to do, naming the streets and describing the manpower at each barricade. When he was done, there was silence on the other end. Nothing at all for what seemed like a long time, not even the sound of breathing. But finally, the voice spoke.

"Good," it said. "You will make one small change in the arrangements."

"Yes, of course."

The voice named one of the streets, a narrow, minor road restricted to one-way traffic. "Leave it open."

"Open? You mean—take away the barricade?" he asked.

"Yes," the voice said. "No barricade, no foot patrol, no surveillance. Can you do that?"

It was not a question; it was a threat. He swallowed. It was harder than it should have been. "Yes," he said. "I can do that. But that means— You want him to get away?"

A chilling pause before the reply came. "No. I want his assistant to get away. That's vitally important."

"But then—the entire setup—and you want one of them to escape? Why?"

"That is not your concern. Just be very certain it happens that way. If you fail—there will be consequences. Extreme consequences."

His mouth went completely dry. Clearly there was some larger plan here, something beyond what he could imagine. And "extreme consequences . . ." There was no mistaking what that meant. And if he failed, he did not doubt that even a ranking police officer like himself could meet with an accident. "All right," he said. "And then I'm clear? My debt is wiped clean?"

The sound that came back at him was probably meant to be a chuckle, but there was nothing amusing about it. It made his flesh crawl.

"It's wiped clean," the voice said. "For now."

And then the line went dead.

His hand ached. He'd been gripping the phone tightly enough to crush a beer can. He relaxed his grip, put the phone in his pocket, and wiped his hands on his pants. Then he took a long, deep breath, feeling the luxury of it, and then let it out slowly.

"Free," he murmured. "I'm going to be free." It felt wonderful to say it, to think it, and to believe it, and he savored that for a minute. Then his mood turned serious and he took another deep breath. "Never again," he said to himself. "That's it. I'm done."

He could almost believe it, too. But then a nasty little voice in his head answered him with, "Done, really? Do you want to bet?"

And he did.

CHAPTER

29

Nigel Blount was rather unhappy. He had been for three days now, and it was not a feeling he was used to—at least not in such a prolonged dose. But it was unavoidable. Nigel loved people, and he loved making them as happy as he was, which he did, generally speaking, by showing them the marvels of the museum and steering them to other wonders they might not have known about.

And for the last week, just the opposite had been happening, over and over, every day. Because he had been ordered to stand at the blocked-off entrance to Room 4 and turn people away, tell them no, sorry, can't see the Rosetta Stone today. No, not even a peek, awfully sorry. Yes, I know, it's a terrible thing to do when folks such as yourself have traveled so far to see it. No, sorry, I really am, but I can't let you look.

He hated it. Hated seeing the expressions of great disappointment on their faces. Hated having to endure the occasional fits of anger directed at *him*—because he agreed with them. It really was a bloody horrible thing for the museum to do, and with no proper explanation why.

But he did his job and turned them all away, as nicely as he could. He might not have if he hadn't known it would soon end. Maugham had assured him it would be over as soon as the new exhibit was in place, and he was quite sure that wouldn't be terribly long, so just grin and bear it, old sod, right?

Nigel bore it. But he didn't grin. However soon they finished their work, whatever they were doing, it wasn't near soon enough for him. He could hear them in there, just the other side of the plywood barrier. They would move about, sometimes talking. There would be brief bouts of hammering and sawing. But he heard nothing that could tell him what they were doing or when they'd be done, and he was bloody well sick of turning people away.

Grin and bear it, he told himself. But he still couldn't manage a grin.

Helmut Schmeisser was a meticulous man. He had very strict standards, and he followed them unwaveringly. They had been instilled in him in his childhood in what was then East Germany, mostly by his father, who had come of age in the war, followed by the brutal Soviet occupation. These principles guided him through his university career, all the way through a PhD in art history. And he believed that it was adherence to those standards that had propelled him through an exemplary career until he landed his dream job, here at the British Museum.

One of those standards stated that if you give your word to a donor, you honor that word. And so even though it was driving him nearly insane with frustration, he kept his word to Dr. Babcock. He kept everyone from even the tiniest peek at the marvelous head of Horus—everyone including himself. And he made sure that no one had any idea what was going on in Room 4. Even he did not really know, and that was causing him to spend far too much time grinding his teeth, and would certainly result in a massive dental bill. But he had given his word, and he would not break it.

Of course, it was quite proper, even laudable, for him to check with Dr. Babcock and his assistant, Miss Farnsworth, now and then—just to make sure that all was well and they had everything they needed. And if he should accidentally get just the tiniest glimpse of the head while doing so—an entirely *accidental* glimpse—well, then, surely that was not actually a breach of his promise.

So far he had not managed even a fleeting peek at the head. And so if that entirely unwanted urge to help popped into his brain more often than it should have, and prompted him to be a bit more frequently helpful than he might have been, could anyone really say he had done wrong?

Today he was feeling more helpful than usual. It had been three days since the arrival of the head, and not only had he failed to catch a glimpse, he had also received no word at all from Dr. Babcock as to when the work might be finished.

But perhaps if he asked a little more insistently he might get an answer. After all, he had to write a press release, plan a major event for the unveiling, inform the media . . . He could not simply have the barricade removed and say, "Come on in."

And so, as he pushed back from his desk and marched out of his office, he was determined to press Dr. Babcock to name a day when the unveiling might take place. Politely, of course—even obsequiously—but press him nonetheless.

He strode to Room 4, mentally turning over various phrases. Obsequious but firm was not easy. And he was well aware that he was more direct than most English people. German bluntness, he supposed. Still, if he said something like, *If at all possible, I really must know*—was that abrasive? Surely not; it couldn't possibly offend.

He had just settled on that phrase when he reached the barrier. With a nod at the guard who stood there, Helmut knocked on the plywood. "Dr. Babcock? Hello, Dr. Babcock? It's Helmut Schmeisser?"

Footsteps echoed inside, and a moment later, a hand slid into the crack between the museum wall and the plywood. The wood bent inward, and Dr. Babcock appeared.

"Yes? What is it now?"

"I, uh—I merely wanted to make certain that everything was satisfactory so far? That you—"

"It's all fine," Babcock said. He started to pull away.

"Wait! Dr. Babcock, please!" Helmut called desperately.

Babcock returned, looking even more peevish. "Yes? What is it now?"

"Ah, I had hoped—that is, I wondered if, ah, actually—there are so many things that need to be done, and—is it at all possible that you could give me a guess about when you might be finished?"

Babcock's face turned red and seemed to swell two sizes larger. For a moment Helmut thought he had gone too far. Then Babcock hissed out a breath.

"I suppose," he said. "I should think we'll be done in one more day. Does that satisfy your many needs?"

"Yes, indeed, very much, thank you, Doctor, and may I say—"

But there was no need to finish his sentence. Dr. Babcock was gone.

Even so, Schmeisser returned to his office in a far better mood. Soon, the waiting would end and he would see it. That wonderful, unmatched, beautiful head of Horus. Here in the museum for the whole world to see at last.

CHAPTER

30

D r. Charles Babcock stood back and looked. He scanned what they'd done, from the tall securely draped object in the middle of the room, to the other similarly-draped objects of assorted size around it. He looked briefly at the large wooden crate that stood close to the door. Then his gaze returned to the covered objects. He moved around checking each one, smoothing out the covering canvas, tugging at the cords that held it in place. He paid particular attention to the one in the middle that covered a bulky rectangular shape.

Finally, he nodded and went to join his companion. "Well, Miss Farnsworth."

Miss Farnsworth smiled at him, not at all the cool and controlled smile she had used on Schmeisser, but something warmer, more intimate. "Yes, Dr. Babcock?" she said.

"I believe we are done here. May I ask you to bring round our lorry?"

"At once, Dr. Babcock," she said, still smiling.

Dr. Babcock watched her go, and any observer might have been astonished to see that he, too, was smiling.

A re you still arsing about with those maps, Delgado?"

Delgado looked up from a map he'd been studying, a street map of London. It was spread out on the table of the small conference room they'd been using as the task force headquarters. It was West, of course. He'd come in with another cup of tea. He seemed to drink it endlessly.

Delgado just nodded. Nothing he said seemed able to penetrate the armor of disdain West wore. The silence grew until it was awkward. "It has been my experience," he said at last, "that something has almost always been overlooked."

"I'm quite sure that's how the FBI does things," West went on. "But our arrangements are quite thorough—you said so yourself. No need for you to hang about on holiday in London." He slumped into a chair and put down his tea mug somewhat forcibly. "Where's fucking Maugham?"

Delgado glanced at his watch. Five after one. They had scheduled an update meeting for one, with just Maugham, Delgado, and West. Maugham was a little late, which didn't seem characteristic for a top sergeant of the Royal Marines. But it was only five minutes. No big deal. There wasn't anything to update anyway.

"He'll be here," Delgado said, and went back to studying the map.

A few minutes later, Maugham breezed in. "Awfully sorry," he said. "Small mix-up back at the office. Nothing serious." He settled into a chair at the table. "Right," he said. "What's the news?"

West made a rude noise, but Delgado just shook his head. "Nothing new on our end," he said. "What about at the museum?"

"Always the same, and we like it that way," Maugham said. "So what happens now?"

Delgado shrugged. "We just have to wait for something unusual to happen."

"Unusual," Maugham said. "That's a rather broad category."

"Riley Wolfe will not do anything we expect," Delgado said. "He succeeds by doing things in a way that we usually can't imagine."

"Yes," Maugham said, "I suppose he would."

"So when he does move, we won't recognize it as a move," Delgado said patiently. "All I can say is it will be something out of the ordinary, even if it seems small."

"Rather vague, though, you must admit," Maugham said.

"It is," he said. "No help for it."

"Right, well then, never mind," Maugham said. "How can I help today?"

"I'd like to go over this map with you, if you don't mind," Delgado said. "Investigator West tells me we've covered all possible routes away from the museum. But I think it's possible you may have some local knowledge that he doesn't."

"Bollocks," West muttered.

Delgado ignored him and tapped the map with a finger. "You're probably familiar with the area?"

"Yes, naturally, I know it well," Maugham said. "I had ought to, after twelve years." He walked around to Delgado's place and leaned over the map. "I suppose we needn't worry about a rooftop getaway," he said. "Not with a great fucking chunk of stone on his back."

Delgado smiled. "Actually, we do need to worry about that a little," he said. "It's covered. Just in case."

"Oh? Well, I suppose," Maugham said. "And even the main entrance, too?"

"I think so," Delgado said. "Although I imagine it's generally kind of crowded."

"Lord, yes," Maugham said. "And if there's some sort of an event, like a new exhibit, the queue can be a regular mob scene."

"We should post someone there, though. Again just in case."

"Right, better safe than sorry," Maugham said. "But I would worry more about one of these side streets." He pointed to the map. "Here, on the back side of the building, and over here as well." He frowned. "Look here, is this one uncovered?"

"Not necessary. I've been informed it's under construction. Impassable," West said, suddenly appearing beside them.

"All right," Delgado said. He turned back to Maugham. "What can you tell us about traffic patterns? That might affect the choice of escape route."

For several minutes they discussed the assorted pros and cons of the different roads and alleys that led away from the British Museum. West didn't join in again. He sat back down and drank his tea moodily, and when he'd drained his mug he got up and went out, presumably to refill it.

Maugham was describing a particular narrow street, when he paused.

He frowned and looked thoughtful for a moment.

Delgado looked up at him and raised an eyebrow.

Maugham nodded. "Just a thought," he said. "Tell me, then, as far as the day-to-day operation of the museum—you know, routine occurrences and so forth—what sort of thing might you consider unusual?"

Delgado pushed down the surge of hope and instead nodded encouragingly. "There are no real guidelines," he said. "Did something happen at the museum that seemed out of the ordinary?"

"I'm not really sure," Maugham said. "But—"

Before Maugham could answer completely, the door slammed open and West came in. "I've just got the call from my informant," he said. "It's happening now."

That's all of it," Miss Farnsworth said, tilting her head to the forklift. It was loaded with a large wooden crate. Protruding from the top of the crate was a heap of trash.

Dr. Babcock looked around the room, frowning. "Let's have another look. Wouldn't do to overlook something, you know," he said. He began to move around, peering under and behind things, and one more time checking the wraps and bindings on the canvas-draped objects.

"I'm sure we've got it all," Miss Farnsworth called from the seat of the forklift.

Dr. Babcock took a last look around and then nodded. "Right," he said. "Then we're off."

Miss Farnsworth turned the forklift around and headed toward the doorway. Babcock followed behind her, past the barrier, down the hall, and onto the loading dock.

CHAPTER
31

The NCA team moved out quickly and efficiently, but to Frank Delgado they all seemed to be moving through molasses. West could not tell them how much of a head start they had to overcome. All they could do was move out and hope.

The basic plan of action had been ready for several days, and everyone knew where to go and what to do. Delgado had hoped to be able to study and refine it a bit more, but it was happening now, and they would have to go with what they had. He went over everything mentally as they deployed, convinced he had overlooked some vital something—all while rushing into a flak jacket with an NCA windbreaker over it. No firearm, of course. The NCA team were all armed, but as a foreigner with adviser status, Delgado did not carry. And in any case, he hoped that weapons would not be needed. He thought it unlikely that there would be violence. Wolfe was more than capable of murder. He'd proved that many times. But his pattern showed that he didn't like firearms. He would most likely count on his ability to escape, and surrender meekly when they cornered him.

If, he mentally corrected himself. *If we corner him.* It was far from a sure thing. The plan was good, the team was a large and competent one—but this was Riley Wolfe. There had been too many times Delgado had been sure, and each time, at the last second, Wolfe slipped away somehow. And now, every second was taking the thief closer to another escape. All Delgado could do was watch as the British team moved into place with what seemed like nightmarish slowness.

He zipped up his windbreaker, wondering if they'd be in time, sure they wouldn't be.

"Coming with us, Delgado?"

The voice jolted him out of his funk. It was West, of course. He wore his NCA windbreaker already and had a pistol on his hip.

He raised an eyebrow at Delgado. "Of course, if you'd rather wait here where it's warm and safe, I completely understand."

"I think I'll come along," Delgado said.

Helmut Schmeisser was just finishing his third draft of the press release when his office phone rang. He'd been stuck on a tricky bit of phrasing. What were the politics of giving the full provenance of the head of Horus? It certainly cast Dr. Babcock's family in a rather bad light. Would it offend if he said that the head had been "hidden away in a private collection"? Should he simply skip over that part of the story and go straight to "Thanks to the unprecedented generosity of Dr. Babcock"?

But the phone kept ringing, and Schmeisser finally gave in and answered. "Yes, hello, Schmeisser here," he said.

It was Maugham. "Schmeisser, get down to Room Four—you must check on the Rosetta Stone immediately!"

"Check on— What on earth could possibly—"

"Schmeisser, the NCA believe it's been stolen. Get down there and see."

"Stolen—the Rosetta Stone?" Schmeisser said. "You must be joking!"

"I am not, nor are the NCA," Maugham said. "Get down there now."

"But, Reggie, see here—"

"Now!" Maugham barked in his master sergeant voice, and rang off. And Schmeisser was up and out the door before he even knew what he was doing.

Schmeisser pushed past the plywood barrier—it was to be up until the grand unveiling—and entered Room 4 still clinging to the certainty that this was some kind of absurd prank—whether by Maugham himself, or someone having Maugham on. It was ridiculous; the Stone weighed nearly a ton. And Dr. Babcock had been right there the whole time. No one could possibly steal something that large with him looking on.

Still, he supposed he had to look, if only so he could have a bit of sport with Maugham afterward. The Rosetta Stone, stolen, you say? Really, Reggie? And what's this enormous thing here, then?

He strode into the room quite confident of what he would find. And sure enough, the Stone was right there in its proper place. Still covered with a protective canvas wrapping, of course. But naturally, he must look under the canvas. He was thorough and meticulous in everything he did, and this would be no exception, no matter how absurd.

It took him a minute to undo the knots that secured the canvas.

They were quite complex, and had been pulled rather tight. But he undid a few of them, enough to pull up one side of the canvas for a quick, reassuring look that would certainly show—

He jerked to a stop. Then he lifted the canvas higher, because what he was seeing was not possible.

Underneath the canvas, where the massive grayish shape of the Rosetta Stone should have been, there was only a wooden framework. It was the right size and shape, but it was not the Rosetta Stone. That appeared to be gone.

"But that's—" Schmeisser couldn't think how to finish the sentence, so he didn't. Schmeisser put a hand through the wooden frame, as if he might somehow feel that it was still there. But it wasn't.

He dropped his hand. It was true. The Rosetta Stone was gone. He could not imagine how anyone could have taken it—and in the middle of the day, with the museum open! And not only how; *who* could have done such a thing? The only people in the room had been—

No, he thought. *Oh no....*

He hurried over to the massive draped shape that hid the head of Horus. That is, it should. Which is to say that certainly the head, at least—

With trembling hands he tugged at the rope bindings and then jerked up the canvas. And there underneath ...

A wooden frame. Not the head of Horus.

For a very long time he stood there, frozen, while all around him his world was melting. And then, he sat down on the floor and put his face in his hands.

CHAPTER

32

Traffic was light, and the lorry moved easily down Bloomsbury. To all appearances, it was just another tradesman's van going about its business on an ordinary London afternoon.

Inside the lorry, things were, for the most part, just as ordinary. There were a few clashing details, however. The driver was not the sort of rough-looking tradesman one would ordinarily expect. Instead, sitting at the wheel was a rather stylish woman, who wore clothing that could only be called blue-collar haute couture; the kind of clothing a rich and pampered woman might wear to work in her garden.

Her companion in the adjacent seat was also clearly a man of substance, and not the sort of worker you might normally see in a tradesman's lorry. Although he was dressed in working clothes, too, they were high quality, nicely tailored to his chubby middle-aged body.

Aside from a tumble of rubbish, there was only one item in the lorry's cargo area. It was large and ponderous-looking, obviously something important, although exactly what was impossible to tell, since it was hidden by a canvas shroud. Stout ropes had been threaded around the object and then securely fastened to the metal cross braces of the lorry's interior, so that a spiderweb of support held the object safe from falling over.

The driver and his passenger sat quietly at first. But when a traffic signal brought them to a halt, the woman turned around and looked at their cargo. A moment later she turned back to face front, and she started to laugh.

The man glanced at her, and she stopped laughing. But still smiling, she said to him, "Well, then, Dr. Babcock."

He smiled back. "Yes, Miss Farnsworth?"

"That was rather easier than it should have been," she said.

He frowned. "Yes," he said. "And that worries me."

"Does it?" she said. "Why on earth would that worry you?"

The man opened his mouth to answer but was cut off by the sound of a police siren a few blocks ahead of them. "That," he said.

For a moment they drove on, silent and noticeably more tense. Then the woman pointed.

"There," she said. "We'll turn down there."

The man nodded, and she steered the lorry down a side street.

t's a buff-colored lorry, probably sixteen feet long," Maugham said, putting down his phone.

"How do you know that?" West snapped.

"Two museum employees saw it," he said. "A woman on the loading dock having a smoke, and a janitor carrying out some rubbish."

"Right," West said.

He turned away and spoke into one of his radios. He had three of them, to communicate with the different law enforcement groups involved. West moved from one transceiver to the other, listening and giving orders, and Delgado could only watch. There was no part for him to play right now, and that made him nervous, much more so than when he was taking an active part in things.

The three of them were in an NCA car, with a uniformed officer at the wheel. The siren screamed at the surrounding traffic, which moved reluctantly aside for them. But it was still taking much too long, and it seemed even longer to Delgado, who could only look out the window of the moving car and listen to voices on the radios.

Finally, he could stand it no longer, and he leaned over toward West. "Has anyone spotted the lorry?" he asked, using the unfamiliar word self-consciously.

West glanced at him with an annoyed expression but didn't answer. Maugham cleared his throat and looked out the window. Delgado realized his anxiety had made him ask a foolish question—but he felt so helpless, so useless, a mere observer when the quarry was Riley Wolfe. He'd devoted most of his career to trying to catch this man, and to be this close while at the same time having no control, no real input—it was maddening.

But it couldn't be helped. All he could do was ride along and hope.

He sighed and looked out the window on his side. One way or another, it would be over soon.

CHAPTER

33

The sirens were getting closer, and there were more of them. Normally that just added a little excitement to things. But now I was in an unfamiliar foreign city, and I didn't know anything about what streets to take and which to avoid. Relying on anybody else is almost always a bad idea, and I don't like it. Still, this time it was Caitlin, and she seemed to know where we were. That's the main reason she was driving; she knew London, I didn't. And I still have a problem driving on the wrong side of the road, which doesn't help.

Caitlin was used to all that, and she clearly knew how to drive a van. She knew the city, too, choosing turns that took us down side streets and very tight alleys, and once—briefly—the wrong way on a one-way street, which finally dumped us back out onto a major boulevard that was not as crowded as Bloomsbury had been.

I looked at Caitlin. She let out a long breath, and her shoulders dropped from around her ears.

"Right," she said. "That should do us oh Christ."

As a sentence, that didn't make a whole lot of sense. But it got very clear when she went rigid again and stared out the windscreen in front of us. I looked, too, and suddenly it all made sense. The reason the traffic was light was that the street ahead was blocked.

By a line of police vehicles.

For a half second I could only blink and hope I was seeing it wrong. I wasn't. They were all still there, and they were looking at us.

Caitlin jerked the wheel over and took us down another tight alley. She stopped beside a dumpster halfway down, overflowing with garbage, and pointed at it. "Push it into the center—quickly!"

She really didn't need to add the "quickly." I mean, I had been paying attention. But I jumped out, and pushed the dumpster into the center of the alley as fast as I could. It wasn't the most fun ever; the dumpster belonged to a restaurant—a seafood restaurant—and it smelled like it was low tide. After three seconds of pushing, I did, too. I climbed back into the van covered with the delightful scent of spoiled bait.

Caitlin stopped me before I was all the way in. "Get out here," she said. "If they see the lorry moving they won't look for you on foot."

"What? No! I won't let you sacrifice—"

"Don't be a fecking eejit! I'm not sacrificing! I have a plan—but it only works for me!"

I started to ask what the hell that meant—and stopped. I'd never asked her about her past or present connections to clandestine organizations, Irish or otherwise, but I was pretty sure she had some. It made sense that they wouldn't help me.

"Caitlin—"

"Never mind that, you fecking gobdaw." She leaned over and gave me a quick kiss. She wrinkled her nose and said, "Christ, you stink. Hurry home, luv."

A siren squealed, very close, like it was trying to underline what Caitlin was saying. "They're here. Run, Harry!"

And then she gunned the engine, and I had to jump clear as she raced ahead, out of the alley, and away.

D elgado realized he was grinding his teeth, but he couldn't stop. They still were moving so slowly, and he was burning to do something—anything—and knew he couldn't. He looked out the window again and took a deep breath. Letting it out slowly, he told himself to relax, be patient.

Halfway through his slow exhale, one of West's radios spat out a burst of static, followed by a voice Delgado couldn't quite hear. West picked it up, listened, and spoke briefly before putting down the radio again. He turned to face Delgado.

"We've got them cornered," West said. "They've cut through an alley and right into our roadblock."

All the tension snapped back into Delgado's shoulders and he leaned forward. "How far?" he said.

West nodded toward the street ahead of them. "Three blocks up, two over," he said. "We'll be there in two shakes." He turned away again.

"West," Delgado said.

West turned halfway back and raised an eyebrow.

"You might move in the special team now."

West nodded. "Right," he said, "good call." He picked up one of his radios.

CHAPTER

34

've been chased by cops many times, and I'm still here on the outside. And that is totally not bragging, because it's nothing to boast about. Having a swarm of gendarmes breathing down your neck is not a good thing, even if they're Keystone Kops. It means you've screwed up, made a dumb mistake, and you are paying for it in adrenaline. And if you are not very careful and very nimble, you will be paying for it with hard time.

The thing was, I couldn't figure out how I'd screwed up this time. How had the cops even figured it out so quickly? And they hadn't just figured it out now, today, as it happened, like from seeing us take the Rosetta Stone and drive away. There were too many of them, and they were too well organized. That takes planning, and it takes time, and I was only fifteen minutes away from the museum. Something was way off here, and I needed to figure out what, how and why.

More immediately, I'd just driven right into a trap, and there wasn't any really obvious way out of it. But like I said, this was not my first rodeo, and I had a few moves to make before the show was over. I jumped on top of the stinky dumpster and launched myself straight up the side of the closest building. Not hard for me, and not something the cops ever expect. Using parkour had saved me many times, and it would now, too. Cops think two-dimensionally. They're chasing somebody on the street, and they expect their perp to stay there, or cut down another street, duck into a building, something like that.

So when that guy they're chasing on flat surfaces is suddenly up a wall and on the roof, waving bye-bye before he races away across the rooftops, they just aren't ready to deal with it.

It was an easy climb. Plenty of window ledges for handholds. The building was four stories high, and it took me less than half a minute to reach the roof. Once I was on top I could just zip away onto the next roof, and the next, until it was safe to come down. Then I could head back to join Caitlin in a more ordinary way, like via the Tube.

I pulled myself up onto the roof and took a step forward—

And stopped.

Because there were four cops lining the far edge of the roof. And just like they were all part of a really tight dance troupe, they stepped toward me in perfect unison.

For a half second my jaw dangled, and the only thought I could manage was *What the fuck . . . ?!*

It just wasn't possible.

It was bad enough if the cops were on to you before you even light the victory cigar. But they weren't just blocking the streets. They were here, on the roof, and that was sending a message that was a whole lot worse, something so bad it put the hair up on my neck and sent a nasty jolt of stomach acid into my mouth. The message was this:

They knew it was me.

Incredibly, somehow, they knew it was me. Putting cops on the roof said that just as clearly as if it were painted in big red letters on a gigantic banner.

That was enough to make me run for my life, straight over the horizon and into a deep dark cave until I figured out how any of that was even possible.

Of course, getting to that nice dark cave looked a little bit problematic at the moment, with four cops coming for me up here, and a whole flock more moving in below. But there was still one thing I could do, so I did it. I went back over the side and down again.

The car turned a corner sharply, causing two of West's radios to slide onto the floor. He ignored them, talking into the third one, listening intently to the response. He put the radio down and leaned forward, said something to the driver, and immediately the car made a U-turn and headed back the way they'd come.

Delgado frowned. They'd been driving straight for the street where Riley was cornered. Why head in the opposite direction? He leaned over and tapped West on the shoulder. "Where are we going?" he asked.

"Headquarters," West said. "It's over."

"What? Over how?" Maugham said.

"The special squad," Delgado guessed. "They caught him on the roof."

"No, they didn't," West said. "I'm trying to make this make sense, and it doesn't quite." He looked at Delgado.

"Tell me what happened," Delgado said. "From the beginning."

West said nothing for a moment, then he nodded. "Right," he said. "The lorry pulled out, saw the trap, and backed into the alley again."

"So they caught him right off," Maugham said happily.

West shook his head. "The squad on the roof reports he came up the side of the alley wall."

"That's Wolfe," Delgado said, feeling the excitement surging up inside. "Got to be him."

"Maybe," West said. "But he came up to the roof, saw the special squad, and went right back down."

"So nicked in the alley, then," Maugham said hopefully.

West just glanced at him and went on. "Not at all. As our team was still moving in, he apparently climbs back into the lorry and drives out of the alley, down another two blocks away, and then back onto the street and straight to the roadblock."

Delgado frowned. Didn't sound like Wolfe. He must have some kind of plan.

"He surrendered?" Delgado said.

"No," West said. "He rolled down the window and said he had a delivery to make and could he please get by."

Maugham laughed aloud. "Really!" he said. "Cheeky bastard."

"They didn't let him by, did they?"

West snorted. "They pulled him out, cuffed him, and he's on his way to headquarters. As are we." He leaned back in his seat.

"What's the part that doesn't quite make sense to you?" Delgado asked.

"In the first place, the lorry had already left the alley," West said.

"What? But—well, I suppose he could've caught it up," Maugham said.

West gave him a withering look but said nothing.

Delgado's stomach felt sour. "There's more," he said.

West nodded. "There is," he said.

"What is it?"

"It's just that the fellow they're bringing in is a Sikh," West said. "He came down from the roof as a chubby, middle-aged man. A minute later he's at the barricade and he's a Sikh." He shook his head. "Rather fast change."

"He could do it," Delgado said.

"Could he?" West asked. And he seemed to be asking sincerely. "Full beard, turban, total change of clothing—and skin several shades darker—all in thirty seconds?"

Delgado hesitated before answering. He had seen Wolfe accomplish things just as seemingly impossible. But this . . . He had a sinking feeling that the man they'd arrested was not Riley Wolfe. It seemed more likely that this was another sleight of hand, a way for Wolfe to say, *Look over there!* And when everyone looked, he escaped in the other direction. If so, that meant Delgado had missed him again.

He wanted the so-called Sikh to be Wolfe, wanted it badly. But it was very hard to believe.

"I don't know," he said at last. "I just don't know."

CHAPTER

35

'Ve been in a lot of traps in my life, and what I've learned is that whoever laid the trap almost always overlooks something. The trick is to learn how to look for that something, because that's always your way out.

This time was no exception. I was already looking when I went back over the edge of the roof. And before I was even halfway down the side of the building I'd found it. I pulled off my jacket, wrapped it around my fist, and smashed a window, knocking away enough glass so I could slide in without shredding myself. They'd be onto me as soon as they saw the broken window, but it would give me a minute or two I didn't have now. That was going to make all the difference.

I swung myself through the window and inside. One glance was enough to see I was in somebody's flat. My luck was running, because it was the middle of the day, and nobody was home. I took a couple of seconds to peel off my Dr. Babcock outfit and stuff it into a closet. I grabbed a coat and hat hanging there, opened the front door, and ran into the hall and down the stairs to the street. By the time I got down I had to be somebody else.

The trick to any quick disguise is to change your profile. With hundreds of people going by, the cops would be looking for somebody who looked like Dr. Babcock. If they were any good—and so far, it looked like they were—they would expect me to change my appearance. But they would be looking for a disguised chubby middle-aged guy. And in a moving crowd, that means looking for that profile.

So I didn't have that shape anymore. I'd already pulled off the padding that made me a chubby middle-aged man. By the time I stepped out into the street I'd pulled on the borrowed coat and hat, and as the building's door closed behind me I slowed to a leisurely walk and slouched over just a little. I moved a little stiffly, like an older man with sore knees, and I kept with a small cluster of people.

I heard shouting behind me, in the alley, but I didn't look, and I didn't pick up my pace. I just trudged on, up the street and around the corner and in no time at all I was going down the stairs to the Tube. I waited three minutes for a train, and rode it across town. There was even a seat available, and I settled into it and tried to think. With the immediate problem of getting me away taken care of, I thought about Caitlin.

Had she gotten clear? She'd been very confident that she would—but was it confidence from experience? Or from not realizing what sort of trap she was in? I didn't really have any idea how deep her background in the Naughty Arts might be. Other than the Otto Dix painting she'd stolen for me, I didn't have anything to go on. Somehow we'd never talked about it. And let's be real here, hiding a van is not easy, even if you call it a lorry. There had been a lot of cops—could she really get past all of them and into some kind of secret hiding place?

It was worth worrying about. In the first place, if she was arrested, I had to assume she would talk eventually. It might be her only way to get some lenient treatment, tell them it was all my fault and I made her do it—*Here's the address where you'll find him.* And I really couldn't blame her if she did that. In fact, I could only blame myself if I was still hanging around waiting to be caught.

Of course, the guy she was giving up would be Harry Metzger, and he would be long gone about fifteen minutes after I got back to my flat. And I'd be gone from Harry's flat, too. That would mean Caitlin would have no way to find me if she did get clear—and that made me realize I wanted her to find me. That, naturally, made me realize I was most worried about her getting caught not for any sane, rational reason like, she might give me up—but because I wanted to be with her, and I couldn't if she was locked up. And that was a whole universe of brand-new problems I still wasn't ready to deal with.

What the hell, it gave me something else to worry about, and worrying passed the time nicely. That large crowd of cops meant one thing—a carefully laid trap. And they were almost on us when we split. What the hell had happened? Someone must have been watching us, figured it out, told the cops—but who?

I switched trains three times, just to be safe. I was certain I hadn't been followed, but better safe than sorry, as Mom used to tell me, although I'm pretty sure she didn't mean it to apply to getting away from cops after committing a major felony. I rode around the city for almost an hour before I finally headed for home. And I'd spent most of that time stewing about Caitlin and realizing, time and time again, that there was no way to know yet, and nothing to do about it even if I did know.

By the time I climbed off the train, I felt like gnashing my teeth. But instead, I spared my teeth and hurried up to the street gnashless. I went to Caitlin's flat first, knocked three or four times, and even called out, "It's me!" which is certainly one of the dumbest things you can say. Because who else would it be? "Hi, it's not me—I'm someone else using this voice!"

It didn't matter which I was. Caitlin didn't answer, so she had probably gone to my flat. If she'd gotten away. I crossed the street and went into my building and up the stairs, and when I saw the door to my flat I stopped dead.

It was open.

Caitlin had a key, but she wouldn't leave the door open, not when the police were looking for us. I had locked it when we left. But somebody had left it open.

A lot of thoughts went through my head in almost no time. My first thought was to keep walking, right on down the hall past my door and out of the building. That was certainly the smart move. But the next wave of thoughts vetoed that. An open door just didn't make sense. If the cops had already traced me to this flat, they could be waiting inside to grab me.

Except they would close and lock the door to make it look like they weren't there. If it was Caitlin, the door would be closed and locked, too. If it was some random burglar, they might leave the door open when they left. But what were the odds of that happening? Especially right now?

Long odds. It didn't make sense, and I couldn't think of anything that did. That made it a lot harder to know what to do.

But there was still common sense. At the moment, anything unknown was an enemy. So the only smart move was to keep walking. Just cruise on by like that open door had nothing to do with me, and keep going until I got someplace far away. Nobody but an idiot would do anything else.

So I walked up to my door, took a deep breath, and went in.

I paused just inside, looked and listened. Nothing. And the place had that empty feeling, the deadness of the air that says nobody else is there.

A quick look around confirmed it. Nobody there; no cops, no burglars . . . And no Caitlin. But someone had been here, and they'd had themselves quite a party. I went back to the front room to survey the damage.

I'll admit, the place had been a mess when I left. Now it was several levels beyond mess. A shambles. Furniture broken, closets and cupboards emptied onto the floor, books and papers ripped up and flung everywhere. There wasn't a single inch of the place that hadn't been trashed.

I prowled the whole flat, poking at the mess, looking for some clue to tell me that Caitlin had been here. And as I kicked through the clutter, I caught a glimpse of something in the closet, and my heart shot up into my throat. It was the shirt she'd been wearing as Miss Farnsworth. I grabbed it up to be sure; it was torn, but yes, that was it. She'd been here. She made it past all the cops, and she'd been safe when she got here, or she wouldn't have stopped to change out of the Farnsworth outfit.

I was so head-smacked with relief that I just stood there holding the shirt for a minute. To my credit, I didn't actually smell it, or cuddle it. I just held it. And then something else occurred to me: Why was it just the shirt? And more than that, Caitlin would not throw the shirt in the closet, even if it was torn. She would throw it away, or maybe put it on a hanger. But not here, not in this closet. She kept her stuff back in the bedroom. This closet was just for storage. And there was one thing in particular I had stored there.

I stuck my head into the closet and searched until I was sure. And then I was. It was gone. I'd stashed all the shiny loot from the pyramid in a gym bag and put it in this closet. It wasn't there now. But I found something where it had been that was pretty interesting.

It was just a piece of paper, and I'd ignored it while I searched. But I saw it now, and I noticed that there was writing on it. Big block letters that looked like they'd been written with a Sharpie. I picked it up.

> You took from me. Now I have taken from you.
> And I will take more.
> Want her back? You know where I am.
> Come get her, if you think you can.
> Better hurry. I'm feeling playful.

Below that was an odd little drawing of a coiled snake. Even without a signature, I knew who had written the note. I'd taken something from someone recently, and when I took it I knew they were the kind of person who would hold a grudge and probably search for me. It looked like they had, and they'd found me, just in time to grab Caitlin. I didn't need to question it even for a second, I just knew.

The Cobra had Caitlin.

CHAPTER

36

The prisoner was waiting in an interrogation room. Delgado glanced through the one-way glass. A sturdy-looking man, mid-thirties. His skin was dark, and he had a thick black beard. He wore cheap, loose-fitting cotton clothing, the kind of clothes one might wear on a hot day in India. On his head he wore the turban worn by all Sikhs.

Delgado's hope dropped a few more notches. This man looked like the real thing. If it was Wolfe, if he had reached this degree of perfection in under a minute—

"If that's a disguise, it's bloody amazing."

Delgado glanced to the side; West stood there looking in, a disgusted expression on his face. "What has he had to say so far?" Delgado asked.

West shook his head. "Nothing," he said. "They were waiting for us to get here. Besides, his English is fucking awful."

Delgado looked back through the glass. The man just sat there, patiently waiting. He turned his head to one side, looking around the room, a puzzled expression on his face. It was either a brilliant act, or genuine.

He turned to West. "What about the Rosetta Stone?" he asked.

West nodded. "Right there in the lorry," he said. "Intact and unharmed."

It was not the relief for Delgado it should have been. What he knew of Wolfe told him that it was almost impossible that he would allow himself to be caught with his loot.

"Investigator West?" A uniformed policeman came in behind them, and West turned to him. The man nodded and said, "Sergeant Anand is here, sir. We're ready to proceed." Delgado saw another officer in the hall, with a beard and turban that marked him, too, as a Sikh.

"Right," West said. "Let's have a go, then."

Inside the interrogation room, West pulled out the chair opposite the prisoner and sat facing him. The Sikh officer, Anand, stood behind him, and Delgado folded his arms and leaned on the wall just inside the door. He was strictly an observer this time.

West said nothing for a minute, just sat and looked at the man. And the prisoner just looked back, the puzzled look on his face slowly morphing to an expression of concern. Finally, without looking away, West spoke.

"What's your name?"

The prisoner responded with a long burst of excited speech—but none of it in English. West glanced up at Sergeant Anand.

The sergeant nodded. "Punjabi, sir," he said. "He wants to know why we have arrested him."

"Is it authentic?" West asked. "Accent and all?"

"Oh, yes, sir," Anand said. "Quite authentic. The accent says probably Amritsar region."

West nodded. "And his name?"

Anand spoke to the prisoner, who answered him. "Talwar, sir. Hardeep Talwar."

West asked several more general questions; standard procedure to get the subject relaxed and used to answering. But finally he asked, "What were you doing in that lorry?"

Talwar shrugged and responded.

"He says he was making a delivery," Anand translated.

"Where was he going?" West asked.

Talwar took a crumpled paper from his pocket and held it up to Anand, who glanced at it, frowned, and asked Talwar something in a more demanding way. Talwar held up his hands helplessly and answered.

"Well? What does he say?" West asked.

Anand shook his head. "He says he was told to deliver to this address, sir," he said, holding up the paper. "But I don't—" He broke off abruptly.

"Sir," he said, and handed the paper to West.

West glanced at the paper, then jerked his head up and stared at the prisoner. "This is Buckingham Palace," he said, waving the paper across the table. "Did you not know that?"

Talwar looked astonished when Anand translated—and much more alarmed. He spoke excitedly until Anand waved him quiet.

"Sir, he says he did not know. He has a great reverence for the king and would never presume. He has just arrived in this country, sir, and he did not know where he was going."

"And yet he was hired to make a delivery," West said.

"Yes, sir. So he says."

West stared at Talwar, then nodded as if it made sense. "Who hired him? And when?"

"He says," Sergeant Anand said, "a woman approached him—"

"What's that? A *woman*?" West interrupted.

"Yes, sir. That's what he says."

West glanced at Delgado. "A woman. And he's quite certain?"

"Yes, sir."

"Describe her."

"Rather small, sir," Anand translated. "Petite, as you might say. Dark red hair, nice clothes, very pale skin."

"Right," West said. "Go on."

"This woman approached him and asked if he knew how to drive. He said of course he could drive, and she gave him a thousand pounds to make the delivery. She said it was very urgent."

"Must have been," West murmured. "And when was this?"

"Right before he was arrested."

"Had he ever seen this woman before?"

"No, sir," Anand translated. "But she was very nice-looking, very upper class. And she seemed in a great hurry."

Anand hesitated, and then added, "And, sir?"

"Yes?" West said.

"He wants to know if he can keep the money."

There was more to the interrogation, but Delgado didn't hear it. He left the room, closing the door behind him, and then paused in the hall. He didn't really have anywhere to go, here in an unfamiliar police station. But he found it painful to hear any more of the Sikh's story, just more hurtful reminders that he had missed out on catching Wolfe. Again. He stood in the hall and tried to see what he might have done differently. He couldn't think of anything. He'd been right about almost everything and the advice he gave West had been spot-on—and still Wolfe had eluded them. And it didn't really matter if it was luck, or his own fault, or some shortcoming of the Brits. They'd missed.

Wolfe had won again.

PART 3

THE COBRA

CHAPTER

37

My first impulse was to jump on a plane and go rescue Caitlin. And there were some really good reasons to hurry. But there's a big difference between rapid response and panicky half-ass full-speed charging at the cannons. Right now there was only me, which is an extremely light brigade, and I couldn't afford to blunder. I needed a plan—and before I could make one, I needed to know a couple of things. The most important was this: Had the Cobra set up the police operation as a way to grab Caitlin and lure me off to his stronghold? Or had the Cobra come for me and walked in just in time to take advantage of something that was already happening by grabbing Caitlin and forcing me to take her back?

You might wonder why that was important. After all, the Cobra had Caitlin either way, and had to know I was coming for her. But I had to know a few things first, starting with this. Why?

If it was coincidence, I was dealing with a basic one-on-one threat, brute force, me against the Cobra. I could handle that. I had done similar things in the past.

But that didn't track. I don't believe in coincidence. And if it was a massive, coordinated operation that involved somehow coercing a police officer or two to help make a large and intricate police trap to catch me? That meant the threat was a lot worse, and there was complex multilayered planning behind it. That made it a whole lot more dangerous—and a lot harder. Because the way I beat a powerful guy with a mean organization is by outthinking and outplanning the opposition. It's a whole lot easier to outplan somebody who thinks hitting something with a hammer is the best strategy. If it all had been planned, my thinking had to be a couple of notches better.

Even more important than that: if it really had been a plan that intricate, it meant I was dealing with somebody who was a whole new level of good. Maybe even almost as good as me. If I was going up against somebody that good, I had to plan very carefully. That was a scary thought, and it meant I had to take my A game. My better-than-A game.

So before I rushed into a rescue plan, I needed a couple of answers. And I thought I knew where to get them. Right here in London.

Investigator Michael West woke up in darkness. That wasn't normal. He usually kept a night-light on in the bathroom of his small flat. It was not possible that it had burned out—it was less than a year old.

And he was cold—it was bone-chilling cold, which it shouldn't be in his flat. But stranger than that, he didn't remember going to sleep. The last memory he had was stopping in a pub on the way home, sipping on a Guinness, and then . . . nothing. Blank, dark nothing. He was fairly sure he hadn't gotten drunk and blacked out. He never had more than one drink.

But here he was, opening his eyes to a very cold, completely dark room. He tried to think it through, remember what had happened, or at least understand why he couldn't recall anything. But nothing came to him.

Well, life was full of mysteries. He would remember eventually, or he wouldn't. Either way, it didn't matter. There was work to do.

He started to get up—and found he couldn't. His arms and legs wouldn't obey him. He jerked hard with his right arm, and was rewarded with pain at the wrist, and a jangle of metal. He pulled slower, experimentally, and heard the soft rattle of steel; his hand was manacled to something very solid. He tried the left arm, then his legs, and it was the same thing. He was tightly shackled in place.

"You're awake. Good."

The voice came from somewhere above and behind him. And it was not a natural human voice—it was coming from a speaker, and filtered through one of those voice-disguising apps.

Just like the voice on the other end of his shameful phone calls.

"What do you want? Where am I?"

He was answered with a chuckle. With the overlay of artificial vocal distortion, it sounded monstrous, inhuman, and definitely not funny. "I hope you don't mind the cliché," the voice said, "but I will ask the questions."

"I did what you asked," West said, fighting to keep panic out of his voice. "You know I won't say a word—I can't!"

There was a short pause. "Tell me exactly what you did," the voice said.

"That's—just what you said! I pulled a barricade, left that one street open! Just as you told me to do!"

"And do you know who I am?"

"You're the fellow who promised to clear my debt with the bookmakers."

"Could you identify me?"

"How could I? I never saw you, I only ever spoke to you by phone, you know that!"

"A policeman has resources," the voice said. "You could have used them to identify me."

"But I didn't! I just wanted to clear my debt!" West found that he was sweating, in spite of the chill in this room.

"And you never tried to follow any clues to my identity?"

"No, I swear, I—all I did was look up that password you gave me, *Beithir-nimh*. But that was just curiosity!"

"Really. And you found out what it means?"

"It's Gaelic, it means 'venomous serpent.' I only—why are you asking me all this?"

There was no answer. West waited, and still nothing.

"Hey!" he finally called. "Let me go!"

Still no answer. West waited, but the silence only grew.

Special Agent Frank Delgado had half a day to spare before his flight home. He'd spent the first part of the day at the British Museum; not out of any real desire to see its many marvels, but because he wanted to see the Rosetta Stone, restored to its proper place. It had been recovered from the lorry and returned as quickly as could be. Aside from the fact that it was the museum's most popular attraction, the NCA and the museum wanted to make the statement that even the most audacious thefts would be foiled, and all was just exactly as it should be.

So Delgado went to the museum, said good-bye to a cheerful Reggie Maugham, and then went down to Room 4. He wanted to look at the Stone in its proper setting and try to understand how Wolfe had stood there in the same place and decided he could and would steal it.

He stood there for fifteen minutes, looking without really seeing as his mind roamed, connecting this to Wolfe's past crimes. Most of them were successful. This one almost had been, too. If not for the timely alert from West's informant, the plan probably would have worked. Wolfe would have taken the Stone and gotten a huge cash payment from the insurance company, as he usually did.

He wondered about the identity of West's informant, too. Wolfe worked alone. But the Sikh driver they'd arrested mentioned a small pale woman. She was obviously part of Wolfe's team. She had vanished, too. So who had informed? Had it been someone connected to this mystery woman? Whoever it was would need to have some reason to be here, at the museum, where they could observe and know when the theft was happening.

If it had been his case, he would have begun by examining the background of museum employees, as soon as the Stone was recovered. It would be a big job, but if a guard, or someone selling tickets, had some past connection that raised suspicion—perhaps even a criminal record—that would be a start.

Delgado shook his head. It wasn't his case. And the only part of the whole affair that interested him was the thing he'd wanted to do his whole career: catching Wolfe. That wasn't going to happen now, not here in London. Wolfe would be far away. And standing here in an attempt to understand was fruitless. The motivation and reasoning eluded him, and probably always would. He would never really learn to fully think like Wolfe. He glanced at his watch and sighed. He had one more stop to make, and he did not anticipate that would be a great deal of fun.

He took a cab to NCA headquarters in Vauxhall. Even though the trip to England had been a failure, he felt he had to say good-bye. He didn't think Investigator West's farewell would be very cordial, but there was also Deputy Director Emma Pullings, and cordial or not, he felt he should close out his trip officially. It was the right thing to do, and it was expected of him. It was very possible that there would be future joint operations with his British counterparts, and maintaining good relations was part of the job.

He found Pullings in her office, and she waved him to a chair facing her.

"Well, then, so you're leaving us, are you?" she greeted him.

"I am," Delgado said.

"Well, I'm sorry it didn't work out a little better," she said. "But we gave it a go—and we got the Rosetta Stone back in one piece, which is the big thing, isn't it?"

Delgado smiled politely and said, "Yes, it is," even though he was thinking that he would have traded a dozen Rosetta Stones to finally collar Riley Wolfe.

Pullings cocked her head to one side, and as if she were reading his thoughts, she said, correctly, "I suppose you'd rather have nabbed Wolfe."

"In truth, ma'am, I would," he said. "I've been chasing him for so long, and I'd like to end his career."

"Yes, quite so, understandable," she said. "At least he doesn't appear to have killed anyone this time."

"I'm not so sure," Delgado said.

Pullings raised an eyebrow. "Really. Who d'you have in mind?"

"The man he was impersonating, Dr. Babcock," Delgado said. "Has there been any sign of him?"

"Ah. There is that, isn't there," she said. "No, not a trace of him. So I suppose one might assume the worst, hm?"

"I think that would be wise," Delgado said. He stood up. "I'd like to say good-bye to West," he said. "Is he in?"

Pullings frowned. "No," she said. "Actually, he isn't. And we're not sure why."

Delgado blinked. "I'm sorry?"

She shrugged. "He had duty this morning and didn't show," she said. "Hasn't answered his phone, either."

"Is that usual?"

"Not at all," Pullings said. "He's never done anything like this before. But I'm sure there's some very ordinary explanation. And if there's no sign of him by tomorrow, we'll run him down, wherever he might have got to."

Delgado was not as optimistic. With anything that involved Riley Wolfe, coincidence was very suspicious. But he didn't say so. "When you do, please tell him I said good-bye."

"Of course," Pullings said. She rose from her chair and reached across the desk to shake his hand. "On behalf of the NCA, thank you for your assistance in the matter. I hope you have a pleasant trip home."

Delgado shook her hand and gave her a brief smile, the best he could manage. "Thank you, ma'am," he said.

CHAPTER

38

Wherever I go, and whoever I am at the time, I always carry a Go Bag. It's just what it sounds like, a bag filled with stuff I might need if I have to run for it in a hurry. It holds some cash in several different currencies—and some gold, too—as well as a handful of spare identities. For each potential New Me there's a passport, a couple of credit cards, usually a driver's license. There's also some basic stuff to change my appearance.

I was pretty sure I had to hurry now. Once they found their missing crooked cop, they'd be even more anxious to catch me. Especially if he was dead when they got to him. I didn't worry about that too much. I'm not real fond of cops, and I figure a cop on the take deserves what he gets.

The things that cop had told me confirmed what I'd been most afraid of. The Cobra had tracked me to London, and then somehow found out I was after the Rosetta Stone, and set up a massive operation to catch me, with the assistance of the British cops.

That told me I needed to make one more stop in the UK before I headed home, and I definitely needed to change what I looked like to get out of London. I flipped through the passports, and settled on one for a Shlomo Berkowitz. He was from Pittsburgh, and an Orthodox Jew, which meant a big bushy beard. He had glasses, too, which always helps the disguise. I've also noticed that the average person tends to avoid talking to or interfering with people who are wearing attire that says they're Orthodox—or any other religion or culture that isn't the cultural majority.

So Shlomo took the train north to Birmingham and rented a car. Then he drove farther north to Manchester, fighting the whole way to remember to stay on the wrong side of the road. It was mostly success-ful, and he/I only came close to killing ourself a couple of times.

If this seems to you like a really bad shortcut for getting home and gearing up to rescue Caitlin, that's because you don't know what I know about Manchester. Or more exactly, about an abandoned indus-trial park on the outskirts of the city. There's an old factory there that's only *mostly* abandoned. One person lives there, a kind of New Age oracle known to the cyber world as Saint Alia of the Knife. Her real name is Tamiqua Coates, and she is the greatest hacker in the world.

Things being what they are nowadays, everybody pretty much needs a hacker. I mean, if you work the late shift at Dunkin', maybe not so much. But if you are the world's greatest thief, you sure as hell do, and that hacker better be the best.

A few years back, I'd gotten myself into something that called for top-of-the-heap computer expertise. I'd gone trolling on the dark web until I got a nibble. Somebody answered me in a snail-mail letter with my birth name and sent it to my supersecret private mailbox. That's two things that, in theory, nobody knows. This somebody found both. Meaning they not only tracked me down—they found out just about everything about me. It was a hell of an audition.

And Tamiqua lived up to it. I'd used her services several times since, and she always came through. And I always paid her about twice what anybody else would, which I've found to be a great way to keep people loyal. We'd gotten to trust each other; we were even pretty close to being friends. So now I was one of the few who knew her name and where she lived, and she was one of the few who knew my birth name, J. R. Weiner. She got a kick out of using it with me, and she was so good at what she did, I let her.

I'd called ahead to let her know I was coming; that was usually a good idea if you wanted to avoid being electrocuted, or worse. I had no idea what new kinds of defensive booby traps she might have put in place around the old factory, but I knew she had them, and I didn't want that kind of surprise.

After making that first contact, I threaded my way in and back to her work area. She has an old IBM mainframe there that she's done frightening things to, and about four tons of electronic stuff in every possible stage of assembly. There's a poster of Bob Marley on one wall, and one of Public Enemy above her workstation. When I came in, she was pounding away on her keyboard. As I crossed the threshold, I heard a soft chime, and Tamiqua turned around to greet me.

She knew it was me—but I hadn't told her what "me" looked like right now, and she was not ready for Shlomo. She took one look, gaped for a second, and then gave a hoot of laughter that collapsed into howling hysteria lasting several minutes.

She finally calmed down just long enough to gasp out, "Oh fuck me twice, J.R.—!" and then she was off into another minute of huge, howling and barking laughter.

I sat down and waited. She came up for air at last, and said, "Oh Christ on a kipper, I think I'm in love. The fucking beard— Oh, J.R., you're a fucking beast."

"Thank you," I said. "I had some heat in London—"

"Must've been a fucking furnace," she snickered.

"It was."

Still smiling, she cocked her head to one side. "Half a mo'—that was your pig's ear with the Rosetta Stone, yes?"

I didn't bother asking how she even knew about it, let alone that it was me. "It was," I said. "And it went very bad very quickly."

"That's bait. Who grassed?"

I shook my head. "I'm not sure," I said. "Somebody who doesn't like me tracked me down somehow."

"Can't be many of those, J.R.," she said.

"Less than five thousand. And I know who it was. I need to know how he found me."

She gave me the sort of pitying look you'd give a little dog who can't quite make the jump up onto a tall chair.

"Have you heard of something called facial recognition, J.R.?"

I opened my mouth, then closed it. Because of course I'd heard of it. Who hasn't? But it hadn't occurred to me that it could be used on me—or, rather, that I could be identified by it.

"I'm pretty careful," I said. "I mean, I was disguised."

She laughed. It was another one of those loud, nothing-held-back laughs that would be contagious—if it weren't aimed at me. Unfortunately, this one was. "No jokes, bruv?"

"No. Why didn't my disguise fool it?"

She sighed, like she was explaining something to a child who didn't quite get it. "J.R., facial recognition programs run through an AI interface and—" She paused, cocked her head. "You've heard of AI, right?"

I let her have that little dig and just nodded.

"Good boy. 'Course you have. Right," she said. "AI is getting geometrically better every day. Mine is dog's bollocks, but there's one or two by hackers near as marvelous. And mine could recognize you with a bucket on your head."

I shook my head. I knew this would be like explaining how a microwave works to a fourteenth-century peasant, but I asked anyway. "How is that possible?"

"Easy, mate. Lookit." She turned and attacked her keyboard. A headshot of me came up on her monitor. "Simple version, awright?"

"Yes, please."

"Here's a few cardinal points, what the AI looks at," she said, moving her cursor to highlight my eyebrows, nose, and forehead. "With me? Right. Those still register with most disguises. But if we change these around, mess with your face a bit—"

She made my nose wider and longer, joined my eyebrows, brought my hairline down on my forehead. It still looked like me—sort of. "That's enough to fool AI?" I asked. "I need to make sure it doesn't happen again," I said.

"'Simple version' I said, J.R." She shook her finger at me. "Listen up, bruv. No worries, I'll send you a bangin' workup, cheers."

"Thanks," I said. "You said there are one or two people who are almost as good as you. Can you figure out which one tracked me? Or who did?"

"'Course I can. Why do you want to know?"

"I need to get into a heavily protected place," I said. "Headquarters of the person who hired that hacker."

"And you think the hacker can tell you how if you ask politely?"

"I do," I said. "Can you find them?"

"It might take some time," she said thoughtfully. "Maybe as much as five minutes."

"I'll wait," I said.

CHAPTER

39

Tamiqua was as good as her word. I left Manchester with the name of the hacker the Cobra used, and it took her four and a half minutes. Tamiqua said the hacker, who used the handle "Cardinal Sin," was very good, though naturally not quite as good as Tamiqua. I had a few questions for the Cardinal before I went into the Cobra's den to get Caitlin, but I had to be quick. I needed to do it before the Cobra did her too much damage. I was pretty sure the whole security setup had been modified since I went in and got the Irish crown jewels. When somebody like me gets in, that's what you do. You make it all better.

So Shlomo drove toward the Manchester Airport. He/I could turn in the rental car, morph into somebody else, and get on the warpath.

On the way I thought about how I would do it.

I knew now that the Cobra had planned a truly devious operation to get me. So I couldn't just show up at his gate and ask nicely; I was pretty sure that wouldn't end well for me—or for Caitlin. And I was just as sure I couldn't bargain for her release. Call me an egotist, but I had a hunch the only thing I had that I could trade for her was me, which would kind of defeat the purpose of rescuing Caitlin, since I would be a little too dead to enjoy the reunion.

I hadn't come up with anything by the time I turned in the rental car. I was still blank when I went into a stall in the airport restroom and got rid of Shlomo. And when I came out as Herve DuChamps, bookshop owner of Marseilles, I still didn't have any good ideas. Normally that's okay. Creating the right plan takes time. But I didn't have that kind of time, not with Caitlin in Cobra's bloody clutches. And, of course, the more I fretted about needing to hurry, the less my brain actually worked on planning.

Herve booked a first-class flight to Oslo; partly because there was a better connection to Atlanta from there, and partly because it's always a good idea to hop around a little when you're fleeing in terror from the cops. It's a short flight, and I only had time for two quick slugs of mediocre cognac. The drinks also failed to flog the gray cells to their duty, and I landed still blank, and starting to get grumpy about it.

Herve bought some new clothes in the airport and then went into the restroom, where he disappeared, replaced by Samuel Akers of White Bluff, Tennessee, owner of a large poultry farm. And Mr. Akers, who was really a simple man of the earth, with a mere high school education, got an idea.

I won't let Sam take all the credit. He was inspired by something he saw outside one of the airport shops. There was a row of posters with travel themes, of all things—in an airport, no less. And one of them urged us all to visit Dublin. The enticement this poster offered was the National Museum.

That certainly wasn't an attractive incentive in my present state. I was pretty sure that things being what they were at the moment, I could live very well without any more exposure to museums. And an Irish museum? No; I turned and walked away. Irish is what started this whole shit show, going back to the crown jewels I'd liberated from the Cobra. Who apparently had some kind of weird fetish about Irish treasures. So there was absolutely no reason for me to go gape at a whole museum full of reminders unless I was going to steal one as a way to—

I stopped so suddenly that four people hurrying to their gate bumped into me. Because what the actual fuck had I just been thinking? I turned around and went back to the poster.

This time, when I thought it again, I got it. And I liked it.

CHAPTER

40

It was winter, and the sun had set hours ago, even before closing time. Now it was full dark, the dead of night. The crowds were long gone, and the chill that was over the land had come into the museum, a gloomy place after midnight with no one about but the ghosts that cling to so many old things, even here on Kildare Street in the heart of Dublin. Because "here" was the antiquities section of the museum, and there were plenty of old things for ghosts to cling to. There were relics left by Viking raiders, old weapons and domestic items from Ireland's early history, and many precious items dug up and recovered from old and destroyed monasteries, churches, convents. All these things had their own ghosts.

Only one living creature shared the darkness with the ghosts, the night watchman. Declan Devany knew they were all about him, the shades of ancient Ireland, but he didn't mind. He'd long ago made his peace with the old spirits. On a night like this, Declan was glad of the company, however ephemeral it might be. Winter has a way of bring-ing us to our low points, and being alone quickly turns into aching loneliness.

But Declan didn't feel it. He'd never married, in part because he didn't feel the need of companionship. Sure, he enjoyed chatting it up over a pint with his friends, but he was perfectly content to go home to the flat he shared with no one. And here in the museum, even on a chilly winter evening, he didn't mind being on his own.

In theory he was here to provide security, to ensure that no one broke in and attempted to steal anything. There was a great deal worth stealing, too, if you were so inclined. In the Treasury exhibition alone there were eyepopping items worth millions and millions of euros. Like the Ardagh Chalice, for example, which was a pure icon of Irish history and a source of national pride for its marvelous and uniquely Irish workmanship. On top of the patriotic value it had, the chalice also carried religious significance. And obviously, a great deal of mon-etary value.

Part of a hoard of eighth- and ninth-century items recovered from an ancient ringfort in County Limerick, the chalice had been used for Eucharistic wine during mass. It's made of spun silver adorned with gold, and ornamented with amber, lovingly crafted with uniquely Celtic artistry. Declan loved it, perhaps a bit more than all the other items in the Treasury exhibit, and he would gladly defend it with his life if anyone were to attempt to steal it.

But there was never any sort of incursion at the museum. Declan passed his working nights in quiet contemplation of the beautiful things under his care. He patrolled the halls in peaceful silence and solitude—except for the ghosts, of course, and if it came to that, Dec-lan was only half convinced they actually existed.

So he strolled through the halls, content, pausing now and again to gaze fondly on a favorite exhibit. He would stand in front of an exhibition of Viking weapons and imagine what it had been like, defending the land against raiders from the North. Or he would picture himself at a tenth-century mass, the beautiful Latin service ringing between the stone walls of the old church, and himself receiving Communion, perhaps from the Ardagh Chalice itself.

He entered the long hall of the treasury exhibit in a state of pleasant reverie, walking down the long gallery with here and there a quick stop to look at old favorites. He arrived at the center of the hall expecting nothing but more of the same. There, in the very middle of the gallery, was the tall and slender case holding the Ardagh Chalice, and Declan strolled up to it for a short visit—and stopped dead as if he'd run into a wall.

For just a moment he felt all the spirits, haunts, and banshees of the museum gather around him and scream, and his mouth went dry and his heart surely stopped—because there was no mark on the display case, and no sign that any actual living human had been anywhere near—

But the Ardagh Chalice was gone.

CHAPTER

41

As a rule, I really dislike taking from the 99.9 percent. They have enough to worry about. And I really, really, dislike smash-and-grab jobs. I think they show a lack of artistry, and a lack of respect for the ancient and honorable profession of stealing stuff. There's no real skill in breaking a piece of glass, snatching something, and running for the exit. So I try not to stoop to that kind of barbaric behavior.

And I hadn't this time. I'd slipped in past the security system, which would definitely get you, so don't get any ideas. I came in on the second floor, because modern security hasn't really caught up to the idea of parkour yet, so the upper floors usually aren't guarded quite as well. And what the hell, I like to climb.

The chalice was on the first floor, in a long hall conveniently labeled TREASURY, just so I couldn't miss it. And I got the case open easily enough, grabbed the big silver thing, and was back out the window I came in by. Then I headed for home.

I landed at JFK as Guillermo Bonavente, a wholesale fruit merchant from Napoli. I had no idea if selling wholesale fruit is even a thing, but it sounded cool. Guillermo got to the taxi stand in front of the terminal just in time to hit the morning rush hour heading into the city. And riding in to Manhattan I said a silent thank-you again to the city's Taxi & Limousine Commission for their fixed-fare policy. I mean, I have plenty of money, I could afford to buy the damn taxi fleet if I wanted. But no matter how rich you are, it's annoying as hell to sit in traffic with nothing moving except the meter.

Ninety minutes later, the cab let me off in Midtown, and I walked down to Port Authority. I took a stall in the men's room, turned myself into a native New Yorker by the name of Vinny Alessandro, and took a train over to Vinny's apartment in Brooklyn.

My place—Vinny's place—was the second floor of a converted warehouse. I'd had it for a couple of years, which usually means it's time to get rid of it and find a new apartment. If you stay in one place too long, sooner or later somebody will track you down, and it will be somebody you would rather avoid. But I wasn't there that often, and it was a really great space: big, an open floor plan, plenty of light from the huge old windows. I'd put a bulletproof film on the windows, reflective on the outside, and it still let in lots of sunshine, when there was any.

Not that I needed any sunlight right now. What I needed was more time, and that was always the hardest thing to get. I had the outline of a plan to keep the Cobra busy while I rescued Caitlin. I knew where Cobra probably was; I'd been there before, when I stole the Irish crown jewels, and it was very far from everything, in the Canadian wilderness. I'd figured a way to make that work for me, and it depended on one simple move: What I had to do was get Cobra out of his super-secure secret hideout, and away to someplace far enough from it to give me time to get in, get Caitlin, and get out. I had the bait to lure the Cobra out, which was the most important part. But God damn it, I needed somebody to stay with it and sell it to the Cobra.

Yeah, that bothered me. Not because I'm that guy who wants to do everything himself to show how great he is. I mean, maybe I am, a little? But there are some very good reasons for it, too. First, I hate having to depend on somebody else. No matter how good they are, no matter how loyal to you they are, something always goes wrong, and you're not there to make it right again. But there was no time to think of a way around it right now, so I didn't have a lot of choice. I needed a helper.

Because I was in New York, I thought of Monique. She lives here, and even though I don't really trust anybody, she is as close to it as I come. But almost-trust wouldn't be enough this time. And anyway, she was still recovering from our last heist together. And what I trust her with had nothing to do with what I needed now. Monique is the greatest art forger in the world. When she copies something, it's better than the original. But her survival skills are pretty much tied to her American Express card. I couldn't put her in a dangerous situation like this. I'd had to do that in the past, and it didn't end well for her.

There were a couple more people I could call, people I'd worked with before, and they were more than able to handle any rough stuff that might come up. The first was T. C. Winston, a totally gung ho ex-Marine, who could handle just about anything. He was also the only pilot I could rely on, and I was going to need him for that. Unless I wanted to hike a few hundred miles through a Canadian wilderness—in winter—I had to go in by plane.

Then there was Arthur Kondor. He was basically a thug for hire. But I liked him because he was a lot more than a simple thug. I mean, he was that: big, strong, fast, and willing and able to turn out the lights on anybody I pointed to. But he was smart, too. He read things, he had thoughts. And even better, he felt like he owed me, because he'd been guarding my mother when a miserable shit bag rogue federal agent grabbed her and let her die.

But Kondor *looked* like a thug. He'd be great, standing in the background backing up my main player. And that was the big problem. For the starring part I needed somebody who could look a little more refined, in a sleazy kind of way. There was really only one person I could semi-trust who could do that. My old partner, Chaz.

Way back when I was starting out, I did something I just don't do. I took a partner. I mean, not just a helper, but somebody in it with me on an equal footing. I hooked up with Chaz, and we worked together for a while. He was older than me, and he'd been in the game a long time when I met him. I was just starting out, and I learned a lot from him. Together we pulled off some very fine jobs that neither one of us could have managed alone. It was fun, but nothing is forever, and we drifted apart.

But recently I'd reconnected with Chaz, and he would be perfect for this. He does a sleazy German art dealer that's almost good enough to fool me, even when I know it's him. With Kondor backing him and T.C. flying me, it was a good team, and they knew each other. It made my stomach churn to think of counting on this many people, but if I had to do it, these three were the best choice I had. And I was out of time.

I started calling.

CHAPTER

42

Kondor and T.C. both said yes without hesitating. I'd been pretty sure they would, but it's always nice to be right about that kind of thing.

My next call was to Tamiqua, even though it wasn't actually a call. She didn't trust phones. It's hard to say she was wrong about that. I mean, I know ways to hack into somebody else's phone, and I'm not a tech genius. So I'm pretty sure the cops, the government, and even savvy private players can tap into anything at all that anybody does with a phone. And if you think I'm being paranoid, look up something called Pegasus. You can apologize to me afterward—just, not by phone.

So I communicate with Tamiqua on the dark web, using a very secure VPN. I did that, giving her the gist of a notice I wanted to put out, and the name of a guy in Germany who needed a really good fictional background. I had bought a mailing address for him. Other than that, the guy didn't actually exist yet, but I hoped he would. I needed him to, for my plan to work. The plan was shaky enough, what my mom would have called slapdash. But there was no time for anything else. Every hour that went by was an hour Caitlin was in danger, and maybe worse.

Tamiqua would get the notice out in the right places, so it would be seen right away by a few discriminating patrons of the stolen arts. And she would build a bio, with documentation, for the sleazy German dealer selling it. I knew Tamiqua would do it up right, better than I could, so I put it out of my mind and moved on to the last piece. I had to do that one in person, because Chaz didn't even have a phone. It was a long flight down to see him, but it was worth it. I knew he'd say yes.

N o. Fuck off."

"Come on, Chaz. Half a million bucks for three days of work."

"God damn it, no! I'm retired!"

"You said that last time."

"And I should've stuck with it. I almost got killed—twice! So no! I'm not getting sucked in to one of your batshit crazy bloodbaths again—fuck you, Riley."

To be perfectly honest, it was going just about as well as I'd expected. Chaz liked to play hard to get. I guess because he was so comfy and secure living in his double-wide in a Florida trailer park. But I knew the guy, better than he knew himself. There were two things he truly loved—money and adrenaline. He wasn't going to get either one in the retirement colony he lived in. So even though Chaz was making it sound like he was staying out and his mind was made up, I knew him too well to buy that. His mind *was* made up: He wanted to do it. He just wanted to be seduced first.

"You'll be perfectly safe," I said, in a voice like you'd use to soothe a spooked horse. "Kondor will be right there with you."

"Kondor is twice as fucking scary as anything we might be up against," he said. "If I need him for backup, I'm in something terrifying. So fuck off, Riley. I'm too old for this shit."

I let out a big, theatrical sigh. "I guess you are too old, Chaz. You never used to get scared like this."

"What? I'm not scared. I'm cautious!"

"Scared. And too old. Probably can't even drink a six-pack anymore without falling asleep."

"Bullshit! Now you're getting personal!"

"Prove me wrong, Chaz," I said. I put a six-pack on his rickety little table—PBR, his drink of choice. I'd showed up with a case of it, because like I said, I know Chaz.

He glared at me. "You think I'll chug a few beers and say, *What the fuck, I'm in?*"

"Yup."

"Well, fuck you twice, Riley." He reached over, pulled out a bottle, and chugged it. Then he reached for another one.

Forty minutes and three six-packs later he was still saying no, but I could tell he was wavering. I mean, he wasn't getting drunk. As far as I could tell, Chaz never got drunk. He was just one of those rare people who can drink beer endlessly without showing any effect. No slurred words, no jerky drunken motions.

But he was getting kind of sentimental. "It's just not the same anymore, Riley," he said, with a big sigh. "In the old days we had something to prove. To the world, to ourselves. Now?" He drained his bottle and reached for another. "Done it all. Nothing left to prove. And fuck it, I am slowing down."

"It's not about proving anything this time, Chaz. I need your help."

"Eh." He waved that off. "You can find somebody else."

"I'm out of time. This has to happen now." I could tell he was weakening, and I leaned in for the kill. "You're the only one I can trust to pull this off, Chaz."

"Trust?! Didn't I teach you anything, dumbfuck?"

"You taught me a lot," I said.

"Then why?" he said. He took a long pull from the bottle. "What's so different this time?"

I hesitated, because I knew what he would do with it if I told him. But if he was going to put his neck on the block, he deserved to know why. "There's this woman . . ."

If you are a fan of comedy, you've probably heard of something called the Danny Thomas Spit Take. It goes like this: Danny takes a sip of coffee just as his wife says something like "I'm pregnant." And Danny's so shocked he spits out the coffee and says, "You're *what*?!"

That's pretty much what Chaz did now, with beer instead of coffee. And instead of shock and outrage, he was laughing his ass off. At me. I wiped the beer off my face and waited for him to slow down.

He finally did. "Holy shit, I should've known. The ones who never fall always fall hardest." And he was off again, laughing like a loon.

Eventually, he wanted beer more than he wanted to laugh at me, so he stopped and took a long sip. "Jesus fuck, Riley. First trust, then a woman." He shook his head. "Tell me all of it."

I told him. I left out a few really personal parts, but I gave him the overall picture. About halfway through I noticed that he was looking at me weird; head tipped to one side, and a kind of puzzled half frown on his face. I told him all of it anyway. And when I finished, he was still looking at me that way. Then he shook his head and looked away.

"What," I said.

He shook his head some more, then looked at me straight. "Is this Cobra person a true badass?"

"One of the worst."

"And his place is surrounded with lethal stuff to kill people like you who try to get in?"

"I mean, yes, but I did get in before, Chaz."

"Which just means, if he's as good as you say, he's got a whole new set of killer shit in place that you don't know about."

I opened my mouth, then closed it again. To be honest, which is okay to be if it's just to yourself, I hadn't really been thinking of that. But I obviously couldn't tell Chaz that.

"I've got to do this, Chaz."

He sighed, a deep and heavy sigh, like a dad disappointed that Sonny Boy just hasn't learned anything. "Dude, this isn't like you. Not at all. Throwing away your life and for what? A woman? They make more, you know."

"Not like this one."

Chaz threw up his hands in despair. "Oh, for fuck's sake, anything you can't sell for six or seven figures is just fucking stupid. And what do you get from this? Sex? I promise you, I can make one phone call and in half an hour you'll be having the best sex of your life. Professional sex, Riley! The best!"

I wanted to tell him that the way Caitlin made me feel was only partly about sex. That when she walked into the room, something inside me lit up, something that had been dark for most of my life. Tell him that just being with her, with or without sex, was better than sex, and she made me feel good in a new way I couldn't really understand.

But this was Chaz. Either he'd never felt like that or, if he had, it had gone horribly wrong. Anything like that I said would just be more ammunition for him to shoot down my plan.

So instead, I just said, "There's a treasure room. It's got some great stuff in it. Seven or even eight figures."

"Right, sure, naturally. And so it makes perfect sense to you that since you're there anyway, why not grab this woman?"

"Chaz, I have to do this. I have to. And I need your help to make it work."

Chaz picked up his beer, realized it was empty, and flipped it over his shoulder without looking. It went right into the little trash can. He didn't seem to notice—he was already opening another. "Riley, this is all bad. Bad setup, bad thinking, bad motivation."

"Doesn't matter," I said. "Gotta do it."

He drained his beer halfway and slammed the bottle on the table. "And God damn it, a bad payoff!"

"Half a million dollars," I said.

Chaz didn't say anything and he wouldn't look at me.

"Your part is easy. You just hand over the item I already have and take the money. You just have to do your German art dealer, and Kondor will be right there with you the whole time."

He drank the last half of his beer and threw the bottle in the general direction of the little trash can. It went right in. "Fuck it," he said. "You're gonna do this anyway. I'm in."

CHAPTER

43

Alex thought the meeting had gone well. Yes, she'd been covered in the cold sweat of terror the entire time. But she was coming to accept that as part of the price she had to pay to keep this particular client. And it was worth it. The Cobra paid twice as much as her usual asking price, and Alex charged a lot for her services, more than anyone else in the field—with the possible exception of that legendary hacker Saint Alia of the Knife.

It was a pain in the ass to get there, though. She had to go in a small, propeller-powered seaplane, because Cobra lived in the Algoma Highlands, an isolated wilderness area in Canada. The plane landed on a remote lake and taxied to a dock on the island that held Cobra's home. There were no airports anywhere near—there was no *anything* near except trees, deer, and bears, as far as Alex could see. That's why Cobra chose the place.

So it was a long trip on a small and loud airplane, which was annoying. And then landing on water, which made her very nervous. It was a little hard to believe that the plane would actually float when it hit the water. It always did, but every time, Alex had a couple of bad moments before she was sure.

And it was much worse now, in winter, when the lake was frozen and the plane skidded into the dock on skis. Alex was sure that the ice would break, and the plane, no longer equipped with floats, would sink like a rock and drag her down into the freezing depths of the lake.

But she was getting used to it. She was even coming to enjoy the scenery, too, the lush wilderness that surrounded Cobra's stronghold. Of course, it was winter now, and the scenery wasn't much more than a whole lot of snow. But the money was just as pretty as when the leaves were green: six figures, wired to her account as soon as she left Cobra, and that warmed her up a hell of a lot more than a cup of cocoa.

This had been a quick trip, too, which was very nice. Getting past the security took longer than the actual meeting, and Cobra had been pleased with what Alex had found, and that she'd delivered it quickly, before anyone else could act on it. So Alex flew up in the morning, and now she was headed home in the afternoon, just ahead of the setting sun. She had been on the island just long enough to make her report, which the Cobra first received with typical frigid silence.

"I found this," Alex had begun, sliding a glossy photograph across the table.

Cobra looked at it and then back at Alex.

"It's, um—it's called the Ardagh Chalice," Alex said, her mouth already dry. "And in Ireland it's considered an incredibly important—"

"I know what it is." If anything, the voice was colder than the stare.

"Right, of course, um—so the thing is?" Alex heard her voice crack. She tried to swallow, couldn't. "It's been stolen, apparently?"

"Apparently?"

"Well, it's definitely missing? And, well, the museum hasn't released a statement yet, but—they're claiming that the room it's in is closed for remodeling? But I hacked into the security cameras? The case that holds it is empty. And that's—I know this is the kind of thing you like? So I did a search, and—"

Alex paused, because Cobra had leaned toward her, and it was frightening. But it was clearly because what Alex was saying had caught Cobra's attention, so Alex went on. "There's a dealer in Frankfurt—Germany, not Kentucky. His name is Jurgen Pfluger. He has a reputation for being, um, sleazy? Dealing in stolen goods and so on."

She paused and took a ragged breath.

"And?"

"He's offering the Ardagh Chalice for quick and discreet sale. It has to be very quick," Alex said. Her throat was dry, and that made her voice raspy, so she could barely recognize it as her own. But the words were clear, and they clearly pleased Cobra.

"Good."

"Um," said Alex, "there's one small condition? Pfluger insists on conducting the transaction face-to-face, with the actual buyer. He says it's for his protection."

Cobra said nothing, didn't move or even blink. The silence stretched and all Alex could think was that she couldn't swallow and she really had to pee.

"Of course," Cobra said at last. "Perfect."

Alex felt a shock as those terrible dead eyes came up and met hers. "Contact information."

Alex had that ready and slid it across the table. Cobra nodded. "You can go."

Alex hurried out and made a beeline for the bathroom. She made it just in time. When she came out, the pilot of the plane was waiting for her.

"I'm supposed to take you back now," he said.

Alex nodded and followed him out, overwhelmed by the feeling that she had narrowly escaped a horrible death. It probably wasn't true, but that was just the way it was with Cobra. And Alex was well aware that it really *was* true for an awful lot of people who didn't please Cobra.

The plane took off from the frozen lake and banked right, climbing as it headed south. Alex dozed for a while, waking when the engine changed pitch. She looked out the window and saw water again—but a large body of water this time. As always they were coming in low over Lake Huron, under the radar. Shortly after, they landed at a small private strip outside of Mackinaw City. Alex got off the little plane and was immediately hit by a wind so cold it went through her coat as if it were a sundress. She hurried across the pavement to where a car was waiting to take her to the airport at Grand Rapids, Gerald R. Ford International.

The car was parked beside the only building, a hangar just big enough for three or four planes and a little office. The car's motor was running to keep the heater on against the bitter Michigan winter and, as Alex approached, the driver jumped out and opened the door for her. He had to be feeling the cold, too. He had a thick wool scarf wrapped around his face from the bridge of his nose down.

Alex climbed into the back seat as the driver closed the door and hurried back around the car to get behind the wheel. They were already rolling as she shrugged her backpack off onto the floor at her feet and rubbed herself to chafe away the cold.

The driver saw her in his mirror and said, "Sorry, miss. I'll turn the heat up."

Alex nodded, and the driver leaned over the dashboard. A moment later she could hear the increased hiss, and a stream of warm air blew at her.

But something wasn't right. "Hey!" she called to the driver. "There's some kind of vapor coming out!"

"Just condensation, miss," he said. "You just relax and enjoy the ride."

"It smells weird," she said. "Kind of medicine-y?"

"That's perfectly all right," the driver said soothingly—and to her mild surprise, Alex decided he was right.

It was fine, a little medicine smell never hurt anybody. She leaned back in her seat and smiled. It was really good to be out of that place and on her way home. She'd be back with Pudge, her cat, soon enough. Everything was fine.

That was the last thing she remembered thinking.

It took Alex a while to wake up, and then a while longer to realize she was awake. Everything seemed so hazy, a little out of focus, and maybe not quite real. But that was okay. She felt good, and if things were a bit blurry, that was fine, too. It made some cool pictures. So she just relaxed and enjoyed it.

After a while it occurred to her that she didn't recognize anything around her. Not because it was blurry; she was in a place that was completely unknown, slumped in a cheesy easy chair. She looked around her; it looked like a sort of cheap hotel room, the kind she would never stay in. But she was here now—how had that happened?

What the hell, she didn't really feel like getting up. The chair was crappy, but she was comfortable, and she felt so good there was no reason to change anything and maybe ruin it by moving.

But it was weird that she was here and didn't know why. She thought about it a little and it started to bother her. Just when she thought maybe she should get up and find out, a man came in. He was smiling, and he looked very nice. Alex decided she liked him.

"Hi, Alex," the man said cheerfully.

"Hi!" Alex answered. "Who are you?" She heard that she was slurring her words, almost like she was drunk.

But the man understood her, so that was okay.

"My name is Thomas," he said, and smiled at her.

"Okay, hi," she said. "Wussup?"

"I wanted to ask you a few things, okay?"

"Sure," she said. "I like to talk."

"Of course you do," Thomas said happily. "So let's talk." He pulled a desk chair up to face her and sat down. "So where have you been?"

"Oh, man," she said, with a giggle. "There's this island? Like way the fuck out in super nowhere. I have to go there sometimes. Just, you know, business."

"That's a funny place to do business," Thomas said.

"Oh, hell yeah, but so not funny, if you know what I mean?"

"I think I do," he said.

Alex nodded. Of course he knew. Thomas was obviously a guy who knew things. "Right, so, then you know it's scary. And I had to pee soooo bad you wouldn't believe."

"That can be awkward," Thomas said, with a really nice smile.

"Yeah, it can," she said. "But hey, I held it and all, so . . ."

"It's such an isolated place," Thomas said. "In a wilderness area—but you do computers, right?"

"Yeah, right, totally," she said. "And you know, I'm really freaking good? I mean, if that's okay to say?"

"Of course it's okay," he said. "Because it's true."

"Yeah, right, it is true," she said.

"But they can't have computers in the wilderness, can they?"

"Oh my God, no, they totally do!" she said. "A new IBM main-frame that runs like everything on the island."

"Wow, even the security system?"

"Hell yes! And—oh! But I'm not supposed to talk about it."

"I know," Thomas said soothingly. "But you can talk to me."

Alex nodded again. That made sense. Of course she could talk to Thomas.

So she did. She talked for a half hour or so, telling Thomas all about the island. Every now and then he would ask a question, and she was glad to answer. She could tell him anything.

Thomas finally stood up to leave. "Thank you, Alex. It's been really nice talking to you." He leaned toward her and she put her arms up for a hug. But instead of hugging her, he took a bottle out of his pocket and sprayed it in her face.

"Hey!" she protested.

"It's all right," Thomas said. "You need to go back to sleep for a while."

"Oh. Okay," she said. And then she did.

CHAPTER

44

Herr Pfluger was sweating, and not just from bustling about making things ready. He was nervous, more so than he should have been. But this was no routine transaction he was preparing for. The item was unique, priceless—although of course he had put a price on it—and the client was said to be rather dangerous. Arranging the shop for such an important transaction took work. And his assistant, Guido, was no help. He just stood there, looking threatening. It is true that this was his primary job, but even so. There was so much to do with this particular client coming, and one aging man was hard-pressed to do it all. Guido could certainly lighten the burden if he would lend a hand. But when Herr Pfluger asked him to help, he shrugged and said, he was doing his job, looking threatening.

And now the time had come and the client would be here momentarily. All was as ready as it was going to be. Herr Pfluger mopped his forehead with a handkerchief and sat for a moment.

"Well," he said.

Before he could utter even one more syllable, he heard the bell above the door of his shop ring. The client was here. Herr Pfluger stood and nodded to Guido.

"Call and tell him," he said. "But come back to me quickly."

Guido nodded and Pfluger hurried to the front of the shop.

Three men stood inside the shop's door. Two of them were clearly cut from the same cloth as Guido; protection for the client who was, after all, carrying a considerable amount of cash.

The third man, the client himself, was a very different sort. Middle-aged, thin, and wearing a very expensive overcoat. His features were rather ordinary—except for his eyes. They were large, pale blue, and lifeless. Those eyes locked on to Pfluger's and somehow radiated a cold menace that Pfluger felt all the way to the marrow of his bones.

Still, they were not meeting to form a friendship. He felt Guido glide into the room behind him, and immediately felt better.

Pfluger swallowed and gave the man a brief bow. "Mr. Colubra, I assume?"

"Yes." The one syllable was spoken quietly, but it felt like a slap to the face.

But Pfluger was used to dealing with hard characters. Seldom quite this hard, but even so, there was business to be done.

"I have the item in the back—if you would please come this way?"

Pfluger and Colubra stepped behind the counter and into the back room, trailed by their three guardians. Pfluger placed a leather case onto a table in the center of the room, pulled on a pair of white cotton gloves, and opened the case. Inside, nestled into a cushion of velvet, lay the Ardagh Chalice. Colubra stepped forward for a better look, and

Pfluger handed him a pair of gloves like the ones he was wearing. Then, with a dramatic flourish, Pfluger lifted the chalice from its case.

"There, you see it," he said, holding the chalice close to Colubra. "The Ardagh Chalice."

Colubra held out a gloved hand. "May I?"

"Of course," Pfluger said, holding the chalice out.

Colubra took it, examined it carefully, turning it to inspect it from every angle. He looked up at last, and said, "It appears to be quite genuine."

Pfluger looked a little hurt. "Of course it is," he said. "I guarantee it."

Colubra held his eyes for an uncomfortable moment. Then he nodded. Without looking away, he said, "Ramon."

One of his guards stepped forward and held out an attaché case. Pfluger took it eagerly and opened it. It was full of euros, all showing the purplish tint of the five-hundred euro bill. Without looking away from his client, Pfluger handed the case to Guido.

"Well, then," he said. But there was no need to say more. Colubra placed the chalice in its case, handed it to one of his men, and left without another word.

For a moment the little shop was utterly silent. Then Guido snorted, a small and disdainful laugh. "Security. Three seconds and I'd have Ramon on the floor. One more and his buddy is lying beside him."

"Maybe," Pfluger answered in the same language. "But I'm fucking thrilled we didn't need to find out how good they are."

Guido shrugged. "No biggy," he said. And then abruptly, he added, "'Colubra' is Latin," he said. "It means 'snake.'"

Pfluger locked eyes with him. "Huh," he said.

CHAPTER

45

The sunsets in the Algoma Highlands are usually really beautiful. Today it wouldn't have mattered if it were the greatest sunset in the history of the world. I wasn't looking. I had a couple of other things on my mind. Little things, like getting into Cobra's place, getting out again with Caitlin—and God damn it, staying alive long enough to do all that, which didn't seem like a gimme right now, because T.C. was flying us in so low I was looking *up* at the treetops. I knew we had to be that low to keep from being detected, and I knew T.C. was really good at what he was doing—but I was still close to wetting my pants at a couple of near misses. Some of those trees were huge.

But T.C. brought us down safely, on a frozen lake about four miles from Cobra's hideout. There were a lot of smallish lakes in the Algoma Highlands, and this one was close enough to Cobra's for me to get there easily on foot, but far enough so they wouldn't detect the plane. I only hoped Caitlin hadn't been hurt, so she could make it back. I mean, she was small enough that I could carry her, but that would definitely slow things down.

T.C. and I had been waiting for the call from Chaz while sitting in the plane, at a clearing in the woods just inland from Whitefish Bay in Michigan. It didn't have to be much of a clearing for T.C. He could set a DC-3 down in a strip mall parking lot, and the little four-seater we had now was a lot smaller. As soon as we got the call, we were back up in the air, cutting across the water to Canada and then up into the Highlands.

The sun was just dipping down to the horizon as T.C. taxied up close to the shore and shut down the engine. He looked at me. "Okay, buddy," he said. "This is it."

"Yup." I zipped up my snowsuit. I know it sounds like something you put on a six-year-old kid, but trust me, it wasn't. This was a state-of-the-art US Army winter camo outfit, and it would keep me warm, even up here where the temperature could go way below zero. Especially at night, which it would be in about fifteen minutes.

As I was shrugging on my tactical pack, T.C. put a hand on my shoulder, and I turned to him. "Let me come with you, Riley. I've done this kind of shit, and you're gonna want backup."

"Thanks, but no," I said. "I need you here in case it's a hot pickup."

He looked unhappy, but he nodded. "I can be there pretty quick if something comes up."

"Let's hope it won't," I said. I opened the door, letting in an arctic blast. "Keep warm, T.C."

"Closing that door would be a good start," he said.

I hopped out onto the ice, shut the door and waved, and then I was off, across the last few yards of ice to the shore.

There was a clear strip of beach about fifteen feet around the edge of the lake. Then the vegetation took over. It was a mix of old growth timber, mostly evergreens, and scrubby brush. And over everything, of course, a deep blanket of snow.

That might sound pretty: idyllic vistas of majestic trees festooned with fluffy snow. Ah, wilderness. It really does look wonderful—when you're sitting by a roaring fire and looking at it out of a window. But trust me, it wasn't pretty when you were in it and had to get across it. For starters, the snow wasn't fluffy. I don't know how much you know about snow, but there are a lot of different kinds. In Scotland they have 421 words for it. I know, you've always heard that Eskimos have the most words for snow. Nope. First of all, don't say Eskimo. They're In-uit, and they don't like the word "Eskimo." And second, at most the Inuit have forty to fifty snow words. Scotland takes the prize.

As far as I was concerned, they could take this snow, too. It was what I call Styrofoam snow, because when you step on it, that's what it sounds like: like you're stepping on one of those cheap coolers. Your feet crunch through it, and it's a struggle to pull them out again—especially when it's deep, which, let's face it, snow usually is in Canadian winters.

I was wearing snowshoes, and it was still tough going. Try walking with tennis rackets strapped to your feet sometime and you'll see what I mean. At least I didn't break through the crust with every step, but there were plenty of other problems. The surface of Styrofoam snow was hard enough to be slick, like walking on ice. Sometimes I'd break through, and sometimes I was practically skating, and on the whole, it was a lot more exercise than I wanted right now. I kind of wished I'd brought a dog sled, or maybe a snowmobile. But what the hell, I was here to rescue Caitlin, and whatever it took, I was going to do it.

I slogged on. Full dark came on, but it wasn't all that dark. When the whole world is solid white from snow, every little bit of light from the moon, or even the stars, gets picked up and reflected and it might as well be high noon. That made it a lot easier to see where I was going. It also made it a lot easier for anybody who might be watching to see where I was going. So I tried to keep in the tree line and move from one shadow to the next. Ninety minutes in I was still only halfway there. That was fine with me. I didn't want to get there too early. I like to hit a guarded place at the witching hour. Or anyway, late at night, when people are getting tired.

I took a quick break to check my GPS. I was still on course. I took a sip of water and ate an energy bar and moved on.

Another hour and a half more and I was in sight of the Cobra's lake. The compound was on an island about a half mile from shore, with a dock on the side I was watching. The perimeter fence was visible beyond that, and the rooftop of one of the buildings in the compound. I stopped well within the tree line and watched it. There was smoke coming from a chimney, but no sign of movement. Not that anybody would be likely to take a moonlight stroll tonight. The temperature was right around zero and dropping, which makes most people think it's a good idea to stay inside.

There was also no sign of the Cobra's plane. It should be waiting somewhere, probably at Sault Ste. Marie, to bring Cobra back here after his return from Germany. Probably a private jet for the long flight across the Atlantic, then the small float plane for the last leg home. Even with a private jet, he couldn't possibly get back for another eight or ten hours.

The important question was, how many people were still here on the island, watching over the place while the boss was away? I didn't think there would be many; in fact, I was kind of counting on that.

And also on the fact that they wouldn't be at their absolute peak of alert watchfulness. Why should they be? When the cat's away, the mice get lazy. My guess was that whoever was left on the island, they'd be a lot more relaxed about security than they usually were. Between Cobra's absence and the freezing weather, I was pretty sure they'd turn on the electronic security, take off their shoes, and open a beer or two. I was betting an awful lot on that—myself. If I was wrong, it would likely be my last mistake.

I watched for almost an hour. Nothing happened. Nobody moved. The only real problem that came up was that I started thinking. And okay, thinking is a great thing to do, and I strongly recommend it— most of the time. But when you are in the middle of a plan, and it's too late to turn back or change things, it's usually not a good idea.

My thoughts were not comforting. I had rushed into this, and when you do that there are always speed bumps, things you didn't think through or plan on. All of those kinds of things jumped into my head now. Most of them were either stupid or totally unlikely, and I just pushed them away. But one of them stuck.

What if Caitlin wasn't here?

What if Cobra had moved her, or taken her to Germany, just to keep an eye on her?

The thought stuck like chewing gum on a hot sidewalk. I couldn't scrape it off. I told myself I was being an idiot, that Caitlin was absolutely here, and when that didn't make the idea go away, I added that one way or another I would know soon enough. And after wrestling with it a little longer I decided that the time to find out was now. I was getting cold anyway.

I took a radio transceiver from my pack. It had a small modification, a USB port on one side. There was a thumb drive stuck into the port. Because, okay, Chaz had been right to worry. There almost certainly would be new security, just because I got through it once. A call to Tamiqua had hopefully taken care of the problem. The thumb drive held a string of code she had sent me, a virus she built based on my chat with Cobra's computer whiz, Alex. Tamiqua guaranteed it would take down the island's security system, everything from cameras to motion detectors and alarms. And it would do that invisibly, leaving whatever image or readout had been there when the virus took over the system.

I turned on the radio, pointed it toward the island, and pushed SEND. Just that simple. The hard part was waiting ten more minutes for me to be sure the virus had wormed its way in and taken over, which Tamiqua said was not necessary. And I believed her, but she wasn't here to apologize if she was wrong.

Ten minutes passed on lead feet, but it passed. I took off my snowshoes and started across the frozen surface of the lake.

CHAPTER

46

I circled halfway around Cobra's island on the ice close to shore before I snuck onto land. Coming in by the main gate would not be smart. Even if the security was down and everybody was half asleep, somebody would be watching that entrance. It was the only way into the compound, unless you cut through the chain-link fence.

Which is what I did. That would absolutely have set off all kinds of alarms if Tamiqua's virus hadn't done the job. But she was the best at what she did, and her worm should have worked by now. So I made one cut in the fence, and then skittered back to cover at the island's shore. I watched for a few minutes. Nothing happened. Just like I knew it would, Tamiqua's virus had worked.

I went back to the fence and snipped until I had a hole big enough to crawl through. I slid through and into the shadows around the nearest building, a storage shed. I knelt and looked around the corner. The main building was about fifty feet away across completely open ground. There was a light in a window at the front of the building, the kind of flickering colored light that comes from a television. Other than that, the other buildings in the compound were dark, and nothing was moving.

It was about like I'd expected; whoever was on guard duty was kicking back and binge-watching something. Probably *SEAL Team*. Either that or porn. All good. Moving at a crouch, I hurried across the open space to the main building.

This was the tricky part. I had to get inside and past whatever guards there were, without alerting anybody else. And then I had to find Caitlin. My guess was that she was locked up in the large area under the compound. It was a lot more than a basement; it was bigger than the building, and it was made to be secure and heavily reenforced with the kind of stuff they make bomb shelters out of. The whole basement area was built to survive just about anything but a direct hit from a nuke. It was obviously meant to be a kind of final hidey-hole in case things went very bad. Cobra's treasure room was down there, too. I'd been there when I grabbed the Irish crown jewels.

Just past that treasure room I had seen a couple of secure steel doors, the kind they have in maximum-security prisons. I knew from the few banged-up bodies that had been found downstream from the place that Cobra took prisoners and then tortured the crap out of them. So I was pretty sure they actually were prison-style cells. I hadn't examined the cells themselves last time I was here, because my only interest in Cobra's lockup was staying out of it. But I remembered those doors, and I was betting that Caitlin would be behind one. The door would be locked pretty securely, but that didn't matter. I've never met a lock I couldn't open.

But first, I had to get inside.

The first, and only other time I'd been to this place, I had found three possible ways in. One of those was the main door, which I ruled out then. I ruled it out now, too. If I lived through a run-in with the guards on duty, the noise would get anyone else on the premises up and shooting.

The time before, I'd gone through a skylight. I thought it would be a bad idea to try the same way. They would have put together something new and nasty to make sure nobody got in that way again. At least not alive. And it might be mechanical, which meant it would still be active despite the electronic security being down. So that left me the third way in. It was slower, and kind of messy, but it would have to work.

I circled carefully around to the back of the building. There was a large heat pump unit there, and an exhaust pipe next to it, just big enough to crawl through. It took me a minute to get the grate off, and then with my fluffy camo on it was a little tighter than I'd thought, so I had to take off my pack. I wormed inside and pulled the pack after me.

I crawled along slowly until I came to a junction. The conduit forked off in two directions, and both ways were too small. Dead end. I would have to go back to a vent I had passed about ten feet back. The space was way too tight to turn around in, so I had to inch along backward until I got back to the vent.

I hadn't paid much attention to it before. Now I did. I wriggled up close and listened for a minute: nothing. I took a peek, and then a longer look. It would be a very tight fit, but I thought I could get through. I looked to see what I would land on. On the other side of the vent was what looked like a store room—lots of canned food, big bags of rice and flour. Good: There wouldn't be anybody coming in for ingredients to make a giant cake at this hour.

It took longer than it should have to get the grate off, because I couldn't grab my pack and pull out the tools in a space this tight. I had to reach back, open it, and get the right tools by feel. But I got the grate off at last, wiggled and struggled to get through the opening, and finally fell through, landing gracefully on my head.

I saw bright stars in a dark sky for a minute. I shook it off and looked around. I'd landed on a pile of grain sacks, which had broken my fall instead of my head. It had also muffled the noise I would have made otherwise, noise like screams of pain. I took that as a sign that luck was with me. I tried not to think that maybe that soft fall had used up my luck.

I got up, dusted off, and stuck an ear to the door. It was all quiet on the other side. I eased the door open and looked out.

I had a pretty good floor plan of the place in my head from my previous visit. I was looking at a corridor, still in the back area of the building, just behind the kitchen and far from the guards at the front. Good. I moved carefully out into the hall.

The stairs down into the sublevel were closer to the front entrance. I snuck along the hallway to a second corridor that went right, to the stairs. It also went past a doorway to the room where the on-duty guards were watching TV. And that door was half-open.

I approached slow and sneaky, flattened myself against the wall, and peeked around.

There were four guys in the room watching TV, and yeah, it wasn't *SEAL Team*, but it was close: *Homeland*. I don't know why, but badass bad guys love those shows. Either they haven't figured out that SEALs would be after people like them, or they had an unconscious desire to be punished for their behavior.

Whichever it was, these four were riveted to the screen, and nobody looked up as I slipped past the door.

Another twenty feet and I was at the door to the sublevel. It was a big steel door with a pressure seal. If it had been closed, I could probably open it—in four or five hours, using explosives and diamond-tip drill bits. But it was open. My luck was still running.

The stairs were wide and dark, with dim safety lights at foot level every ten steps or so. They led down about twice as far as you would go to get down to an average home basement. At the bottom was another steel door, like the one at the top. And it was open, too.

I stepped through and into the basement. I stood there for a minute, just listening. I didn't hear anything, except the soft sighing of the ventilation system. I slipped down the corridor to the treasure room, and I couldn't help sneaking a quick look.

Any normal bad guy would have his stuff in a vault, even if it was in his Fortress of Solitude. Not Cobra. He had his stuff on display; in this room he'd set everything up like it was a museum. There were soft lights shining down on the display cases, and some of the stuff was impressive. A lot of it stuck with the Irish theme, which was Cobra's thing. But from the doorway I could see one item that wasn't Irish, and it hadn't been there before. It was in the very center of the room, on a raised plinth. This was clearly Cobra's brand-new Most Prized Treasure. And I could see why. It was a gorgeous thing, a unique and beautiful piece of work. It also had a gold cobra on it, which would make it more valuable to somebody who called himself Cobra. And I loved it the second I saw it. Of course, that second had been a while ago. Because guess what it was?

The *wesekh* I took from the pyramid. And then Cobra took from me, when he took Caitlin. He obviously saw it and thought, *Hey, I'm here anyway, so—hell yeah!* And grabbed it on the way out.

Right away a picture popped into my head: Caitlin, naked, except for that *wesekh*. It had been one of the greatest sights of my life. And I remembered the lust she had shown to hold it, wear it, keep it. I thought of how happy she would be when I got her out of here to safety, and then said, "Oh, by the way," and handed her the *wesekh*. And she deserved it, too, for what she'd gone through—which was, after all, my fault. Cobra only took her to get at me. That wonderful *wesekh* would make a great apology.

Of course it would be stupid to take the time and the added risk to steal it now.

So I did. I was pretty sure Tamiqua's virus had taken out any alarms there might be here in the treasure room, too. I looked the display over carefully anyway, saw nothing tricky, and lifted the plexiglass case off. Nothing happened: no clanging bells, no shrieking siren, no clatter of boots as the guards rushed to respond. Nada.

I put the *wesekh* into my pack and went on down the hall.

There were the four prison-style steel doors, two on each side of the corridor. There was a small window high up on each one, made of two-inch-thick glass, with wire mesh embedded in the middle of it. I looked through the first one on the left; it was dark except for one dim light on the back wall. The cell was empty.

I tried the one on the right; also empty. I crossed back to door number three, on the left. And my luck was still in.

Because there she was. Caitlin.

CHAPTER

47

She was on the floor, half slumped and half lying down, leaning on the cement bench that passed for a bed. Her face was in profile, her eyes closed. The cell was lit only by the same dim light the others had. By its light I could see that she still wore the shreds of her Miss Farnsworth costume, except for the blouse they'd ripped off her in London. There was a manacle attached to one leg, the chain running to a big U-bolt embedded in the floor.

Even in the dimness I could see bruises—on her arms, her neck, her face. The eye I could see was swollen and purple. She'd been beaten, and it looked bad. For no reason except to get at me, and since there was nothing I could do about it, just to make me crazy.

It worked.

I started tearing at the locks on the door without even seeing what I was doing. I broke a fingernail, but I didn't care. I had it open in a couple of seconds, and then I was on my knees beside her.

I put a hand on her carotid artery. Her pulse was strong.

"Caitlin," I said softly. I patted her face gently. "Come on, Caitlin, wake up."

Her eyelids fluttered but didn't open.

"Caitlin," I said, a little urgently. "Wake up."

She scrunched her eyes tighter and whimpered. "Please," she said, a terrible soft broken sound. "Please . . . ?"

I put an arm around her and she tried to flinch away, but I held on. "Caitlin, it's me. I'm here to get you out. But you have to wake up."

The panicked clenched face morphed into confusion. "Out . . . ? Who . . . ?" Her eyes opened at last. For a moment she just stared blankly. Then her eyes went wide. Very slowly she reached a hand up to my face, as if she were afraid that if she touched me I would turn out to be a hallucination.

But I wasn't. Her fingertips brushed my cheek and I heard her gasp. "It's you," she said.

"It is. Can you stand?"

"I . . . think so . . . ? But the leg iron . . ."

"I'll get it," I said. I glanced at it. It was a pretty basic manacle, just one simple lock. I had it open in a few seconds. I pulled it off her leg and dropped it to the floor.

"Now," I said. "Let's get out of here." I put a hand on her cheek, stroking softly over an awful purple bruise. "I'm taking you home."

Suddenly her eyes got very big. She pointed at the door. "Did you hear? They're coming!"

I jumped to the door and listened. I didn't hear anything. Very carefully, I peeked out into the corridor.

There was no sign of life. Just the same dim, empty hallway.

"It's all right," I said. "Nobody's coming."

"But they will! I know they will!" she said. She gave a kind of whimper and folded up into a ball.

I went back to her. Caitlin had been strong, fearless, and fierce, and now? I tried not to think what they'd done to break her like this.

"It's all right now," I said. "I'm here, and I'm going to take you out of here."

"I—I can't. I just— Please, just hold me, just for a minute," she said.

I knelt and held her, stroking her face again and making soothing noises. I held her for a minute, but I started to feel time running out.

I unwrapped myself from Caitlin. "Come on, we've got to go."

"Yes, all right," she said.

I stood and held out my hand. "Come on," I said. And as I did I happened to see my fingertips, right where I'd stroked her cheek.

They were purple.

The exact color of the bruise on her face. Makeup? But—

Sometimes the nickel drops right away. Sometimes it takes a little longer. This time it took just long enough for Caitlin to snatch up the leg iron. Her hands moved very fast. I heard the rattle of a chain, felt something clamp on to my ankle, and then Caitlin was across the room and standing at the door with a broad smile on her face.

"Actually, I think I shall stay," she said. "And I believe you might stay for a while as well." The smile got bigger, but it was the coldest expression I'd ever seen.

"What—" I took a step toward her. Or anyway, I tried to. I only got about half a step, and then I was jerked to a stop.

By the leg iron.

Which Caitlin had apparently clamped on to my leg.

An awful lot of things went through my brain, really fast. None of them actually made sense. My purple fingers, the leg iron, her smile. I just blinked at her.

"Did you—did they—"

"No, dear boy, they didn't. You've not sorted it, have you? Poor thing. Let me explain." She took a small step forward, close enough for me to see how pleased she was. Not close enough to do anything about it. "They didn't—for a very basic reason. They didn't—because I am 'They.'" She gave me a very small bow.

I shook my head. I couldn't think of anything to say.

"Oh no. Really?" She shook her head and made a pitying, clucking sound. "Aren't you supposed to be clever? Come on, guess. Have a go."

There was only one guess that made sense of it, and that didn't make any sense. It just wasn't possible. I shook my head. "You're not . . ."

"Yes, I'm afraid so," she said. "I am the Cobra."

CHAPTER

48

Have you ever had one of those dreams where everything goes along totally normal, like you're actually awake—and then something so bizarre happens that you couldn't possibly believe it, except that all that normal stuff has set you up, and now you have to believe the unbelievable things, too?

For a minute, I was pretty sure that's what was happening. Because it was absolutely impossible to think that Caitlin—I mean, after all we had—I mean shit, it just wasn't possible.

Except it was. Little pieces dropped into place, and every one of them said, *Yeah, of course, now it makes sense.* And every one of them tacked on, *How could you miss it?*

Piece one: Somebody told the cops what we were doing, way ahead of time, far enough for them to set up an elaborate trap. It wasn't me. Who else had known?

Piece two: The only reason I went through with it was because *she* wanted to do it.

Piece three: Why else would she separate from me when the cops cornered us?

Piece four: The British cop, West, had been scared, meaning somebody scary had made him leave a way out of the trap. Somebody Cobra-scary.

There was more, but Caitlin the Cobra wasn't finished with me. "I see it's starting to jell in your wee nasty noggin. Yes, I am the Cobra. Yes, even in spite of all the grand shagging. Yes, you totally bought into it." The not-funny smile got bigger. "Scarlet for you, innit?"

Not much I could say. So I didn't.

"You've done the exact same in your time, now, haven't you? Pretended to be in love with some poor chit until you got to their prize trinket. And you thought you were the only one clever-cold enough. Oh, you really are a manky wanker." She shook her head pityingly.

I guess I was. Because I did think all that, and I was clearly wrong. So I didn't need her to explain it all. But because our brains are basically stupid things, one thing that was totally idiotic and unimportant bothered me.

"Why Cobra?" I asked. "Why not Banshee, or something else to stick with your whole Ireland-forever motif?"

She cocked her head to one side. "Stuck on that, are you? It's rather simple. And if you weren't so molly-eyed you'd have seen it." She looked down, frowned. "It was the nuns," she said.

I thought that was a great start to something, but it didn't tell me much, so I gave a little nudge. "It's always the nuns," I said.

She looked up, and I saw the Cobra face—eyes so cold they went right through my snowsuit.

"It always is in Ireland," she said. "I went to convent school, of course. It happened first day, when they read the roster. I was entered as 'C. O'Brian.' Sister Brigid was not of the brightest. She read it as 'Cobran.' Children being the wicked lot they are, they took to calling me Cobra."

Her eyes and her smile got colder, which I wouldn't have thought was possible.

"I made it stick," she said.

I nodded. "The name suits you."

The cold smile again. "It does," she said. "And you've earned a bite."

She opened the door to the cell. "Conal!" she called.

Two seconds later a very large man stepped in. At least six foot five, and massive muscles popping out all over. His nose was flattened in a kind of sideways mush, and there was scar tissue all around his eyes and cheeks. All sure signs that he had an advanced degree in Hitting People. He handed her a robe, which she shrugged on.

Then she turned to Conal and nodded. "Let's begin," she said.

The beating wasn't all that bad. I mean, I've had much worse. Conal cut the snowsuit off me and worked me over slowly and carefully. Nothing was broken, or permanently damaged. And yeah, I knew they were just doing it that way so it would last awhile, maybe a few weeks. That was fine with me. The more time they gave me, the more certain it was I would get out.

Conal really enjoyed his work. Always nice to see. He smiled as he hammered at me, and he was humming softly in rhythm to his workout. "One Singular Sensation," from *A Chorus Line*. When I recognized the tune, I almost laughed—except that right then he slammed a hand into my side that made me see stars.

It hurt. Most of what he did hurt. But this wasn't my first rodeo, and I'd learned to focus my mind away from the pain. I mean, not all of it, but it helped. What really hurt was that Caitlin—I mean, Cobra—sat and watched it all with an eager and happy smile on her face. Every now and then she'd make a suggestion: hit him *there*, or *a little harder now*. She even had a chair and a cup of tea brought, so she could sit and sip while she watched. See Riley bleed. Watch bruises form on his face. Lovely. Better than TV any day.

When I started to fade into unconsciousness, she called a halt. She came over and examined my face, and then nodded happily. "A fine start," she said. "We'll have another go later."

Conal stooped and picked up my tac pack. He looked at Caitlin inquiringly.

"Put it by the door," she said. "So he can see it and never reach it."

She patted my face and gave me one last smile. "And so he'll know he's here for the rest of his short and painful life." The pat turned into a slap, and it was as hard as anything Conal had done.

"Later, luv," she said. Then she leaned forward and gave me a hard and passionate kiss. She pulled back and stared for a moment. She laughed, and the sound of it was worse than the beating. "This is going to be grand fun," she said.

Then she was gone.

I slept for a while. Not really peacefully. That wasn't possible. But there was a concrete bench along the back wall, just wide enough to lie on without hanging off the edge. If you like a really firm mattress, I'd recommend it. Otherwise, you might as well sleep on the floor.

I don't know how long I slept. There was no way to tell time in here. The light didn't waver, there were no sounds or odors to indicate anything at all. But it was at least long enough for my body to stiffen, just to make sure everything hurt a little more. I tried to stretch a little, get some blood flowing, and that helped a little. It also reminded me of all the places Conal had hit me.

I did a quick inventory of what hurt the most. The pains on each side of my chest said Conal had broken a couple of ribs. It hurt to breathe, but at least I could still do it. My right knee was about twice its normal size. One eye was swollen shut, but it didn't hurt too much. Altogether, I'd gotten off easy. I probably wouldn't next time.

I stretched. The chain rattled along with me. Once, I moved a little too far and the chain pulled me back. That hurt, too; the manacle attached to my ankle was a real classic, a fine piece of heavy steel that really bit into you if you pulled against it. One more little ouchy.

After a few minutes of stretching I sat back down on my nice firm bed and looked things over. On the plus side, I was alive, and everything I needed to get out of here was only a few feet away in my pack. On the minus side, I wasn't going to be alive, or even mobile, for very long. And as close as my pack was, I couldn't reach it.

I tried. I stretched myself out on the floor, as far as the chain on my leg iron would let me. Nope. It was still about four feet away, and there was no way I could ever stretch that far, at least without removing some of my bones. But what the hell, Conal would do that for me, sooner or later. By then it would be too late.

I sat back down and thought some more. I was pretty sure that more beatings were coming, and other things, too, probably involving gardening utensils and power tools. I was also sure that each session was going to leave me weaker and less able to do anything about it.

So if I was going to escape, this was the time to do it. And yeah, of course I was going to escape. I just had to figure out how. That was challenging, since on the face of things, it was impossible. Of course, they said that to Edmond Dantès, too, and look how that turned out. He escaped anyway, and with a treasure and the title of Count of Monte Cristo, too.

I didn't need a title. I just needed to get out. And I would, too. Somehow.

I looked around the cell for inspiration. Apparently, nobody had put any of that in the room. Concrete-block walls, steel door. And then my shredded snowsuit, a bucket in reach for a privy—and my tac pack out of reach. My eyes kept going back to that. Everything I needed was there. I could almost smell it. And no disrespect to Conal, but seeing the pack right there out of reach was indeed worse than the beating. Nice touch, Caitlin. Turns out she was really good at the whole super-villain thing.

I thought some more. I looked around some more. Snowsuit, bucket, tac pack. Nothing helpful had materialized since I'd looked two minutes ago. Nothing beamed into the room for the next half hour, either. Snowsuit, bucket, tac pack. Period.

I tried to figure out how long it might be before Caitlin and friends came back for another round. The longer I sat thinking about it, the more important it got. I couldn't be sure how long I'd slept, but it didn't feel like very long. Say two hours at most. That would make it some-where in the early A.M. now. Two or three o'clock at most. There would still be a couple of guards lounging around and polishing their bullets. But would Caitlin be asleep? That's all that mattered—nothing would happen to me if she wasn't there to see it.

Okay; assume she kept a normal schedule. She was asleep, along with Conal, and most of her people. Just guessing, but that should give me a couple of hours to get out. Plenty of time. If I just knew how.

I looked around again. No changes. Snowsuit, bucket, tac pack. Same three pieces of absolutely no freaking help at all. Snowsuit, bucket—

A little bell rang in the back of my head. I answered. *Hello, Riley? This is your brain.* Oh, hi, brain, how're you doing? *Not bad, thanks. Better than you, anyhow. Listen, do you have a minute?* Sure, brain. What's up? *Snowsuit, bucket, tac pack.* Yeah, thanks, I got that already.

My brain sighed. *No, dummy: Snowsuit, PLUS bucket, EQUALS tac pack.*

Oh.

A minute later I was scrabbling for my shredded snowsuit. The longest piece of it was almost half the suit, from the leg up to the chest. I pulled that out of the shredded mess, dropped the rest and picked up the bucket.

I tied the leg piece of the snowsuit around the handle of the bucket, a good solid constrictor knot. Then I laid out on the floor again and tossed the bucket at my pack. It bounced off and hit the floor with the loudest clang I've ever heard.

I lay there sweating in fear for two minutes. Anybody within half a mile had to have heard it. But there was no alarm, no clatter of boots on the stairs, nothing. I counted to one hundred; still nothing. Deep breath; try again.

And again. And twice more. Like shooting a basketball, but in reverse—throwing the hoop at the ball. One more time. And then finally, the bucket dropped over the pack. I gave a slow and steady pull. The pack moved—and the bucket fell to the floor.

But the pack had fallen over. It now lay flat on the floor, the top of it facing me. There was about a four-inch gap between the bottom of the pack and the wall beside the door. Perfect: Change of plan.

I picked up one end of my "rope" in each hand, making a loop of the rest of it, and stretched forward as close as I could get. I threw the loop, trying to drop it over the pack so it caught on the bottom, the part closest to the wall. It only took me two tries and my snowsuit loop was hooked around the pack. Slowly, gently, carefully, I pulled it toward me. Closer, almost close enough to touch, closer—

Gotcha.

Thirty seconds later the leg iron was off.

CHAPTER

49

The lock on the door was a good one. It took me almost a full minute to pick it. It was a little harder, too, because one of my hands wasn't working right; Conal had sort of accidentally stomped on it on his way to beating a different part of me. I eased the door open and stuck my head out for a cautious look up the hallway, toward the stairs. That's why I didn't see Conal, on the other side of the doorway. But I felt his presence. Painfully.

Because of course Caitlin posted a guard outside my cell. She knew me. And of course it would be Conal, because he knew the places that already hurt, and he could get right back to work on them.

The first hint I had that anybody was there was when my head exploded with pain and I fell to one knee—the bad one, of course. Before I could chase away all the little birdies in my head, I was joining them up in the air, lifted effortlessly by the big brute. He drop-kicked me back into the cell, catching me square on the butt. That sounds funny, but not so much when it's your butt. The pain went all the way up into my spine, and I fell face-first onto the floor and just lay there gasping.

Which didn't slow down Conal at all. He just hopped in after me and got to work. He didn't bother to bend over. He just went at me. I think what he was doing is known as "putting the boot in" in the UK. Like all truly great foreign art forms, it translated really well to my American sensibilities. Brand-new body parts started to scream with pain. And Conal was humming again. This time it was "Popular" from *Wicked*. What a wry wit he had. And a strong kicker, too. I felt another rib crack, and then my left hip went numb, and I knew that if I didn't stop him soon, I wouldn't be going anywhere unless they carried me.

Under the circumstances, it was a very good thought to have. Of course, stop the beating. Absolutely. Terrific idea. But like always, the question was "How?" It's really hard to think creatively when you're being kicked into small pieces by a really strong thug—even if he supplies a charming sound track of Broadway musicals.

I tried to crawl away. Conal just reached down and grabbed one of my ankles. He pulled, and I started to slide backward. I scrabbled frantically for something to grab, to pull me back away from him. I felt three fingernails break on the rough concrete floor, but my hands didn't come into contact with anything, except the chain for the leg iron. Useless, but I grabbed it anyway.

I held tight and jerked to a halt for just a second as the chain came taut. I didn't let go, even when Conal really leaned into the pull, stretching me so my whole body was hanging six inches off the floor. I've never been strapped to the rack, but I'm guessing it feels something like that. The stretching gives your body a larger surface area, and everything hurts just a little more. I wanted to cry. I didn't, and I didn't let go.

Conal dropped me, no doubt to move in and get a grip on my hair or something equally pleasant. I took the few seconds of relief to pull myself farther away, using the chain. I even managed to get up on one knee—the good one this time—and face Conal. He was watching me with a big smile. He switched to humming, "My Boy Bill" from *Carousel*. What a wonderfully cultured man he was.

He stepped forward, grabbed me around the neck, and lifted straight up. I was still reflexively clutching the chain from the leg iron, and as I went up, my hand slid along the chain until I stopped rising six inches from the manacle on the end of the chain. I was nose to nose with Conal, and he looked very happy about it. He raised a fist the size of a Thanksgiving turkey. I guessed he'd run out of songs, and this was going to be lights out.

I didn't actually think to do this. It just sort of happened by instinct. But as his fist went back, I swung the chain. The iron manacle on the end of it hit Conal—right on the temple. He dropped me and swayed a little, and I swung again, with some real snap this time. Hit him in the same spot.

He took a step back and shook his head, but I was already on him. I hit him with the manacle three more times before he dropped to his knees. Even then he started to get back up. So I showed him that we have soccer in America now, too. I drew my good leg back and put the hardest kick I have right on the point of his chin.

Conal stopped humming. He looked a little confused, like he just couldn't decide what to do. I kicked him again, and he made up his mind. He fell over backward, landing in an awkward sprawl, and he was out. I had a hard time believing it, so I kicked him one more time, in the side of the head, but it was true. The giant was sleeping. I hoped it was forever, but I'd settle for a few hours.

I fastened the leg iron to his ankle, took a quick survey of what wasn't working—most of my body parts—and picked up my pack.

CHAPTER

50

I t took a couple of minutes to get all the moving parts working again. Conal was a real artist, and there wasn't much of me that wasn't throbbing, swelling, broken, or bleeding. A few parts were doing all these things simultaneously. I moved around a little in the cell, pausing once to kick Conal again, just in case. Everything hurt, but it was all working, just enough.

This time I went through the cell door carefully and low. Nothing stirring that I could see or hear. I moved forward toward the stairway. I went slowly, because there might be another surprise or two waiting for me. And anyway, I was not actually capable of moving fast. But I was moving, and that's what mattered.

The stairs hurt a little more than the level floor, especially in my swollen knee. But I made it to the top without whimpering out loud or falling over, which was kind of a triumph, considering.

I paused at the top of the stairs. The door was open just a crack, which could mean anything. I put an ear to the opening. I didn't hear anything except the TV playing off to the left in the guard room. It sounded like *Jack Ryan* this time.

I leaned away from the door and thought. There was no way in the entire goddamned world I was going to get out the way I came in. Not in the shape I was in. There was a back door, away from the guard room—but I had to believe that Caitlin put the security back online once I was locked up.

Besides, once I was out, there was the question of what I was out *in*. Which was a winter night somewhere around twenty below zero. If there was a wind it would be a lot worse. I needed some kind of jacket or I wouldn't make it back to T.C.'s plane.

There had to be all kinds of coats and even gloves for the guards to use on their patrols. The front door at the guard room would probably not have an active alarm. If these guys were any good—and I was pretty sure they were—they would go out at random intervals to patrol the perimeter. An alarm on the door they used would be a nuisance.

If you're thinking, *Gee, the guard room sounds like the way to go. Except*—guards?! Okay, you're right. But I had my tac pack now, and it had some really cool toys in it—including a couple of sleepy grenades. They worked very fast, and the only disadvantage was that sometimes they killed people instead of just putting them to sleep. Right now that didn't seem like a disadvantage. I pulled one out of my pack, along with a very small rebreather. I'd have to pinch my nose for a minute, but that seemed like a pretty good trade-off for taking out a roomful of nasty people with dangerous accessories.

I limped quietly to the door where good old Jack Ryan was happily blazing away with a grenade launcher. Good: lots of noise to cover the noise I was going to cause. I bit down on the rebreather's mouthpiece, rolled the grenade into the room, and pinched my nose.

It took five or six seconds for anybody to notice what was happening. You can't really blame them; they weren't expecting trouble from inside the building. And to be fair, *Jack Ryan* was a really good show.

But finally somebody said, "What the fuck—" and I heard boots hitting the floor. Normally a good move, but this time? Not so much. Because when you're startled and you jump to your feet, guess what else you do at the same time? That's right—you take a big breath. Moments after I heard boots hit the floor, I heard bodies hit. There were a couple of very satisfying melon-thump sounds; heads hitting the floor or furniture really hard. It made me very happy. I hoped they were friends of Conal's.

I waited for a minute. Then I stuck my head around the doorframe for a look. They were all laid out across the floor and the furniture, out cold. It was a beautiful picture: *Still Life with Thugs.*

Even prettier, beside the door was a row of heavy parkas. Still pinching my nose, I limped over and around the bodies, grabbed a big down parka that looked like it would fit, pulled on some gloves that were in the pocket, and struggled into the parka. I grabbed a rifle from a rack by the door, an HK416. I slung it over my shoulder by its strap and staggered out the front door. I put away the rebreather in a night that was so cold it froze my nostrils shut, and I zipped the parka closed, pulling the hood over my head.

I hoped that with the parka on I would look like one of the regular watch dogs. I tried not to limp, figuring that would probably give me away, but it was tough going. I made my way slowly around the perimeter until I got to the hole I'd made in the fence. I figured that would be the easiest way to slip out.

Unfortunately, I wasn't the only one who figured that out.

I had just bent down to worm my way through the cut in the fence, when a man's voice came from behind me.

"Is it you, Lawrence?"

The voice was a man's, and thick with an Irish accent, which I used to think was beautiful. Lately, not so much. And it hit me square on with a very tricky choice. If I turned around, they'd see me and know I wasn't Lawrence. I couldn't rack a shot into the chamber of my rifle before they shot me. And if I dove through the hole in the fence and tried to run for it—first, I wasn't running anywhere tonight in the shape I was in. Second, even at my best I couldn't outrun a bullet. So I could either turn around and surrender, which seemed like a really bad idea, or I could try to fake my way out. There wasn't much of a fake I could try, but it was better than staying here and finding out if Conal's replacement had the same gentle touch and soothing repertoire of show tunes.

"Uh," I said, and I started to cough.

I let it rip for a couple of really good coughs, and then, with my voice roughened—from coughing—I said, "Yeah. It's me."

"All right, then, I thought so," the voice said.

And then something hard slammed into the back of my head and I was face down in the snow. A steel boot toe thudded into my side, just missing the broken rib, and judging by the feeling, breaking another one. I made a noise that sounded like somebody strangling a sheep, and the boot flipped me onto my back.

I was looking up at a large and ugly guy in a parka, holding a Colt Canada C8 assault rifle.

"There's nobody here named Lawrence, dryshite," he said. And instead of laughing like a normal evil henchman, he kicked me again, several times. I raised my arm to block one, which was a mistake, because that steel toe caught me on the wrist and I heard the bone crunch.

"Stay outside, there's a good lad, they told me," he said, kicking in rhythm to his words. "Just to be sure, they said. And will you look at this? They were right." He gave me a couple of extra hard kicks for emphasis.

And then his leg must have gotten tired, because he squatted beside me. "Off on holiday, are you, you cheeky wee fucker?" He slapped me a few times, just for punctuation. He wasn't really putting a lot into it, but he loosened a few teeth anyway.

"Now, then," he said. He slung his rifle over a shoulder and drew a large and wicked-looking knife.

"Let's give you a small little trim," he said. And I was sure he didn't mean a haircut.

"Wait," I said.

He cocked his head to one side. "Why?"

"Your boss wants me alive," I said.

"And you will be, mucker," he said. "Just only missing a part or two, hm?" He raised the knife up with a melodramatic flourish.

His head exploded.

Blood and brains spattered onto me, and then he toppled over—right on top of me. I was still struggling to get him off me, which was a bit more difficult with a broken wrist, when I heard more footsteps. *Shit*, I thought, *it's all over now.*

Except it wasn't. "Riley—you all right?" The voice came in a loud and urgent whisper, and it was a voice I knew: T.C.

"Not really," I whispered back. And then I felt a strong grip on my ankle and I was sliding through the hole in the fence. Using my good

hand, I got the weight of the headless body off me and then I was looking up at T.C.'s anxious face. He carried an M40 with a suppressor and
he was about the best-looking thing I had ever seen.

"I know you said not to come," he said apologetically.

"Never listen to me ever again," I said. "Let's get out of here."

CHAPTER

51

'm not sure how we got back to the plane. I think T.C. carried me part of the way, and dragged me across the snow a few times, too. I tried to walk on my own, but my legs didn't want to hold my weight, let alone move around with it. The adrenaline that had gotten me out to the fence was long gone, and I was feeling the second beating. On top of the damage Conal's workover did, I was in rough shape. So it must have been slow going. I don't remember much of it, but I'm pretty sure about that.

But we made it. When we got back to the plane, T.C. got me inside and strapped me in. Then he reached behind his pilot's seat and retrieved a combat medic's kit. He zipped it open and took something out. I didn't see what it was; that didn't seem quite as important as paying attention to all the pain I was feeling. I did pay attention, very briefly, when he jabbed something into my arm. I managed to say "Oww," and that was it. Lights out.

I came to in a car moving at a smooth, steady speed. It was bright daylight now, so I'd been out for a while. I turned my head just enough to see a big green sign go by. I couldn't read what it said, but I knew what it meant. We were on a US interstate highway. I turned my head the other way, just to make sure that "we" still meant me and T.C. It did. I went back to sleep.

I woke up again when the car came to a halt. The sun was going down, but there was still enough light to see that we were in the parking lot of a one-story concrete-block building.

"Hey, buddy," T.C. said. "You got to see a doctor now."

"No," I said. To be honest, I croaked more than said. Doctors were a bad idea. T.C. should have known that.

He did. He patted my shoulder. It hurt, but I got the idea that he was trying to tell me it was okay.

"I know this guy," he said. "We served in the sandbox together. He won't talk."

He got out of the car, came around to my side, and helped me out. That was a very good idea, because when I was finally up on my feet, it was obvious right away that those were some really good drugs T.C. had shot me up with. The pain was much less, and kind of far away. But my body had somehow become very tall and fragile. I felt like I was standing on a very high tower in a strong wind. T.C. held me up and led me toward the concrete-block building. There was a sign on the door. It said, DR. BIRUNGI, and under that, DVM.

T.C. was taking me to a veterinarian. I wondered if I should bark.

"It's okay, buddy," T.C. said. "Freddy was the medic in my unit. He knows his shit, no worries."

And Birungi clearly knew what he was doing. He also had some really great drugs, and I was feeling a whole lot better when I got back in the car. I even stayed awake for several hours of the drive home. Which was New York City right now, since T.C. knew my apartment there.

I spent a week doing mostly nothing except getting better; reading, listening to music, sleeping a lot. T.C. and Chaz came by once or twice, to laugh at me and drink up my booze. It helped a little—it was almost like having friends. Even Kondor came once. He drank half a bottle of Scotch with no visible effect, and the son of a bitch even gave me a present. A beautiful leather-bound edition of *Leaves of Grass* by Walt Whitman. How's that for a thug?

I read it while I healed. Kondor had put a bookmark in at "Song of Myself" and underlined, "Do I contradict myself? Very well then I contradict myself. (I am large, I contain multitudes.)" Weird, I know, but it kind of helped. And at the end of that week I felt strong enough to leave, and I did. I'd had this apartment too long. Caitlin could almost certainly find it.

I drove down to a place I had in North Carolina. It was on a mountaintop and secured, like I do with all my places. It was also stocked with nonperishable food and drink, a good library, and a good sound system. I hunkered down and spent a few more weeks putting myself back together.

Most of that repair work was physical—at least at first. But once I was able to move around without crying, the emotional storm hit. It was about what you'd expect: depression, anxiety, all of that. That almost always happens when you're recovering from physical injuries. I mean, if I have to be honest, some of it was about Caitlin, too. Not just that she'd gamed me so completely. Which she had, and that hurt. It was the breakup part, too. I'm sorry if that sounds like high school romance; I don't know how else to describe it. I thought we had something going, and it turned out that was just part of her game.

Mostly. There had to be something real going on under all that, too. For her as well as for me. Right? If I'm being delusional, too bad. I've earned it. But I really believe she had some feelings about me, even if it was only the kind of fondness you have for a really good pet turtle.

Anyway, I had some of those feelings. I still didn't know what to do with that part, all those feelings I'd had, and maybe still had in some warped corner of my twisted insides. I wasn't really ready to sit down and think about that yet. For now, the backlash of all the physical healing was enough to keep me busy. I'd dealt with it before, and I did this time. But when the pain really receded, I had time to think again. I did, and I didn't like the thoughts that came. And yeah, again, they were mostly about Caitlin.

I could admit that I had started to care about her because, hey; look what I went through to try to rescue her. And when it turned out that she didn't need rescuing and I did, it was crystal clear that I'd been a huge idiot. So that hurt.

But more than that, one really nasty thought kept coming back at me. Not what you'd expect, either. I mean, all the obvious stuff was there, and I tossed it away pretty quick; I fell for somebody—bad enough—and she turned out to be my enemy—worse. She fooled me; she outthought and outplanned me; I was a moron; all of that came and went, and it didn't bother me as much as you might think.

But that one nasty thought that wouldn't go away? It bothered the hell out of me. It was this:

I escaped.

You're thinking, *Hey, isn't that a* good *thing? Doesn't it prove that* in the end, I was still top dog? She made her best try, and I beat it. I got away.

And, okay, sure, getting away was a good thing. But . . .

How was that possible? It shouldn't have been.

Yes, I am very damn good. Yes, I always find a way. And yes, it hadn't been easy. But the thing is, it shouldn't have just been hard. It should have been impossible. If the positions were reversed, I would sure as shit be able to keep somebody from escaping, no matter how freaking good they were. Maybe I would have got to killing me a little faster. But I would definitely have made sure.

Caitlin the Cobra hadn't done that. And looking back at all of it, I find it really hard to believe that she didn't. Was it an oversight? Over-confidence? Maybe she relied on the electronic stuff and Tamiqua's virus was still working?

Whatever it was, I got away, and all I could feel was grateful at first. But, the more I had time to think, the more I kept coming back to that and wondering. Because none of the explanations made sense, not with her. I'm smart enough to know when I'm overmatched, and this time I was. I knew damn well that for the first time ever, I had finally come up against somebody who was just as good at deception and deep planning as I was. I mean, yeah, she'd fooled me—but come on, I wasn't expecting it.

And that started to sound pretty feeble very quickly. Nobody ever expects it. Nobody I'd pulled the big con on expected it. The trick to staying in the game is that you *always* expect it. Always look over your shoulder, always expect something to come at you all the time. It's even in the Rules I live by; Riley's Fourth Law states, Even if you're the best there is, watch your back. Because somebody better is coming. Better watch for them, because they are coming for you.

This time I hadn't. Mostly because she knocked me off center, with the most perfect setup I'd ever seen. She figured out exactly what would draw me in—me specifically and nobody else—and she played it perfectly. Starting at the art gallery, moving on to leaving me hanging with the "maybe" that I could see her again—every step of Caitlin's game was custom-tailored to catch Riley Wolfe and nobody else. And I walked right into it.

I'd been the unchallenged king of the heap for so long that it was hard to swallow, but there it was. She beat me. Every single damn stage of the way she beat me, got ahead of me, outthought and outmaneuvered me. She knew me better than I did, and she used it on me to perfection, from the first time she "accidentally" met me to her final good night kiss with me shackled in a cell and beaten to a pulp.

And then I got away. How?

How did somebody that good make such a bad mistake?

I kept coming back to that one nagging thought: If she was good enough to do what she had done—which, duh, she was, she did it—then other than having the crap kicked out of me twice, how did she let me get away so easily? I mean, if I had set it up, and I *wanted* somebody to escape for whatever reason, that's exactly how I would have done it—make it *just hard enough* so it's believable. And if Caitlin had done that, then—

Why? Seriously—*why?*

Was she telling me I really wasn't all that, so it didn't matter if I got away? Or was she saying she could come back and finish me any time at all and I couldn't stop her? Maybe make the psychological torture last longer, with me always wondering when the hammer would fall? Was it a test, to see if I could get past a series of obstacles and escape? If so, again, why, damn it? And way out there past the outfield, something so impossible that it just couldn't be—was it because . . .

No. I didn't believe it. I couldn't. I mean, if it actually was true, then all the boxes lined up and fit together so it made the most sense of all—except it didn't really make any sense. But if I was going to be all cold and calculating about things, I had to consider it, even if it did sound stupid. So—

What if she, you know, *liked* me?

I won't say that other "l" word because that's not even plausible enough to be stupid. Neither one of us is really capable of that other "l." But what if she left a couple of doors open to see if I could get through them, because she *wanted* me to get away? It couldn't have been unconsciously, because one of her thugs would have pointed it out to her and closed the doors. And if she did do it on purpose—if she wanted me to escape and be alive and well out there in the world—again, why? What possible future could there ever be for us together, except trying to kill each other?

I don't know. I couldn't figure it out then, and I still haven't, and it's eating away at me. And maybe that was her whole purpose. The Cobra. She took what she wanted, bit me, and put the venom in my veins, and sooner or later it would finish me.

I don't know, and I don't know any way I can figure it out. What I do know is this; sooner or later, she'll be coming for me again. I don't know when or what she will want or what she'll do, but she will come. I know it like I know the sun comes up in the east. Not just because I'm unfinished business, and not because she has a deep and tragic yearning to melt in my arms and smother me with kisses. No, she'll come for an even better, more practical reason.

The *wesekh*. The one with the cobra rising up on it. The one she said she wanted to hold and keep forever and ever. That's one thing she said that I still believe. She wants it. She knows I have it. She will come for it.

So I have to get ready for her. And I need to stay ready, 24-7, 365. She made me feel that target on my back for the first time ever, and she showed me she can hit the bull's-eye every time. She's coming, no doubt about it.

I just don't know what I'm going to do about her when she comes.

ACKNOWLEDGMENTS

My thanks to Isabella Mulhall of the Irish Antiquities Division at the National Museum of Ireland, who answered my questions quickly and fully. The British Museum chose not to answer any of my queries.

ABOUT THE AUTHOR

JEFF LINDSAY is the award-winning author of the *New York Times* best-selling Dexter novels, upon which the international hit TV show *Dexter* is based. This is the fourth book in his Riley Wolfe series. He has also written two dozen plays and, among many other things, he has worked as an actor, comic, voice-over artist, screenwriter, columnist, singer, musician, bouncer, DJ, teacher, waiter, chop-saw operator in a foundry, TV and radio host, gardener, sailing instructor, and girls' soccer coach. Jeff is married to writer-filmmaker Hilary Hemingway. They have three daughters.